Good Enough to Eat

Stacey Ballis

BERKLEY BOOKS, NEW YORK

THE BERKLEY PUBLISHING GROUP
Published by the Penguin Group
Penguin Group (USA) Inc.
375 Hudson Street, New York, New York 10014, USA

Penguin Group (Canada), 90 Eglinton Avenue East, Suite 700, Toronto, Ontario M4P 2Y3, Canada
(a division of Pearson Penguin Canada Inc.)
Penguin Books Ltd., 80 Strand, London WC2R 0RL, England
Penguin Group Ireland, 25 St. Stephen's Green, Dublin 2, Ireland (a division of Penguin Books Ltd.)
Penguin Group (Australia), 250 Camberwell Road, Camberwell, Victoria 3124, Australia
(a division of Pearson Australia Group Pty. Ltd.)
Penguin Books India Pvt. Ltd., 11 Community Centre, Panchsheel Park, New Delhi—110 017, India
Penguin Group (NZ), 67 Apollo Drive, Rosedale, North Shore 0632, New Zealand
(a division of Pearson New Zealand Ltd.)
Penguin Books (South Africa) (Pty.) Ltd., 24 Sturdee Avenue, Rosebank, Johannesburg 2196,
South Africa

Penguin Books Ltd., Registered Offices: 80 Strand, London WC2R 0RL, England

This is an original publication of The Berkley Publishing Group.

PUBLISHER'S NOTE: The recipes contained in this book are to be followed exactly as written. The publisher is not responsible for your specific health or allergy needs that may require medical supervision. The publisher is not responsible for any adverse reactions to the recipes contained in this book.

This is a work of fiction. Names, characters, places, and incidents either are the product of the author's imagination or are used fictitiously, and any resemblance to actual persons, living or dead, business establishments, events, or locales is entirely coincidental. The publisher does not have any control over and does not assume any responsibility for author or third-party websites or their content.

PRINTING HISTORY
Berkley trade paperback edition / September 2010

Library of Congress Cataloging-in-Publication Data

Ballis, Stacey.
  Good enough to eat / Stacey Ballis.—Berkley trade pbk. ed.
    p. cm.
  ISBN 978-0-425-22963-7
  1. Businesswomen—Fiction. 2. Restaurateurs—Fiction. 3. Natural food restaurants—
Fiction. 4. Life change events—Fiction. 5. Man-woman relationships—Fiction.
6. Domestic fiction. I. Title.
  PS3602.A624G66 2010
  813'.6—dc22

                                                                          2010018841

PRINTED IN THE UNITED STATES OF AMERICA

10 9 8 7 6 5 4 3 2 1

For Jen,
whose friendship makes everything
more delicious!

For Bill,
who makes me believe every day

ACKNOWLEDGMENTS

As always, my loving family: Mom, Dad, Deb, and Jonnie. None of this would be nearly as much fun without you around me.

My wonderful agent and partner, Scott Mendel, for being not only such a terrific navigator on this journey but excellent company as well.

My amazing friends (you know who you are and how much I love and treasure you), who are the best support system any girl could ask for and who are all blissfully good eaters . . . with extra props for the Uzes gang!

Carey Peters, for your friendship and guidance, and for giving so freely of your wisdom during the writing of this book. You not only helped Melanie change her life; you helped me change mine.

Everyone at Penguin/Berkley, especially Leslie Gelbman, Wendy McCurdy, and Melissa Broder.

My friend and trainer, Gabe, for helping keep me healthy, however hard I may fight against it. (I still hate the f***ing squats. I'm not saying; I'm just saying.)

My fantastic gaggle of girls—most especially Rachel, Sue, Denise, Tracey, Gina, Caprice, Laura, Liz, Stephanie, Serena, Ellen, Tracy, Margie, and Peggy—you guys keep me sane! (Or insane, as the case may be . . .)

My NYC BFF, Penny, who showed up right when I needed her, for showing me that less is indeed more, that bringing beauty into your life every day is neither extraneous nor impossible, and that one is never finished finding old dear friends. (And that I can survive quite happily with half the number of occasional tables as previously assumed.)

For Bill, an unexpected gift from the universe. I am so very, very lucky to know you and have you in my life.

Last but definitely not least, the extraordinary Jen Lancaster, who is a daily blessing and an endless source of inspiration. Thank you for all the laughter and adventures and support. Wednesday nights will always belong to you. Team Stennifer rules!

PROLOGUE

The firm close of the door, despite not having been remotely slammed, nevertheless reverberates through the profound emptiness of my house. The sheer force of it pushes me down into a chair at the kitchen table, coffee and shards of pottery at the floor by my feet, the now-cold liquid soaking into my slippers. I wait for the front door to open again. I wait for the alarm clock to go off, waking me from this unreal dream. It is only when the sparkles appear before my eyes that I realize I'm listening so hard for one of these sounds that I have forgotten to breathe. Something vibrates near my arm, and I glance down at my BlackBerry, which is reminding me that I have a phone meeting scheduled with my nutritional counselor.

How ironic.

In the past two years I have lost about 145 pounds. Half my body weight.

And twenty minutes ago, my husband of nearly ten years announced that he is leaving me.

For a woman twice my size.

Carey answers the phone on the second ring. "Hello?"

I can't even reply with a basic greeting. I launch directly into the information I need to impart. "He left. He's in love with someone else. He's in love with someone else and he left me." The words flood out of my mouth, out into the phone, into the ether, the still air in the house crackling with the electric departure of my husband.

"Hold on, hold on, slow down, Mel. Start at the beginning." Carey's voice is calm and assured, a tiny lifeline.

I take a deep breath. "Andrew has just announced, in the most matter-of-fact way, that he is no longer in love with me, and no longer wants to be married to me, and is in love with someone else and wants to be with her. He doesn't want to do any counseling, he knows his heart, he says. He says he's sorry, that he knows it's a blow, that he never meant to hurt me, but that all the changes I've been going through have made him realize what he wants and needs and it just isn't me." I rattle this off as if it is a series of recipe instructions. Sift dry ingredients. Cream butter and sugar. Add eggs one at a time. Mix in dry ingredients. Leave your wife of nearly ten years for your mistress. Tell her that she isn't worth fighting for, that the marriage is permanently broken beyond repair, and the fact that she didn't even notice anything was wrong is completely beside the point. Grab your suitcase and briefcase and tell her you'll come back for your stuff tomorrow while she is at work.

"Oh, honey. I'm so sorry. I thought . . . Well, it's just a

shock. You've never given me any indication that things were bad at home."

"I wasn't aware that things were bad at home. We don't fight, never did. I mean, yes, the sex had sort of become minimal, but we've both been so busy and I've been so tired with getting the store open and on its feet and I just thought it was a phase. . . . It's not like it's been years or something, just a brief dry spell. Well. Apparently a dry spell for me—he's clearly been getting plenty of it elsewhere!"

"When did it happen?"

"About twenty minutes ago."

"Wow. Do you think, I mean, that's very recent, maybe it's just in the heat of the moment?"

I laugh, brittle and coppery tasting. "There was no heat. There wasn't a fight, this wasn't some passionate blow-up. He got up. He showered, he got dressed, he made the coffee, and then he announced that he has been seeing someone else for a while now, and he is in love with her and he knows that I'll eventually understand and that he hopes someday we'll be friends. And I yelled and threw a coffee cup at him, and he stood there and took it and apologized and grabbed a suitcase out of the front closet that he had apparently packed up while I was in the shower or something, and headed out the door."

"I can't even imagine."

"Neither can I. It's like it didn't happen. It's like I'm in some weird dream, and I'm going to wake up any minute . . . and . . . I . . ." My breath seems lodged in my throat. I know I'm breathing but I can't feel it in my lungs. I start making some gurgling choking noises.

"Mel? MEL! Are you okay?"

"I . . . can't . . ."

"Breathe, honey, just slow, deep breaths. Slow, now. You're probably going into some sort of shock."

"Mmm hmmm." Slow. Breathing. I shake my head side to side, feeling the tears start, impossibly hot, stinging my skin, trying to force the air past the stone in my throat.

"That's it, Mel. Now, I want you to yell. Loud. Let it out."

"No, I can't, I . . ." I sound like I swallowed a fistful of peanut butter.

"Trust me. I know you're trying to be strong, but you can't breathe because your bravery is in the way. You have to get it out. Yell. Loud as you can, just . . ."

Suddenly an air-raid siren goes off, shocking me. Shocking especially since it appears to have generated in my chest and is coming out of my mouth. And for some reason, the movie *The Princess Bride* pops into my mind. The sound of ultimate suffering. I'm suddenly farm-boy-turned-pirate Westley, paralyzed by pain as my one true love goes off to marry someone else. And who has more cause to make the sound of ultimate suffering? Through the din I can hear Carey on the phone, offering gentle encouragement, telling me to get it out. The blast dwindles as my lungs empty, and I begin to breathe again.

"That was good, kiddo, really good," Carey says. "Now, I want you to give me Kai's number and I'm going to call him and send him to your house."

"Oh, no, I don't want to see anyone. At least Andrew was good enough to drop this bomb on my day off, I . . ."

"Mel, I'm not asking. You should not be alone right now. Even if you're just going to go get in bed and sleep all day, someone should be there. If you don't want it to be Kai, then give me someone else's number, but since I can't come myself, I'm sending someone to be with you." Carey is in Los Angeles. And frankly, I think if I don't put her in touch with Kai, she is likely to jump on a plane.

I rattle off the number.

"Good. I'm going to put you on hold, and call Kai, and then I'm going to come right back and stay on the phone with you till he gets there, okay?"

"Okay."

"Good. Keep breathing. I'll be right back."

The phone clicks, and I stand up from the kitchen table, squishing in my soggy slippers, which I kick off into the corner of the room, and head over to the living room and plop on the couch. There is no way that this is my life. This doesn't happen to women like me. I'm smart and successful and educated and I was never a harpy or high maintenance. Andrew never lacked for a friendly ear or sage advice or passionate sex. I still wore decent lingerie, I still gave head joyfully and without being asked. I never belittled him or emasculated him or acted like his mother or made fun of his foibles. We used to shake our heads when we heard about those couples that were breaking up because of infidelity. We concluded that either the guys were so shitty and selfish they couldn't keep it in their pants, or so henpecked we sort of couldn't blame them. We were always shocked that the wives didn't know. How do you not notice the signs? Baffling. But not us. Not me and Andrew. Nothing about this makes any sort of sense, and for the life of me I can't begin to figure out why I didn't know I was losing him, how I became exactly the wife I used to pity. I hear more phone clicks, and Carey's voice is back. "Mel? You still there, honey?"

"What's left of me, yeah."

"Kai is going to be there in half an hour to take care of you, and I'm going to stay right on the—"

"She's fat," I blurt out on top of her kindness.

"Who's fat?"

"The woman, whoever she is, he wouldn't say, he said it wasn't the right time to get into that, but she's fat. Fat like I used to be."

"Oh." Carey clearly hasn't expected this.

"Yeah, I know. Kind of a kick in the head, huh?" I start chuckling, although it sounds more like I'm gargling chowder. Then the chuckle turns into a laugh. "SHE'S FAT! A big old roly-poly just like I was! You know, I was always so goddamned IMPRESSED with him for falling in love with me despite my girth. I always thought he was one of those guys who just sees that size doesn't matter, who recognizes all the benefits of not being with some stick. I gave him such credit, the handsome, fit guy who is so self-confident he can show off his whale of a wife without blinking an eye."

"Mel . . ."

"No, I know I was deserving of love when I was big, but I always knew that the love I deserved was because of who I was, not because of how I looked. And the whole time, it was the FAT he loved. It was the FAT he wanted. That asshole was just a chubby chaser the whole time, and all his praise of my endless QUALITIES was bullshit!" The laughter segues into tears as the truth of what is happening really begins to sink in. "I worked so hard, I sacrificed so much for this body, this stupid body that is my lifelong nemesis, and all I did with the sweat and deprivation and aches and pains and frustration was create a body that made my husband fall out of love with me."

"Oh, Melanie. I'm so sorry."

I wipe my cheeks. "Carey, what am I going to do?"

"You're going to suffer what you have to suffer and know that at the other end you are going to be better and stronger and ultimately happier as a result. I know it probably doesn't feel that way now. But think about it. Would you really rather be with someone who was so deceitful, who couldn't even discuss his concerns with you? You didn't just wake up one day thin, honey. You worked really hard for a really long time and it never occurred to him to have a conversation with you about how your changing body was affecting him? He never considered getting some counseling to see if it wasn't something you guys could work through? He just found someone else and bailed on you? You deserve so much better than that, and I know that deep down, you know it."

"I know." But I don't. Not really.

"It's going to suck for a while, but then it won't. That much I know."

"Okay."

"Okay."

"I should probably put some clothes on if Kai is coming over."

"Want to put me on speakerphone?"

"No. Thanks though. I'm not going to do myself a mischief, I'm just going to put on my sweats and throw my hair in a ponytail. I'll be fine. Kai will be here soon."

"Okay, I'll call in a bit to check in on you."

"Thanks, Carey."

"Chin up, kiddo. You'll get through it."

"Sure. Talk to you later."

"Okay, bye, sweetie."

I put down the phone and trudge upstairs. I look at the rumpled bed, where not even an hour ago I lay slipping into waking next to my husband, who loved me and was my soul mate and playmate and partner in all things, not at all aware that everything was about to change forever.

MASHED POTATOES

The first conscious memory I have of food being significant was the Thanksgiving after Dad died. I was four. We gathered at my grandparents' house, made all the right noises; there was football on the television and a fire in the fireplace. But no one seemed to really be there. My mom was still nursing Gillian, and spent most of the day off in the guest bedroom with her. And the food was awful. Overcooked, underseasoned. I remember thinking that Daddy would have hated it. He loved to eat. It's what killed him. Well, sort of. The police found a half-eaten Big Mac in his lap after the accident. They assumed that he was distracted by eating when he ran the red light and into the truck. I remember looking at my family and feeling like Daddy would be so mad at us for not having a good time, for not having a good meal. And halfway through dinner my grandmother said, "Oh my god, I forgot

the mashed potatoes. They were Abraham's favorite. How could I forget!" And then she ran off crying. And I thought, I'd better learn how to make mashed potatoes quickly or the family would completely disintegrate.

"Okay, Mel, let's start with something good," Carey says. "What happened this week that was really great?"

I have to think about this for a moment. "Well, the store showed a small profit this week. . . ."

"Wow, that's like three weeks in a row, right?"

"Yeah. Not anything huge, but my accountant says that all we need is a trend. If I can do three more consecutive weeks in the black, we should be able to project the rest of the year's income. You know, since this is the slow season."

"Why slow?" Carey asks.

"Well, it's February. The New Year's resolutions to eat healthy and exercise have worn off, it's four degrees below zero, and everyone wants comfort food. Chicago in February is no time to run a healthy take-out establishment. No one wants to get out of their cars to pick up a decent good-for-you meal, they want stick-to-your-ribs fare and they want it delivered." I'm babbling.

"Well, then, I'm even more proud of you that you're doing so well in such a tough time." Carey is unflaggingly supportive. She's so much more than a nutritional counselor; she is like my life guru, friend, and therapist all rolled into one bundle of positive energy, and I'd never have gotten through the last three months without her. "But I'd like to hear about something good for you personally, not related to the business. Did *you* have anything good this week?"

"Well." I take a deep breath. "I threw out my bed. I just put it out in the alley, along with all the pillows and bedding, and went and bought a new one."

"Well, that sounds like fun! A little shopping spree for your new place, right?"

"Yeah. I mean, when I moved out it seemed logical to take the bed, since Andrew was staying at Charlene's." I hate having to say their names out loud. "But, I don't know, it just felt like . . ."

"Bad ex-husband juju in the bedroom."

"Yeah. Exactly. I got home from the store, exhausted, went to go collapse, and couldn't bring myself to get in the bed. It was like his fucking ghost was in the fibers or something. And I know that he said he never brought her there, I mean they never did it in our bed, but still. I slept on the couch. In the morning I remembered that the nice woman who did all my window treatments had given me her husband's card. He's over at American Mattress on Clybourn, and she said that he would hook me up if I ever needed a bed, so I just went over there and picked out the tallest, biggest, squishiest, most indulgent bed they had. And then went to Bed Bath and Beyond to fit it out with down pillows and eight-hundred-thread-count sheets."

"That's awesome!"

"It was ridiculous. And I couldn't really afford it, but I felt like I couldn't afford not to either. Wanna know the weird thing? The bed is named Waking Hours. And at first, I wasn't really sure why Serta would name a bed that, since the point of a bed is supposed to be sleeping hours. Except that after the first night, I wanted to spend all my waking hours in it too!"

"And how has the sleeping been since?"

"Better. Much better. But I'm dreaming about cakes again."

Never fails. Stress or sadness, my dream life is all about food. When I decided to lose the weight two years ago, I left the law and went to culinary school, and then got a degree in holistic nutrition. That's where I met Carey. She was one of my teachers in the nutrition program. My store, Dining by Design, is a healthy gourmet take-out café, amazing food that is amazingly good for you.

But no matter how much I feel in control of my relationship with food, my subconscious craves the habits of my former life. The days when Andrew and I would eat spaghetti carbonara as a midnight snack after sex, when there were always cookies in the cookie jar and a cake under the glass dome in the kitchen. The days when food was celebration and joy and reason for living and cure-all. A substitute for two dead parents and a little sister who lives in London and rarely calls. A replacement for the children I never got around to having, and now don't have the energy, money, or husband to make feasible. A way to patch the holes created by a soulless job. A way to fill up that empty pit of hunger that seemed never satisfied.

"And how do you feel about these dreams?" Carey asks. "Are they still about denial, or are you getting to eat the cakes?"

Carey has been with me through everything, the hardest-to-lose last twenty-five pounds, the purchase and opening of the store, the surprising end of my marriage. She knows my dreams almost as well as I do.

"I don't get to eat the cake. I'm just in the room with the buffet, and the cakes are everywhere, and I'm loading up plates with every possible flavor, and putting them aside to take home, to eat in secret, but then there are people and I have to mingle, and then I can't find the plates I put aside. It's extraordinarily pathetic."

"Not pathetic. Natural. You're feeling deprived, physically and emotionally. It's February in Chicago, and your desire is for comfort food. And you're working very hard and going home to a place you haven't fully embraced as home yet. And you are probably a little lonely . . ."

"And horny." If we're going to be honest about it.

Carey laughs. "Of course, and horny. Will you do something for me?"

"You know I will."

"Get your butt over to Sweet Mandy B's tomorrow. Buy every flavor of their mini cupcakes that appeals to you. Go home, pour a glass of champagne, light a candle, and eat every one, slowly. Lick the crumbs off the plate; savor the different flavor combinations, the texture of the frosting. Eat until you are full, and then stop and throw the rest away. We have talked about this before; sometimes you have to eat what you crave purposefully so that you don't fall into a binge of fog-eating."

"I know. And I know I'm in a dangerous spot. But you're right, I do need to address the cake craving soon or I'm going to jump off the wagon and land in a vat of frosting and eat my way out."

It doesn't matter how much I know about this process, how

much I am able to counsel others, being a compulsive overeater is no different from being an alcoholic or drug addict. The only difference is that you can avoid drugs and alcohol completely and you have to have a relationship with food every day for the rest of your life. It's actually the hardest addiction to live with. If you were an alcoholic and someone said to you that you were required to have a single drink three to five times a day every day, but were not supposed to ever drink to excess, or a drug addict who was required to take just one pill several times a day every day, but you're not supposed to ever take more than that . . . no one would ever make it through rehab.

"You're doing great," Carey says. "I'll send you an e-mail about our major stuff from today. Keep up the good work, and don't forget to call or e-mail me if you have any questions."

"Thanks, honey."

"Thank you! Great session today. I'll talk to you in a couple of weeks."

"Okay, Carey. Talk to you later."

I hang up the phone and stretch my arms above my head. I head to the bathroom, where I throw my thick, straight chestnut hair into a ponytail to get it out of my way. I wash my face carefully, my skin being my one vanity, and slide a lightly tinted moisturizer on, surprised as I am every day to find that I own cheekbones, and have only one chin. A coat of mascara on my lashes, making my slightly close-set gold-flecked hazel eyes look bigger. This is as cute as I intend to get today. I check my watch. Eleven a.m. A long day stretches ahead of me. I know I should love Mondays, my one day off, but they always scare me a little bit. Especially since Andrew left me on a Monday. I always wake up feeling like something bad is going to happen, like a Vietnam flashback. Tuesday through Sunday I'm up at five for a forty-five-minute workout, and am in the store by six thirty. By the time I open the doors at eleven, Kai and I have cooked in a frenetic burst of energy, and the cases are full of delectables.

Half Japanese, half African American, and only twenty-two years old, Kai was the star of our graduating class from culinary school. He has better knife skills than anyone I have ever seen, and a cutting wit to match. And along with Carey has kept me sane and functioning these past weeks. Not only did he come sit with me that horrible day, which he refers to as our Abominable Snow Day, but he also essentially did all the heavy lifting at the store for the first week while I walked around in a numb haze, burning things and giving people the wrong items. At the end of that week he came over after work, made me pack a bag, and forced me to move in with him and his boyfriend, Phil, a successful trader. Phil pays the bills, but is out of the house from about five in the morning till about three in the afternoon, which was why Kai could afford to take the job with me for essentially minimum wage, since it is only six hours a day, and only four days a week. On Tuesdays and Saturdays I have an extern from the culinary institute: every other month a new fresh-faced budding chef to train, currently a slightly dim thirty-year-old former dental assistant named Ashley who thought cooking would be more fun than poking around people's mouths all day, and forgot to find out if she had any real passion for food.

In the afternoons and on Sundays I have Delia, who lives

in the women's shelter up the block. It's part of a job-training program they started with the local business owners. Delia escaped her abusive husband in Columbus, and a sort of Underground Railroad for battered women moved her to Chicago for her own safety. New in town, with no contacts, she has been living in the shelter for the past nine months. When she started taking over in their kitchen, the shelter volunteers recognized her love of cooking, and approached me about the program. I pay her minimum wage on weekdays and time and a half for the Sunday hours. She's a homegrown soul-food goddess who learned at her grandmother's knee, and it's been a struggle to hamper her desire to cook things in bacon fat, but she works like a dog and is a fast learner, and reluctantly admits that the food tastes good, even if she thinks the whole idea of cooking healthy is a little silly. "Sisterfriend," she says to me at least once a day, "at my house, it is going to be fried chicken like the good lord intended. None of this oven-baked-skinless nonsense."

All week long there is work to do from sunup till way past sundown, and lovely people to help. There are regular customers to catch up with, and new customers to convert, and bills to pay, and products to order, and precise cleaning to do to keep within sanitation regulations. Occasionally on Wednesday nights there are cooking classes to teach, and on Friday nights there are special events. The other nights there are new recipes to test and perfect.

But Mondays. Mondays are long. Do the laundry. Change the sheets on the dream bed. Clean the condo that never gets very dirty since I'm at the store six days a week for sixteen hours a day. Go to the grocery store and make sure that the fridge is filled with washed and cut-up veggies, fresh fruit, yogurts, and cottage cheese and easy makings for salads and healthy snacks. Try not to think about what Andrew and Charlene might be doing. What sort of plans they are making, if they are talking about me, wondering if they have spent these last three months in a haze of sex and food and happiness while I have uprooted my entire life. Or rather, while they have uprooted it.

When Andrew finally confessed that it was Charlene he had fallen in love with, Charlene he had been sleeping with, it doubled the betrayal, made the humiliation exponentially worse. Charlene is the managing partner at the law firm where I worked in my former life as a medical malpractice attorney. The life where I made a substantial six-figure income, was married to the man I thought was my soul mate, and lived in a gorgeous brick house in Lincoln Park that was built in 1872, right after the Great Chicago Fire. The life where I leased a new BMW every two years, put fabulous designer shoes on my feet, and ate whatever my 289-pound self desired. The life where I had ridiculous amounts of energetic sex with a man who reveled in every soft curve of my ample frame.

Charlene was more than my boss; she was a friend. At about 275 pounds herself, she was my partner in crime, quick with a midday candy bar or cookie, the first to suggest an order of onion rings to accompany the after-work martinis. The one who celebrated every one of our wins and commiserated about our losses by taking us to lunch somewhere decadent, where we would order half the menu on the firm's generous expense account.

But when I decided to take control of my eating, to try to

reverse the diabetes I had acquired, to ease the pain in my joints, to prevent further health issues and hopefully ward off a heart attack, Charlene pulled away from me. And when I left the firm to go to culinary school, she essentially dropped off the face of my earth. I tried to maintain the friendship, never preaching about my program or even suggesting she make changes herself, knowing firsthand that there is nothing more irritating than someone currently successfully managing her weight trying to get a fat person to drink whatever Kool-Aid is the flavor of the day.

I even tried to get together with her at nonmeal times so that she never had to listen to me order something healthy and feel pressure to do so herself. Because you know what sucks? Sitting across from little Miss Egg White Omelet with Tomato Slices Instead of Potatoes, when what you want is a stack of pancakes dripping with butter and syrup and a side of sausage. If you order what you want, you feel judged, and if you order something healthy, you feel like a phony, not to mention disappointed. I suggested spa dates instead, afternoon shopping, theater matinees. She found a million excuses to avoid me, and eventually I stopped trying.

You'd have thought that as I started to shrink, Andrew's ardor would have increased. After all, while there was less and less of me to love, what was there was more and more strong and flexible. We could have managed positions that would have been impossible before, but the smaller I got, the less interest Andrew had in sex, and what had been a three- or four-night-a-week habit dwindled first to once a week, then every other week, then once a month. By the end, it had been so rare I stopped keeping track. He supported me through culinary school, helped me buy and open the store, and then he left.

It was a month after he left me, at the final walk-through when we sold our house, that I found out it was Charlene he had been sleeping with for nearly two years. He left his phone on the counter, and when it rang, I saw it was her on the caller ID, and everything fell into place.

"CHARLENE?" I had screamed. "You've been fucking Charlene?!?"

"Lower your voice, the real estate brokers are right upstairs."

"I don't care if the goddamned queen of goddamned England is upstairs. It's Charlene, isn't it?"

Andrew sighed, as if it were very inconvenient to have to deal with me. "Yes, all right? Is that what you need to hear? Yes. I'm in love with Charlene, I'm moving in with her. Please don't be a drama queen about this."

"*I'm* the drama queen? You're the one behaving like you're starring in some afternoon soap opera. Really, Andrew, you couldn't have gone more cliché if you tried. It's pathetic."

"I had really hoped we could be friends, Mel, after all this time, but you're making it very hard."

That was when I realized fully that I hated him. That I hated who he was and what he had done to me and what he had turned me into: some shrill ex-wife berating him in public, embarrassing herself more than him. I would not let him turn me into the worst version of myself.

"Andrew, I don't think I want to be friends. In fact, I'm pretty sure that if I met you today at a party I'd not want to know you."

"Have it your way."

"Don't you worry. I intend to."

I'm not the only woman to lose her man, and certainly not the only one to lose him to someone she thought was a good friend. But I do believe I'm the only woman I've ever heard of who got thin, and then had her husband leave her for a big girl. If it wasn't so humiliating and hurtful, it would be almost funny.

So now, I focus on my new life. The life where I make barely enough to keep my head above water. The life where I'm divorced from the man I thought was my soul mate, who turned out to just be a lying, cheating piece of shit with a serious fat-girl fetish. The life where I live in a little two-bedroom condo in Ravenswood Manor, a quarter the size of my old house, but all I could afford to buy outright with my settlement from the sale of the Lincoln Park house, since with the cost of the business, I couldn't afford to carry a mortgage as well. The life where I drive a Honda, wear Crocs instead of Jimmy Choos, and eat the way a normal person is supposed to, while trying every day to quiet the demons in my head that crave butter and cream and sugar. The life where I am diabetes-free, fit, and strong, with a healthy heart and a prognosis of a long life, and every day hoping that I'm getting closer to believing it can also be a happy one.

I look around me, at the haven I've tried to create for myself. When I bought the condo, I'd done it fast, because I'd needed a place to be, and I couldn't stay at Phil and Kai's forever with my belongings languishing in storage. Andrew and

I, being lawyers, knew exactly how to get around the legal issue of separation, signed affidavits that we had been living separate lives under the same roof, which unbeknownst to me, we had, and got the Chicago version of a quickie divorce the same week we sold our house. My broker luckily found out about the condo before it was listed, and I made a full-price cash offer. We closed within two weeks, and I moved in right away.

I purposefully attempted to make it a sacred, healing space. I decorated in shades of dove gray, silver, and ivory, with touches of robin's egg blue. I picked soft textures and natural elements: mohair on the down-filled sofa, chunky tables of waxed driftwood. I built on my collection of bird's nest–themed art, finding prints and small sculptures to scatter around, focusing on the symbolism. The work that goes into the creation of a simple and functional place of safety and comfort. The life-affirming message of making a nest. The life that might happen within.

I get off the couch and stretch, the warm light coming through the tall windows reflected in the wall of muted silver-leaf, a major splurge requiring two artisans to work for three days to painstakingly apply the six-by-six squares of delicate leaf and then burnish and seal the wall with a darkening agent, so that the whole thing glows like moonlight under a gossamer pewter veil.

I head to the kitchen, which had been the thing I fell in love with the first time I saw it, a bright space with stainless-steel appliances, treated concrete counters, white subway tiles on the walls and a subtle blue floor. It's a third the size of the kitchen in my former house, but economical use of space makes it a cozy place to work. Everything I need is within reach: my best knives on the counter, spices and herbs in a specially installed wall unit, pots and pans hanging overhead from a wrought-iron rack.

I need to shake off the morose thoughts, and nothing does that as well as testing new recipes. With Chicago in the throes of comfort-food cravings, I have been working diligently to find ways to create some healthier versions.

And today, what I need, what I want, is mashed potatoes.

CHOCOLATE CUPCAKES WITH VANILLA FROSTING

Pink and lavender, with a black plastic door, and one 60-watt lightbulb. I was the queen of the Easy-Bake Oven. And no different from a drug addict who buys in bulk and sells at a profit to feed his own habit, I sold my little cakes and cookies to my classmates at school to supplement the mixes my mom bought for me. I was the only eight-year-old I knew who had figured out exactly how to convert a large box of cake mix into the appropriate measurements to work with the limitations of my equipment. The only one who quickly abandoned the frosting mixes and learned how to make her own from scratch with confectioners' sugar and butter and flavorings. I had good experiments, adding walnuts and chocolate chips to batters, trying flaked almonds on top of caramel icing. And bad experiments; root beer–flavored cake with vanilla frosting does not, despite one's best intentions, ever taste like

a float. But chocolate cupcakes with vanilla frosting, those are always somehow exactly what one needs, and quickly became my go-to combination for every occasion. Through these experiments it became clear to me, and to my mom, that cooking was something I was instinctively good at, and brought me great pleasure. Beyond the eating, which had an element of uncontrollable necessity that never fully sated, the cooking was serene, calm, and soul satisfying.

"T-minus three minutes," Kai calls out from the front of the store.

"Okay!" I call back. We've been knocking out the basics all morning. . . . Asian chicken salad, fruit medley with mint, wheat berry pilaf with dried cherries and almonds. Kai roasted six chickens and a turkey breast, and grilled a whole flank steak, which he sliced thin across the grain. We have green beans in a spicy garlic marinade, braised black kale with smoked turkey, and roasted brussels sprouts. Our signature Morning Energy muffins, bursting with golden raisins and walnuts, sunflower seeds, millet, flax, and sweet with honey are cooling on a rack. We have thawed today's soup specials, which we cook over the weekends and freeze for the week, a golden butternut squash, smooth as velvet, and a chunky pasta fagioli, with whole wheat pasta, white beans, and loads of veggies.

While we will continue to cook throughout the day, adding new things to the case, and replenishing items as they sell, having this basic work finished is always a relief. Especially since Ashley called to say that her car locks were iced over, and she might not make it in at all today.

Kai bounces into the kitchen, his crazy hair spiked in all directions. He is a tiny man, shorter than my five-five by at least two inches, with delicate features. The almond eyes and straight jet-black hair are the only clue to his Japanese heritage. His skin is deep caramel and his lips have his African American father's fullness. He showed up last Halloween dressed as Tina Turner, and damned if he didn't pull it off. His legs are spectacular.

"Okay, the door, she is unlock-ed," he says dramatically. "The people, they are not lined up. But they come, I know that they come."

"I hope that they come, grasshopper. Or we will be eating chicken all week," I say, gesturing to the six glistening birds in the case.

"Better too many than too few," he says, shrugging. "After all, you'll just use the leftovers for chicken salad and wraps and stuff tomorrow."

"True enough. Did you and Phil have a good weekend?"

Kai stretches his lithe arms over his head, the sleeves of his spotless chef's coat sliding down around his elbows, revealing forearms riddled with the burns and scars that are the hallmark of our craft. "We did indeed. Had some of our friends over for dinner on Saturday night."

This is my favorite part of Tuesday morning, hearing what Kai cooked over the weekend. He is a fearless and inventive chef, and Phil is a serious foodie, so they entertain constantly.

"Tell me. Slowly," I beg him.

"Well, darling . . ." Kai purrs. "First, a little plate of nibbles. Gingersnaps with a chunk of Port Salut drizzled with white truffle honey and chopped chili, a recipe I absconded from Phil's friends Peter and David when we visited them in New York last year." I can feel the mix of sweet heat and creamy cheese on my tongue. "Then, little espresso cups with kari squash soup. Braised short ribs with a pomegranate bourbon glaze, your famous asparagus salad, smashed fingerling potatoes with mascarpone and lobster chunks and chervil, and vanilla panna cotta with mixed berries macerated in elderflower liqueur and chocolate tuiles."

"You bitch." I'm literally salivating.

"Don't be a hater. You never say yes when we invite you. So you don't get to eat the magical meal."

It's true that I have consistently declined almost all of Kai's invites. But not, as I have allowed him to believe, because I'm concerned about the decadence of the food. I know that even the most luscious meal can be balanced with a few days of healthy eating and a little extra exercise. I just can't bring myself to see how he and Phil interact, the powerful love between them, the way they look at each other. Living with them after the separation was so hard, even though they were beyond sensitive to my condition. Their friends are a lively group of fun and interesting folks, but I don't do well at parties. I love to listen to people, and forget to speak, and come off as either bored or aloof. I always end up hiding in the kitchen, and on more than one occasion have been mistaken for hired help. I've always been something of a social loner, preferring to gradually build trust with a small group of friends. I can put on social skills when I need them, at business events and meetings and such. I've been told I'm a dynamic teacher; get me started talking about how to cook something and I'm off to the races, but it's a façade, carefully adopted, and emotionally draining.

When Andrew and I were together, we preferred our own company to that of others. We both worked so hard and such long hours, what little time we had was spent cocooned together. We didn't really have a "group," rarely entertained, and mostly ended up either home alone, or as the last addition to someone's table at a fund-raiser. I have a couple friends from college, a couple from law school, only Kai from culinary school. Slowly I am getting friendly with customers, but so far those relationships are kept well within the walls of the store.

"Kai, you know one of your dinner parties would put me in a butter coma for a week." I laugh it off and pretend that it doesn't sting, that I don't wish I could just be free and easy with a group of boisterous strangers, hanging out and talking about nothing. That I could be in a room with two people who are deeply in love with each other and not think that there is potentially something sinister and damaged just beneath the surface. "Besides, I was here till nine thirty, and even I can't justify being that unfashionably late to a dinner party."

"You kill me, Slim."

Kai always calls me Skinny Minny, or Slim, or Little Bittle, among other nicknames. It is lovely and endearing, but still shocks me that he says it without irony. I'm still a fat girl on the inside.

The door opens, bringing with it the bitter chill air, and the tinny scent of impending snow. A tall, lithe woman in a long tweed coat flies in the door.

"Hey, Melanie, hey, Kai!" She huffs, rubbing her hands together and heading for the food cases.

"Not-so-plain-Jane in the house," Kai chirps.

"Hi, Janey, how's the yoga business?" Janey owns Stretch, a yoga and Pilates studio a block away, and has become not only a regular customer, but one of those almost-friends as well. She refers a lot of her clients to the store, and we have done a couple of joint events that have been very successful.

"Bendy. Very bendy. I'm going to need lunch and dinner today. One of my instructors called in sick, so I'm teaching double classes. I need some serious protein and whole-grain carb action."

I walk over to the case and help her select a balanced set of dishes to get her through her day, including half a chicken, much to Kai's smirking delight. As I ring her up, we chat about the weather and business. A couple of other customers wander in, and I mentally prepare for the lunch hour.

There are enough local small businesses that we do a decent lunch business from about eleven thirty to one thirty. And more and more people are also picking up things to either eat for dinner or to supplement whatever they are cooking at home. The day gets into a groove, people in and people out, the explanations of ingredients and health benefits, referrals to specialists. A mother whose son was diagnosed with celiac disease, a newly minted vegetarian worried about getting enough protein. And the inevitable defeated large woman searching for the next way to try to get control, praying for magic, with deep down surety of failure.

I try to be open and encouraging of everyone, but take special time with the big gals. I share my own story, recommend inspirational books, and give them the numbers for Carey or other nutritionists. I show them the framed fat picture I keep behind the counter to remind me where I have been. I look them deep in the eyes and tell them that they can do it. They usually leave with a stack of books and pamphlets, a sack full of food, and, at least I want to believe, a glimmer of hope in their hearts.

I'm happy to see them walk through the door, and also sad. Because only about 10 percent of them ever come back. Usually they check out the nutritionist websites, and see that it can be an expensive proposition. So they decide that they can do it on their own, just eating the food they have bought from me, and reading the books. They feel energized and motivated.

But motivation without support lasts about three days. Then the desire to celebrate kicks in, and once you are off the wagon for one meal, you inevitably decide to bail on the day. One day of decadence and the week seems shot, and the mental decision to "start again on Monday" seems almost logical. Knowing that Monday is coming means the rest of the week is a mindless binge. And now you are back where you were. And no matter how much I share that this was and is my struggle, no matter how much I say that I gained two pounds for every four I lost, up and down, two steps forward and three steps back, these women I try to bond with, they don't come back. As if I will judge them, or be disappointed in them. On the one hand, I'm thrilled that they come in. On average they double or even triple the spending of any other customer, but I write them off, even though I don't want to.

We usually have a lull around two, allowing Kai and me to take stock of what we think we will need to get through the day, clean up and prep, and get ready for the shift change, when I lose Kai's exuberant and slightly manic energy for Delia's comforting warmth and wry observations.

I always take the time to sit down and eat something, even though I'm rarely hungry then. But if I don't, I'll be randomly snacking, picking at the ends and scraps of things, not even realizing what I am doing. Carey once had me set up a video camera in the corner of the store for an afternoon and then watch and write down everything I ate. Nearly four hundred mindless calories, eked out in single bites and little nibbles—a half a piece of this and a quarter piece of that. I was astounded. Nearly 20 percent of what should be my ideal daily intake, without ever really tasting or enjoying the food. So now, I make a plate, balancing some protein, some whole-grain carbs, and some healthy fats so that I have a slow, steady burn of energy in the afternoon, and don't let hunger creep up on me.

I'm enjoying a piece of Kai's chicken and some of the wheat berry pilaf when Delia flies through the door, buoyed on a gust of wind. She pulls the bright red knit cap off her head, and shakes her braids Medusa-like.

"Children, it is colder than a witch's tit out there. Please tell me there is coffee in the pot."

I look at Kai, and he looks at me, and then we both look at Delia sheepishly.

"Good lord, I don't know what the hell I am going to do with you two!" she blusters, heading back to the kitchen, stripping off her parka and dumping it in the closet on her way past, muttering to herself. Neither Kai nor I drink coffee, both of us preferring tea. He never acquired a taste for it, and I can't drink it without remembering that Andrew used to make the coffee every morning, that we used to sit and have breakfast together and discuss our upcoming day, and that when he would kiss me goodbye—real lingering kisses, often with tongue, not the usual married morning peck most couples offer—he would taste of deep-roasted brew. My thirst for coffee seems to have disappeared from the moment I pitched that coffee cup at his head.

Since neither of us indulge, we only remember to put a pot on for Delia about every third day. Kai and I laugh, listening to her mumbling rant, which is still going in the kitchen. "I swear!" we hear, and Kai says, "I think that is my exit cue."

"Don't leave me with her," I beg in false fear. "Ashley isn't coming, I'll be all alone at her mercy."

"You should have thought of that and remembered to make the diva her coffee," he says, going to the closet and getting his coat, winding an endless blue scarf around his delicate neck. "I need to head over to Paulina Meat Market and pick up a hanger steak for dinner, Phil has been craving red meat lately."

"Say hi to the guys for me." I love the butchers at Paulina. They know their business, wouldn't dream of selling you something less than perfect, and can eyeball a ten-ounce New York strip like no one else. Plus they make all their own sausages, and like to slip me a salami stick with a wink when I leave. If I weren't so sure it would be the death of me, I'd be very tempted to marry one of them.

"Will do." Kai pulls on his gloves, and shouts back toward the kitchen. "Bye, Delicious!"

Delia pokes her head out and smiles at him. "Stay warm, baby boy."

He bows. "Have a good night, Mini Mel."

"See you tomorrow, Kai. Thanks for everything."

"You got it. And Melanie?"

"Yeah?"

"Next Sunday, come to dinner. I'll cook light and healthy, I promise. Just you and me and Phil, okay?"

I look at his earnest face, the effort he is making. "Okay. I'll come. Let me know what I can bring."

His grin lights the room. "Will do. We can talk menu tomorrow, you get final approval on everything!"

I laugh at him. "You are a kook. Go buy dinner for your man."

"Later!" he says, and bounces out the door.

"That boy gone yet?" Delia calls out.

"Yep," I call back.

Delia comes out of the kitchen, carrying a steaming cup, and sits beside me at the table. "I cannot handle that child without some caffeine, you hear me? Can-not-han-dle-him." She takes a deep swig, and I can't believe it doesn't scorch the inside of her mouth. Then again, I always assume with her history that she must have a very high tolerance for pain. She sighs delightedly. "Ahhh. So much better. How was the morning?"

"Good," I say around a mouthful of chicken. "Slow at first, but a pretty good lunch rush. But this quiet right now doesn't bode well." I look out the large front windows into the street, where there is already the sense of impending darkness. Minimal foot traffic. We are likely to be dead all afternoon. Which means I have to pray for a really big after-work rush from the people who get off the El a block away.

"Doesn't look like we need to do much back there, the case seems pretty stocked."

"Yeah, we should be fine. We can do some prep for tomorrow morning, but it should be quiet."

Delia takes another deep draught of her coffee. "Good. I can use a quiet afternoon. Those kids at the shelter are making me crazy. Christ, I never saw such a passel of devils in my life."

"Are there a lot of kids over there?" I never really thought much about it, but obviously if women run away from their husbands, they are going to take their kids with them.

"Oh, child, about twenty or so. And most of them hateful little monsters."

"Well, I have to assume, with what they have been through, what they have seen . . ." I'm at a loss to fully understand what the experience would do to anyone, let alone a child.

"Yes, well. That may be true. But that doesn't mean they don't get on my last nerve."

"You never wanted kids of your own, D?"

It is a casual question, but personal nonetheless, and we are only slowly finding our way to that kind of trust. She gets very still, and looks down at her hands. I almost take back the question, not wanting to offend her or make her uncomfortable, but then she starts to answer me.

"I had a beautiful baby boy. Walter. He died. We were at the park, and he got stung by a bee. He was really allergic, that ana-whatever-shock reaction. Just rolled his little eyes back and stopped breathing. By the time the ambulance came he was gone. Just two years old. I got pregnant again, but Deon got into one of his fits, and I lost the baby. Nothing ever took again. Probably better, wouldn't have wanted to put kids through what I been through."

There is tightness in my chest. I reach a hand out and take hers. It is callused and rough, the hand of someone who has known many hours of hard labor. I squeeze. She squeezes back.

"What about you, missy? Why didn't you and that no-good asshole you were married to have a munchkin or two your own selves?"

"There was no time, there was no urgency, no pressing need. And now I'm too old and there is no husband. I was never sure I really wanted them, and just let the time go by. Andrew and I were so driven to get to a certain place in our careers, and whenever we would talk about it, we would talk about how great our life was together, and not wanting to upset the balance. But I think on my end it was all a front for me not wanting to take on a pregnancy at that weight, and on his end a basic deep-rooted selfishness. By the time I got healthy enough to believe my body could handle it and produce healthy offspring, I was starting the business, and now Andrew is gone . . ." I drift off.

"And good riddance to bad rubbish, I always say! God has a purpose, honey. For both of us. If we were supposed to be mothers, we would be. And if we weren't meant to be mothers, it is because we need to be free for some other plan." I envy Delia's faith. Religion was never a major part of our lives. Dad was Jewish, Mom was Lutheran, neither practiced. As kids we did Chanukah and Passover with Dad's folks and Christmas and Easter with Mom's folks, and never did much of anything ourselves, and by the time I got to college, all four grandparents were gone, and we hadn't really taken much to any of their traditions, throwing our energy instead into secular holidays like Halloween and Thanksgiving. I try to put faith into the universe as a general practice, but I see the strength Delia has when she gets here Sunday afternoons straight from church. The way she really means it when she says she believes God has a purpose.

"So, what shall we do with this afternoon?" she says.

I think about my past and hers. The lives we are trying to reclaim.

"Why don't we work on cupcakes? Chocolate cupcakes with vanilla icing."

MACARONI AND CHEESE

The directions on the blue box were so easy. Boil the water, and salt it. Put in the pasta. Cook till the noodles are done. Drain. Put the butter in the still-hot pan and add the noodles back on top. A quarter cup of milk, the bright orange powder from the package, a vigorous stir, and into a bowl. Try to wait a few excruciating minutes, because the sauce thickens if you can stand to wait. Which I never could. Mom only rarely allowed it in the house, decrying it as entirely without nutritional value, and only buying it when there was going to be a babysitter for a special treat. But at sixty-eight cents a box at any convenience store or gas station, a young girl with even a modest allowance can afford to pick up a box on her way home from school. It was our secret, the macaroni-and-cheese afternoons. At least once a week Gillian and I would sit with our warm bowls in front of Tom and Jerry *cartoons and* Brady Bunch *reruns, then carefully wash the pot and bowls and spoons and put them away, laughing at how much fun it was.*

The letter was taped to my door when I got home. One sheet, on the condo association letterhead.

Dear Melanie,

As you are aware, several owners have complained about the heating situation this winter, prompting the association to hire a HVAC specialist to do a full inspection of the building. We have discovered that the problem is a combination of the age and size of our original equipment, insufficient insulation in the "G" and "H" units, and an improper venting situation in the building's systems. Since none of the units are in the hands of original owners, there is no legal recourse with the developer. We have, as the bylaws require, received three different estimates for the repairs, and have chosen a contractor to begin making the repairs on the first of next month. This work will require a special assessment of $15,000 per unit, which has been approved by the association. The assessment is due no later than March 5. Please make the check out to the association.

We will get in touch when the work is scheduled for your unit, no less than five business days before the workers are scheduled.

I know that this unexpected expense is an unfortunate thing, but I assure you that the money you will save in the

*long run on your heating costs, as well as the improved
equity in your unit, will make up for it. We understand
that not all of you may have the amount liquid at this
time, and we are happy to discuss the association making a loan to you for up to two-thirds of the assessment
amount, at a reasonable interest rate, with a twelve-
month repayment plan.*

*If you have any questions or concerns, please feel free
to contact me.*

*Kurt Jacobs, President
Ravenswood Manor Condo Association*

Fifteen thousand dollars. Due in three weeks. My arm is
shaking, and the letter drops from my hand. The store is net-
ting less than five hundred dollars a week after expenses. I have
just under twelve thousand dollars in my checking account,
the last of the divorce settlement after buying the condo. This
assessment will mean giving up a huge percentage of my liquid cash, and would also mean that a slow month at the store
would bankrupt what little I would have to reserve for protec-
tion in the blink of an eye. It also means that I'll have to get
the difference somewhere. Even at a low interest rate, it will
still be nearly a thousand unexpected dollars a month to pay
back the association if I decide to take their money. I have
some retirement savings, but between early withdrawal penal-
ties and the tax burden, not to mention the very real possibility that without them in my old age I would become a ward of
the state, I'd have to be close to living on the street before I'd
dream of tapping into them.

I collapse on my couch, feeling the tightness in my chest, the sting in my eyes. Just when I am feeling like maybe my life is going to be okay, life has other plans. I think about the thousands and thousands of dollars I spent on spa treatments and clothes and handbags and vacations at fifteen-hundred-dollar-a-night hotels. I think about the money that flew through my hands: fresh flowers all over the house every week, a full-time housekeeper, extravagant gifts to everyone in the office at the holidays. And stupid me, never fancy jewelry that you get to keep and has resale value, not antiques or art that you can auction off in tough times. Oh no, just massages and six-hundred-dollar-a-pair shoes, and fancy restaurant dinners with two-hundred-dollar bottles of wine. I own the store and this condo outright, same with my car. But in this economy, with my tiny profit margin and the crappy real estate market, I'm not qualified for much of an equity line on either property. I was too proud to take alimony from Andrew. I didn't want the constant reminder of him, even in check form.

"What would you like to do about maintenance payments, Melanie? The law is clear, you'd be entitled to a percentage of Andrew's income," Bill, the attorney handling our collaborative divorce, asks me.

I look across the table at Andrew, whose glare is steely. He clearly thinks I'm about to nail him to the wall. "I won't be needing maintenance."

Both Bill and Andrew look surprised. "Are you quite sure?" Bill says, in a voice that seems to imply he thinks I'm an idiot, especially now that there is such a marked discrepancy between my income and Andrew's. I love the feeling of surprising them both, of being strong and independent. "I'm absolutely sure." Andrew can keep his money to spend on Charlene. I'd rather have less and know it is mine.

I look around my sanctuary, which now has the taint of being flawed. Broken. Somehow, it makes me love it more, knowing that just under the surface things are amiss. Just like me.

I breathe deep, trying not to lose it. Trying to stem the anger that is building. I get up and start to pace around, rudderless and suddenly starving. Fuck it. Fuck it all.

I call Philly's Best and order a large cheesesteak sandwich, extra meat and extra cheese, a side of garlic bread, and an order of onion rings. By the time I take my shower, getting the day's grime off me while sobbing into the steaming sting of the water, and get into my sweats, the doorbell is ringing.

Soft, chewy buttery bread, steaming seasoned meat, gooey cheese, crispy, salty onion rings. I eat standing at the kitchen counter, barely pausing between bites. In less than fifteen minutes there are only crumbs left. This is always the point when I sort of wake up, when the self-loathing kicks in. The anticipation of the food, gloriously bad for me, high in fat, calories, sodium, and guilt. The first bite the only one that fully registers.

If picking up the phone to call for food is the easiest call to make, the next one is the hardest.

"Hello?"

"Carey. It's Melanie."

"Eleven thirty your time, so are we attempting to prevent

the binge or are we seeking absolution for the binge?" There is no accusation in this, just a genuine interest in my status.

"Bless me, sister, for I have sinned. I have had wanton congress with a Philadelphia cheesesteak and a bushel of onion rings."

"Wow, Philly's Best binge. That is serious. What happened?" Carey knows all my binges. She knows that if I have PMS I turn to chocolate and if I'm horny I turn to carbs. She knows that if I'm lonely for family or friendships I bake, and that if I'm stressed about the business I make rice pudding or crème caramel. And she knows that if the whole world explodes, I turn to the one place that not only delivers till midnight, but takes me back to my undergrad days at UPenn, when I gained the freshman forty while making straight A's and sleeping with an endless series of slightly malnourished geeky grad students.

"Just found out that my condo is doing a special assessment of fifteen thousand dollars, due in three little weeks, to cover some necessary building repairs. This after I got home from the store, where I had to tell Ashley, the extern, that I couldn't give her much of a recommendation, based on her performance, which made her cry. For three hours. Sniffling and wheezing all over the kitchen till I finally just sent her home. All I wanted was a hot bath, a glass of wine, a decent meal, and some *Without a Trace* reruns on TiVo. And instead there is a note taped to my door telling me that I'm about to be even more completely broke than I currently am, and before I knew it . . ."

"Cheesesteak and onion rings," she says.

"And garlic bread," I admit.

"And how did it feel? Eating all that?"

"I didn't feel much of anything. I mean, it tasted amazing for a couple of bites, and then blind mechanics until it was just gone."

"And now?"

"And now I am overstuffed, bloating, retaining water as we speak, and relieved to be living alone, because not only was no one here to witness a truly disgusting spectacle, but the attack of toxic Philly farts that is going to hit in about fifteen minutes is going to make even me wish I didn't live with me."

Carey laughs. And I laugh at the enormity of my own ridiculousness.

"Honey, I can't speak to how your colon is going to react to what you ate, but how long do we have to work on you forgiving yourself when you have a difficult meal?"

"I know, I know. I should have put it on my good china and lit a candle and savored every mouthful, stopped when I started to feel full, and then moved the hell on. Damn you, Philly's Best!"

"See, you know what you should do. Food isn't the enemy, Mel. Philly's Best isn't the enemy. There is no such thing as a bad food, just an inappropriate amount of food. There is nothing you can't eat, if you eat it in moderation. And you know that better than anyone in the world. You know you can always call me when you want to talk, but don't feel like you have to call me to confess your sins, because there is no sin in eating. Ever. And the more you fill your life with primary food, the more love and laughter and good work you have, the less you will need the other food. But when life throws you a curve, like it clearly did today, and you don't have time or energy to go to a museum or watch your favorite movie, or go on a date, then eat what you want, just eat it purposefully and with joy."

"Thanks, Carey. I needed to hear it for the millionth time."

"It's what I'm here for."

"I'll talk to you at our usual time on Thursday."

"Unless you need me before then . . ."

"I'll be okay. Have a good night."

"Good night, sweetie. I'm proud of you."

My stomach gurgles menacingly as I hang up the phone. I go to the computer and check my e-mail. There is a note from Gillian.

Hey, Mel.

Been crazy with work, but it is paying off. They made me a partner! Of course it is going to mean more travel and responsibility, so I'll have to postpone my visit this spring. Maybe I'll be able to get there in the fall. I know you understand, especially since I was just there a couple months ago.

Hope the store is good, got to run!

Cheers,
G

Gilly. I'm so proud of her. And so disappointed that she isn't coming to visit. She keeps offering to fly me in to visit her in London, but I'm too mortified at not being able to afford the trip myself, and too scared to leave the store for any length of time. We were never as close when she got older as we were when we had our secret mac-and-cheese club. In high school she got popular, and I got fatter. I went away for college, and when I came back for law school, we barely knew each other. Her consistent dislike of Andrew solidified the distance between us for a long time, and we only really reconnected when Mom got sick, getting to know each other again and finding reasons to bond. By the time Mom died, things were pretty good between us, but she and Andrew never really got along, so we kept our tentative newfound relationship to lunches or Sunday brunches. When she got transferred to London, we began communicating almost entirely through e-mail. When Andrew and I split, she flew in to help me move, which was probably the nicest thing she ever did for me. Our first night in my new condo, surrounded by the disaster of my circumstances, she made a family-size box of macaroni and cheese, and we ate it sitting on the floor, in the middle of my messy life.

Gilly—

Honey, I'm so proud of you! I know how hard you've worked for that partnership, and I know that you deserve it. I totally understand about the visit, and while I'm of course disappointed, I'm behind you. Go get 'em! Come when you can, I miss you, kiddo. When you get a chance, give me a call to tell me all the details. I want to hear all about it. And everything else. Things here are fine, the store is doing pretty well, and my

place is finally feeling like home. You won't recognize it when
you come! If I wasn't such an idiot I would send you pics but I
haven't figured out how to get them out of my new digital camera and into my computer yet. ☺

Love you, hope to talk to you soon.
Mel

I get out my notebook and begin planning tomorrow.
Because no matter what happens, whether we are ready for it
or not, there is always tomorrow.

MEAT LOAF

My paternal grandmother was an indifferent cook. Not bad, the food tasted good and was nutritious, but was prepared with little joy, and there was no passion in the experience for her. She cooked because it was her responsibility to do so, because people needed feeding. She had a repertoire of exactly seven regular meals—one for every day of the week—one fancy meal for special occasions, and the basic holiday staples. Thursday night was meat loaf night, and the night Gilly and I spent with her and my grandfather to give my mom a night off. Even though she didn't love to cook, and wasn't enormously creative when she did, she did make an effort on those nights, altering the meat loaf week to week to surprise us. Sometimes with hard-boiled eggs or a hot dog hidden in the middle, a little circular bit of excitement in the center of each slice. Sometimes with a glaze of ketchup and

Worcestershire sauce, or a crisp crust of Dijon and bread crumbs. The rest of the meal never changed: green peas with pearl onions, steamed white rice with a pat of butter melting on top, soft knot rolls, and for dessert, chocolate pudding, with the skin for me, without for Gilly. But the ever-changing meat loaf was her way of trying to amuse us, to delight us.

I just sat down for the littlest second. It had been such a long morning. Near-blizzard conditions had kept Kai from coming in, so I was prepping and cooking everything on my own. I had barely slept last night, obsessing about the assessment, which is due in six days, and about whether the association is going to approve my loan. I put the turkey meat loaf in the oven, unlock the door for any customer who might brave the weather, and sit at the little table in the window just for a second. But my eyes close and don't open until the smoke alarm in the kitchen starts beeping. I leap up, and run to save the meat loaf from a fiery grave. It is too late. I dump it in the garbage, thinking about the lost income it represents, and as I am distracted, catch my inner arm with a corner of the hot sheet pan, burning myself.

It is the last straw.

I throw the pan onto the counter and run my arm under the cold water. The burn won't be that bad. The pain barely registers. But I can feel everything welling up inside me. The sobs choke out of me, the tears hot on my cheeks, every sorrow in the world seeming to be mine.

"Um, hello? Are you all right?"

I wipe my face quickly and poke my head out of the kitchen.

Standing at the counter is a young woman, wrapped in what appears to be fourteen different scarves, the angular brows above her bright green eyes furrowed in concern.

"Sorry," I choke out. "How may I help you?"

The girl starts to unwind the first scarf, revealing sharp cheekbones, a generous mouth, calico blonde hair with random pieces of pink. The unwinding continues, and I realize that what had seemed to be several scarves of different colors and textures is actually just one monstrously long scarf, cobbled together in a series of mismatched yarns and patterns, as if someone took one-foot segments of a bunch of different scarves and sewed them together. For some reason it tickles me, this ridiculous accessory, and I begin to laugh. The girl tilts her head at me.

"I'm so sorry," I gasp. "You must think I am insane. Or bipolar or something. You'll have to forgive me; it's been a long morning."

"That's okay. I laugh and cry all the time, sometimes at the same time. Are you all right?"

"I'm fine. I just ruined something in the kitchen and burned myself, which is why I was crying, and then, well, your scarf is so, um . . ."

"Insane?" She chuckles. "I know. I wanted to learn how to knit, but I don't have much patience, so when I wanted to figure out different patterns and stuff I just started right away. And it just kept growing. Like a weird fungus. But in this weather, it is really useful."

"It's very fun," I offer.

"It's manic," she says. "But I'm glad it amuses you. You should have it." She finishes unwinding the thing, and gathers it into a bundle, trying to hand it to me.

"I couldn't," I say, not wanting to be rude, but wondering what the hell I would do with such a thing. It appears to be about twenty feet long!

"Please," she insists. "I know it's silly, but it is a sort of happy piece of something. I don't ever feel blue when I wear it. It would make me very honored if you would take it."

I don't know what else to do, so I accept the pile she is handing me, still warm from her body and breath. "Thank you."

"I'm Nadia," she says.

"Melanie."

"I'm a friend of Janey's, I'm crashing at her place for a bit, and she is feeling a cold coming on and wanted to have some of your famous soup on hand."

I take a deep breath, the powerful emotions I have been through this morning not quite dissipating, but at least moving into a further recess of my brain. I can feel my shoulders unclench. "I'm so sorry to hear Janey is coming down with something. I have just the thing." I move around behind the counter. I fill one container with hearty vegetable soup, and another with a Japanese-style broth, bok choy, scallions, and udon noodles. I pack up a roasted chicken breast, and some plain steamed brown rice. Some orange slices in honey vinegar with mint. A couple of corn muffins. I put everything together in a bag, and hand it over to Nadia.

"Wow. A feast. What do I owe you?"

"On the house. Janey brings me a lot of business; just tell her to rest up so that hopefully it won't be too bad."

"That is very generous."

She hesitates, and I do something completely out of character. "Would you like some tea? Maybe a muffin?" I blurt out in a rush, nervous and self-conscious.

She smiles, her wide mouth revealing slightly crooked eye-teeth. "That sounds great."

"Great."

I reach for a teapot, and wonder why I want her to stay.

I'm an idiot.

I can't imagine what I was thinking.

I pick up the phone, and then put it down.

I get into bed, and then get out again.

I wander up the hall and look into the second bedroom, currently serving as a storage room for the boxes I still haven't unpacked, all the things from my former life I keep meaning to sell or give away, my fat clothes and designer bags and fancy shoes.

I had sat with Nadia for nearly two hours as the storm outside boiled. I offered up my life toils, the weight struggles, the demise of my marriage, the tenuous nature of the retail food business. She dropped in tiny snippets here and there. She was bulimic as a teenager, but hasn't purged in years. She has notoriously bad taste in men, and came to Chicago from Minneapolis with the latest, a musician who dumped her three weeks after arriving, hence her time on Janey's couch. She has a very minor income from a trust left to her by a grandmother, but not quite enough to fully support her. She needs a job, an apartment, a way to get back on her feet.

The offer came out of me unbidden.

"What if you worked here, and rented my extra bedroom?"

"What?" Nadia asked around a mouthful of muffin, a few crumbs dropping onto the front of her ratty Mexican sweater.

I speak in a rush. "I have some temporary financial difficulties, and you need a temporary home. I have a two-bedroom, two-bathroom apartment, and I'm only one person. I'll rent you my extra room for five hundred dollars a month plus half of the utilities. And I'll give you a part-time job here in the store, twenty hours a week, minimum wage. The rent you can pay from your trust, and utilities would come directly out of your paycheck, then you keep the rest. And I'll keep the hours somewhat flexible so that if you want to get another part-time job somewhere else, we can work around it."

Her face lights up. "Really?"

I take a slow breath. Renting the room would help get me over the hump, give me some breathing room. Ashley had left, and because of her indifferent work, I had requested a semester off from participation in the extern program, so I was short a part-time minimum-wage helper. Nadia could use the job and housing to get on her feet and learn the city, and help me out in the process.

"Really."

"I'll take it!" She jumps up from her seat and throws her wiry little body into my lap in a half-hug, half-maul. I am both comforted by her genuine affectionate gratitude and completely thrown by my own un-me-like behavior. She removes her minimal weight from my lap, and sheepishly returns to her chair. "I mean," she says, as if her Flying Wallenda act hadn't happened, "I am very grateful for the opportunity and would love to work here and rent your room." She grins and holds up her teacup for a toast. "To new friends and roomies!" I touch my cup to hers and feel my stomach twist itself into a pretzel.

"Cheers."

I'm almost forty years old. I haven't lived with anyone except Andrew since college. Nadia is twenty-four. I could practically be her mother, or at least her aunt. She is quirky and odd and has no background in food besides the eating disorder she conquered. We have nothing in common.

But she is going to move into my home, into my business.

It is the craziest thing I have ever done, and I'm regretting it with every fiber of my being. I don't want to come home to some twentysomething and her boy problems. I don't want to have to be someone's boss and roommate at the same time. I don't want to be in a life where it would even occur to me to make such an offer.

And strangely, I'm scared to death that Nadia is regretting saying yes. That she is over at Janey's in a cold sweat wondering how long she will be able to stand inhabiting the guest bedroom of some emotional premenopausal divorcee.

We must both be crazy.

But yet, there is also something exhilarating about having reached out to her. To be fighting my own urges to be alone, and forcing myself to do something against my nature.

I turn off the light in the room, and head back to bed. And blissfully, sleep comes.

PANCAKES

Andrew was never a great cook. When it came to meals, he had four go-to dishes. The famous late-night carbonara, a treat whipped up in the burst of energy he always got after sex. In a gender cliché turnaround, I was usually the one practically in a coma after sex. He would kiss my forehead, bounce out of bed, effortless in his body, and come back with an apron around his slim waist, and a bowl with two forks. He was a whiz at cheeseburgers, having essentially lived on them in college. He made a reasonably decent black bean soup picked up from the Ecuadorian nanny who raised him, a little fiery for my more delicate palate, but well-balanced and filling. And pancakes. Andrew made the best pancakes I have ever tasted. Lazy Sunday mornings in bed with the New York Times Magazine *crossword puzzle, light-as-air pancakes doused in butter and swimming in syrup,*

with crispy bacon on the side. Crisp around the edges, tender within, warm stacks of sweet heaven. I may miss the comfort and security of being married, however false it turned out to be, but I almost never miss Andrew himself, just the idea of him. Except on Sunday mornings. When I wonder if there will ever be pancakes, both real and metaphorical, again.

"So, Bitsy, tomorrow is the big day, yes?" Kai says, tossing a pinch of salt into the pot he is stirring and tasting the result.

"Yep. Nadia's moving in." We agreed to have her work for a week at the store to be sure that part of the arrangement would work for us both before having her move in, and while she doesn't have the kind of inherent knowledge about food that Kai and I do, she is warm and kind with the customers, quick to refer questions to me, and I think that she and Delia have bonded in a surprising way. She's an odd duck, and doesn't talk much except to elicit information about you in such a way that after an hour you feel as if you have had this great talk with her, except you realize you don't know any more about her than you did before.

"She's a strange little kitten, but I like her. And I think it's good for you to have a pet."

"She's not a pet, Kai. That's a terrible thing to say!"

"I mean it in only the best sense of the word *pet*, something warm and furry to come home to, something to be a little bit responsible for, something that will remind you not to get too into yourself."

"Is that the patented Kai-finition of pet?"

"Oh, yes indeed. And a much better description than some

creature of lesser intellect and power that you own by control-
ling food and cleaning up poop."

I laugh. "Well, when you put it like that!"

"I do, that is exactly how I put it."

"It's not terribly gay of you, you know. Shouldn't you and
Phil be adopting pugs and Siamese cats and writing them into
your will?"

"Phil is allergic to both dogs and cats, also to walking
around with plastic bags full of crap in one's hand or having a
sandbox full of crap in one's house, and especially allergic to
hair on the Montauk sofa."

"Good to know. I'll try not to shed the next time I'm
over."

"See that you do. Meantime, how are you doing with the
whole Nadia thing? Really."

I think, wanting to word it carefully. "I think I'm fine.
It's unexpected. But not entirely unwelcome. I do think you
are right about the having something warm to come home to
part. I can get too reclusive and this will help. Also, it's very
temporary, so that helps."

"You know that if things are that tight, Phil and I could
make you a loan . . ."

"Kai, don't even finish that sentence. I love you, and I love
Phil, and it's a generous offer that in a million years I could
never take you up on. And I'm not letting her move in because
I'm on the brink of financial disaster." I try to say this lightly,
as if it were true. "I'm letting her move in because it will give
me just a bit of breathing room money-wise in the remaining
slow winter weeks, and because I like her and want to help
her out."

"Glad to know. So tomorrow morning she's moving in; how about tomorrow night Phil and I bring dinner by, just for a short visit? That way if she arrives with a sack of severed heads, or shows up wearing your haircut and a matching outfit, we can save you like the big strong queens we are."

"Well, I guess that depends on what you are thinking of bringing for dinner!"

"How about we pick up Homemade Pizza Co.? We'll get one with the whole-wheat crust and loads of veggies and light on the cheese for you, and one with eight kinds of meat for the rest of us."

"Six o'clock?"

"We'll be there."

"You're the best. Can you hold down the fort till Delia gets here? I want to go to the gym since I probably won't get to work out tomorrow with all the bustle, and I overslept today."

"You got it. Go sweat."

I grab my coat and head out. I keep a packed gym bag in my car at all times. As much as I know that it has saved my life, as much as I appreciate what my body can do now that I have lost the weight and exercise is a regular part of my life, I still hate working out. I go to the gym five or six days a week, where I alternate between either forty-five minutes of cardio or forty-five of weight lifting. And I dread it every time, and check my watch a million times and am always glad when it's over. I love to take a long walk, or do something active, but going to the gym and exercising are still the most hateful hours of my week. All those people who always told me that you get addicted to it, that endorphins kick in, that eventually you crave it and look forward to it are sick lying fucks and I want to choke them with a protein bar and pummel them about the head with a bottle of SmartWater.

I pull into the parking lot of my gym, and am immediately irritated that the only parking spaces are at the opposite end from the entrance. Because lord knows that just because I'm about to work out for forty minutes doesn't mean I want to walk an extra fifty steps if I don't have to.

I grab my gym bag out of the trunk and take a deep breath. In less than an hour it will be over and I won't have to come back till the day after tomorrow. Bolstered by the thought of not having to exercise tomorrow puts a little pep in my step and I head in to get it over with.

"I think that is the last of it," Nadia says, dropping a large floral suitcase on the floor and collapsing on top of it.

I laugh. "The last of what? Two garbage bags, two suit-cases, a backpack and a sleeping bag? Not exactly a lot of stuff." Nadia was able to move out of Janey's and into my apartment in one trip in her battered ancient orange Saab, and three trips up the stairs. I take out more garbage in a week than the entire scope of her worldly possessions. I think she is grateful that my spare room was already fitted with a pull-out couch, or I imagine she would have been sleeping on the floor.

"I travel light. Never know when you have to pick up and go!" There is false bravado in her voice, and her eyes are dark.

"Barry kept the apartment and all your stuff?"

She smiles a winsome smile, the crooked teeth endearing. "Every pot, pan, dish, and curtain. The towels, the sheets, the lamps, and rugs. I got out with my clothes, and not much else, certainly not my furniture or my dignity."

Nadia is otherworldly in many ways. She speaks in snippets of poetry, and is at once very childlike and very old. Her hands are always busy, fidgeting in her long, wavy strawberry-blond hair, streaked with pink. Her green eyes tend to dart around when she speaks, but lock on yours with deep intensity when you speak to her. She touches a lot, a hand on your shoulder as she passes by, an arm slipped through yours when you walk. I'm getting better at not flinching when she does this.

She is like no one I've ever known, and even though she has been working at the store for a week, and has just moved into my home, I'm keenly aware of not knowing her, not being fully comfortable with her, and yet, feeling somehow better when she is around, which instead of being a comfort, worries me. The last time I felt generically better in someone's company was with Andrew, and that sense was so misplaced, that security so false, I'm now fairly certain that I'm somehow the worst barometer of human trustworthiness in the universe. I was the stupid wife offering to bring snacks to the office when he was "pulling an all-nighter with the associates" for some big case, never even suspecting that he declined my generosity because he wasn't really at the office, but instead was sleeping around. I thought he was dedicated. Turns out, he was, but not to work, and certainly not to me.

Nadia heads to the small second bathroom, and I can hear her pee, a very strange and intimate sound that startles me.

I'd forgotten what it was to have another person around, not just superficially, but deeply embedded, intimate. I hear the flush, and for some reason it embarrasses me, this awareness of her personal activity. I turn on the TV just to have some background noise.

When she comes back into the room, she is wiping wet hands on her battered cargo pants. This odd little stranger in my life.

"Mel, this place is amazing. It is the nicest place I have ever lived. I can't believe there is a real tub in there! When I was growing up, I only had this little weird corner tub that was too small for soaking, and all the places I've lived since then have either had shower stalls, or tubs so disgusting you would never want to sit in them!"

I laugh at this outpouring of tub-love. "Well, I'm glad that I can provide a good tub."

"Not a GOOD tub, Mellifluous, a MAJOR tub."

The endearment grates the tiniest bit. I think being around Kai with his little nicknames is maybe rubbing off, but there is something about when Nadia does it that sits strange for me. I shrug it off. "Sorry, I'm glad I can provide a MAJOR tub."

"If you ever wonder where I am, I can tell you right now . . . I am going to LIVE in that tub. I'm going to get in today and not get out till Sunday morning!"

"Let me help get all this stuff into your room," I offer. Nadia raises a hand to stop me from getting off the couch, and then gestures for me to sit back down.

"Do not move. Sit right there. I'm going to make us some tea." She glides into the kitchen and fills the electric kettle. I look at the pile of stuff in my living room. My clean, simple, spare living room. Nadia is babbling about some customer at the store she was talking to yesterday, but I can't focus. Why would she just dump all the stuff here and not move it down the hall to her room? What would it take, two trips? And with my offer to help, it would have been thirty seconds! What is the immediate need for tea? I love tea, but I get tea when everything is done, reward and relaxation at the completion of a task. What is the point of relaxing when you are in the middle of something? It won't actually be restful.

"Honey? Lemon? Agave nectar?" Nadia rouses me from my inner struggle with my more anal tendencies.

"Splash of milk, thanks," is all I can spit out.

I take a deep breath, find rationality. She isn't planning on leaving her stuff in the middle of the room forever. We will have a cup of tea and then she will move her stuff, and the earth will not stop turning and nothing will be amiss and my living room will still be my living room. Except it also sort of has to be her living room. And her mess, her mess in my home, is reminding me of my mess, the mess that is me, and that is troubling on a much deeper level.

"Here you go." She hands me a steaming mug. The tea is fragrant, and the warmth from the cup generates a heat that spreads through my whole body. I take a cautious sip, and look at my new roommate. "So," she says, "how much are you regretting ever letting me set foot in here?"

I choke slightly on my tea. "I don't . . . I mean . . . I wouldn't . . . You're . . . You know . . ."

Nadia laughs, a much deeper, more knowing guttural laugh than you would expect from someone so elfin. "C'mon. If we're going to be living together, even for just a time, we're

going to have to address the elephant in the room." She waves
her arm around and then points down at her own head. "You
wouldn't have me here if it weren't for a desperate situation or
at least something minorly desperate, and I wouldn't be here
without my own desperation. We are strangers relying on the
kindness of other strangers. We are sitting in a pile of broken
glass from the break-in-case-of-an-emergency box. You don't
want me here, and I don't want to be here. Not because of us, I
mean, not because we are bad people or don't like each other,
but because we don't want to be in the situations that make
us have to be here together. You're afraid that I will mess the
place up . . ." She gestures to the pile that is plaguing me.
"And I'm afraid that I'll break something or ruin something
or let you down. You're afraid that you might have to both fire
and evict me, and I'm afraid that I might just do something
that would give you ample cause for one or both. So I figure,
let's talk about the stuff we are both really scared of, and get
it out in the open, and then if we fuck it up, at least we'll
know what we're fucking up and why. You know. If you're up
for that . . ." She lets the thought trail off, and takes a deep
draught of her tea.

And I start to laugh. Really laugh, like I haven't laughed
since I don't know when, tears rolling down my cheeks. "Oh
my god!" I say, wiping the wet from my face and trying to get
my breath back. "I am so fucking freaked out!"

"I KNOW!" she yelps.

"You're twenty-four! I have wooden spoons older than
you!"

"You are going to hate all my music and not want to watch
any of my shows!"

"I'm going to need to take care of you, and I can barely take care of myself."

"You're going to try and mother me."

"You're going to mess up my apartment, and I need it to be my safe place."

"I'm always going to feel like I am walking on eggshells and am going to have to hide in my room all the time."

"You're going to bring boys home without any consideration about how that will affect me."

"You're going to never bring anyone home because you're embarrassed that I'm here."

"You're going to hate me."

"You're going to hate me."

This last sentiment is expressed almost simultaneously, and we stare at each other. And then she smiles. And somehow, even though I know it will be weird and probably uncomfortable at times, I also know it will be okay. At least, I want to believe that I know this.

"We'll be okay," she says.

"Yeah."

"I'll take my stuff to my room."

I think about it. "Leave it for now, I'm starving. How do you feel about pancakes?"

"Love them."

"Perfect."

RISOTTO

I hate those books where the heroine faces loss and despera-
tion with a total lack of appetite. Because when my husband
announced that he was leaving me for my former friend,
when he admitted, with not nearly enough regret in his voice,
that he had been sleeping with her for nearly two years while
I toiled at the gym in an effort to save my own life after full
days of school and finally opening the store . . . all I wanted
was food. The binge was epic. Five pounds in ten days, junk
food and takeout, anything fried or salty or sweet that I could
get my hands on. On the eleventh night of my abandonment,
sitting in my huge living room surrounded by Andrew's art
collection, I broke down. I sobbed until my sides ached and
my cheeks were chapped. And when I was spent, I took a
long hot shower, and then went to the kitchen to cook for
myself. I focused on deep, slow breaths as I chopped an onion

and grated Parmesan. I heated the chicken stock, and stirred the rice, and watched as the grains that were separate and distinct joined together, bonded, became a unified whole. I was undone, unconnected, but at least dinner came together. I stirred in the cheese, some parsley, some lemon zest. I ate it all, cradling the warm bowl to my bosom like a life preserver.

"I'd like to propose a toast." I'm trying to gather my thoughts as I look down at my champagne flute. "When I first found out that I had to lose weight for my health, I was terrified. Not that I couldn't do it. I knew that I could and would. But I was afraid I would never eat another decent meal again!"

The assembled group laughs. I look around the room. Kai and Phil are standing, Kai nestled in the crook of Phil's arm in the most natural and loving pose. Delia is sitting at a table with Benny, her favorite customer, an enormous wall of a woman with skin the exact color of chocolate pudding. Benny comes in at least once a week to tell us that she has lost a half a pound, and then buys half the display case. She is always smiling, always has a funny story about her boyfriend, Andre, a slight, light-skinned man, who sometimes stops in to pick up something to surprise her with. Nadia and Janey are sitting at the other table with Carey, who flew in for the occasion, and about ten other people are scattered around.

I take a deep breath and continue. "The idea for this store was a lifeline for me. I knew that I had to eat healthy to continue to live, but I also knew that food still had to be a delight for me if I wanted any life in that living. When I bemoaned the lack of a place like this to Carey"—I raise my glass at her and she smiles and raises hers back at me—"she told me if there wasn't a place that was the right place, I should make one. And so I did. But I could never have done it without you. One year ago today, on a blustery March morning with a blizzard on the horizon, I walked through those doors for the first time, and I knew that this was the right space. Six months later, Dining by Design was open for business. Kai was here with me"—I tilt my glass at him and he makes a small bow—"and he brought a bottle of champagne and a bottle of bourbon, figuring that we would either be celebrating or commiserating at the end of the day. Janey was the first one to come in the door." I smile over at her and she grins back. "And she was literally jumping up and down at what we had to offer and promised to send all her clients, and came back again at the end of the day and helped us drink that bottle of champagne. We have had plenty of days when we broke out that bottle of bourbon, but more days have been champagne days, and I'm so grateful to all of you for that. We may not be getting rich, but in a tough economy, and at a tough time of the year, we have made it through the first six months. I know most people would wait for the one-year anniversary of the opening day, but for me this dream began the first time I set foot in this room. Tonight isn't just an anniversary for the store, it is in many ways my birthday. Because the day I committed to open this store is the day I was completely reborn. And I couldn't have had a more wonderful group of people to spend this past year with, and I hope that you will all be here for next year's celebration, and the tenth year, and the twentieth! Cheers!"

Everyone toasts, clinks glasses, and the hum of conversation starts up again. I'm surrounded by good people, people who love me, and who stand by me. These are good friends, family by choice, and their warmth and happiness buoy me.

"I'm so proud of you, girl!" Carey comes over and gives me a hug.

"I can't believe you came in for this. You are so sneaky!"

"I wasn't going to miss this, I haven't been back to Chicago to visit in ages, and I've been dying to see the place. You did such an amazing job on it, Mel, truly. You should be very happy."

"I am, you know, I really am." Which is true. I thought it might be weird to celebrate the store. It was only six weeks after the grand opening that Andrew left me, and it was the madness of the six months of work to get the place ready that was the time my marriage fell apart without my even noticing. Andrew had been blindly supportive of my decision to buy the space, had given me carte blanche with the home equity line and the savings account to get it finished, and insisted that his name not appear anywhere, claiming at the time that it was because he wanted the store to really be my baby.

Strangely, I'm not at all resentful of the store. I don't blame it, even though I know now that the reason Andrew's good buddy Jeff told him to keep everything in my name was because he knew that Andrew was sleeping with Charlene, and that if he left me, half ownership of the store could have made him liable for half of the store's expenses or debts in a divorce settlement. That the only reason he was so supportive of my buying a fixer-upper and spending endless hours on-site stripping floors and restoring the tin ceiling and supervising installation was that it kept me distracted and exhausted, the perfect combo for a guy who was stepping out on his clueless wife. It would have been so easy to place all the blame, at least for my cluelessness, if not for the ruination of my marriage, on this place and the time I invested here. But I'm proud of what I have accomplished, proud that we are here, and hopeful for the future.

"Hey, Skinny, should we get the rest of the food out?" Kai comes over and places a delicate hand on my shoulder.

"You go," Carey says. "We'll hang later."

Kai and I head back into the kitchen, where the platters and trays are set up. Grilled vegetable skewers with a lemon dressing. Beef tenderloin, roasted medium rare, sliced thin, with a grainy mustard sauce. Orzo salad with spinach, red onion, and feta. Dilled cucumbers and pickled carrots. White beans with sage. Saffron risotto with artichokes and chicken. Mini pavlovas and poached pears and poppy-seed cookies.

"It's a great party, Mellie Mel," Kai says, sprinkling chopped parsley on anything that he can reach.

"I really couldn't have done any of this without you, Kai, you know that. I have no words to properly thank you."

"I'll tell you a secret, Melanie. You saved my life. I owe you, not the other way around. I was a silly little twink at the Cooking and Hospitality Institute of Chicago, was only there because I couldn't get into a decent college, and at least had some skills from hanging out at my grandmother's restaurant as a kid. And then my folks disowned me when I came out first quarter. I was living with Phil, who hadn't anticipated that the boy toy he picked up at Sidetrack would show up with a suitcase two months into the relationship. I knew I didn't just want to be a little housewife. I was so scared and defensive, but you looked at me like I was something, like I was a force to be reckoned with, and you made me see that part of myself. You were so good that you made me want to be even better than you so that you would still look at me like that. When we graduated, I was stuck. Phil and I were so great, and had fallen into a nice routine that neither of us wanted to let go of, but the only places that had the fine dining sensibility I like all wanted someone full-time, a million hours a week and home at two in the morning. This job is everything I want, and the fact that I get to do it with one of my best friends is a daily gift. Don't ever forget that."

The tears swim in my eyes as I look at this young man, young enough almost to be my son, and I see the respect and love in his face.

"Don't streak your mascara!" he yelps, throwing me a side towel.

"I love you, Kai. Always."

"I love you too, Ittie Bittie. Let's feed the people."

We take the platters out to the crowd, setting up the buffet, milling around, refilling glasses and accepting compliments and well wishes. People wander in and out, the platters slowly emptying, the glasses filling the wash sink. Before I know it, most of the guests have straggled out, and I am sitting with Kai, Phil, Delia, and Nadia, surrounded by the detritus of a good party.

Kai goes into the back and gets a bottle of Krug he and Phil brought, and pops it open. He fills our glasses.

"A great party!" Phil says.

"A great year!" Kai adds.

"Cheers to that," Delia pipes in.

"To new friends," Nadia offers.

"To lots of life in our living." I raise my glass and clink around the table. We all drink, savoring the light sparkle on our tongues, and I completely understand what that famous monk said upon drinking his first-ever glass of champagne, "I'm drinking stars!"

"Nadia, will you escort our fearless leader home?" Kai says. "Our gift to you, we are cleaning up!"

"No way." I shake my head. "This place is a wreck, I can't let you do that!"

Phil laughs, running a hand through his short dark hair. "Way!" he says. "You go home and relax, and let the three of us take care of it. We want to. Besides, with this whirling dervish at home wreaking havoc in the kitchen, I've become a really good dishwasher."

I was so prepared to hate Phil, way back when. I was so protective of Kai, and wondered what this man eleven years older than Kai was thinking, and worried that he was using my young friend. When Kai came rolling into knife skills class five minutes late, clearly still wearing the clothes he had been wearing the day before, and regaled me with the tale of the handsome man who had wooed him with frothy frozen drinks and hearty, if somewhat off-key, renditions of show tunes, I laughed at the easy fun of his hookup. But a few short weeks later, when Kai came out to his family and was summarily dumped on the street and chose to land on Phil's doorstep, I was worried. A one-night stand, no big deal if everyone is safe and in it for fun. A couple months of fun, also no big deal. But a boy of twenty, just out of his parents' house for the first time, adrift without family, is easy prey for an older Svengali type, especially a Svengali with money. And then what happens if things go south? I was fiercely protective, tried to get Kai to come stay with me and Andrew, cautioned him against being overly reliant, emotionally and financially.

And then I met Phil.

Phil is so kind and wonderful, and so clearly in love with Kai, not in a desperate or possessive way, but loving him with an amazing openness. He credits Kai with bringing depth and joy into a life that was already full and rich. He has never tried to change Kai, but revels in who his lover is; the manic energy, quirky voices, club fashion, and frenetic activity level. Despite the age difference and financial discrepancy, they feel to me at all times like equal partners, perfectly balanced, and at ease in each other's love. He is a dear man, and I can see that he and Kai and Delia have been planning this for a while. So, even though it goes against every control-freak cell in my body, I acquiesce.

"You guys are the best. Thank you so much for everything."

"C'mon, roomie. Let's go home!" Nadia says, handing me my coat and purse.

"Get out of here, gal, or it will be time to come back and open up in the morning already!" Delia swats my butt. I hug her, and Kai and Phil, and Nadia and I head out to my car.

"That was so amazing, Melanie, really. All those great people. Are you happy?"

"Yeah. It's kind of overwhelming, you know? So much has happened in this year, good and bad and great and awful, I'm just trying to get my head around it all. Thank you, for your help these past few weeks. I know it has been crazy."

"It's the best job I've ever had," she says, playing with a pink strand of hair. "And the best roommate too!"

I laugh. "Well, that is a dubious honor considering your history, but I'll take it."

She laughs, and we sit in companionable silence on the short drive home. I park the car, and we head into the building, stopping to get the mail. Bills, junk mail, the ubiquitous 20 percent off coupon from Bed Bath & Beyond, which never fails to excite me, despite the fact that one seems to arrive every other day. And something from the Washington, D.C., chapter of the Jewish United Fund, forwarded from my old address. Nadia heads straight for her room, always desperate to check her e-mail the second she gets home. I drop my bag on the table and open the JUF letter.

Melanie—

Don't know if you will remember me, but I was in your class at UPenn, and we took Arthurian Lit together Junior year. I was the other fat girl in the back row, and we used to buy those bags of Gummi Worms and malted milk balls at the union and share them during class.

Anyway, I'm now living in D.C. with my husband and three (!) kids, and doing some volunteer work for the local JUF chapter. I saw the article about you in the Penn magazine a few months back, and was so amazed at all you have done! I was frankly thinking about the gastric bypass surgery, since I'm still heavy, but your story inspired me, so now I'm working with a trainer and a

local nutritionist and having some sllllllooooooooooooow
success.

I'm chairing a fund-raising luncheon for the local
women in a couple of weeks, and my keynote speaker just
informed me that she is having a family emergency, and
cancelled on me. So I had a great idea (I hope!). Would you
be available to come to D.C. from March 23–25? Women,
especially Jewish women, in my experience, seem to have
such issues with body image and relationships with food,
and just reading that article about you and the way you talk
about food and cooking and your body and your health was
so inspirational to me, and I know it would be amazing to
have this group of women hear from you, so I was thinking
we could do a combination of you overseeing the cooking
of the lunch, so that we are eating your best and healthiest
recipes (I have a great local caterer who you could work
with), and then you could be the keynote speaker!

My budget is $1,500 for the honorarium for the
speaker, and then $1,000 to oversee the menu and food
prep. And of course we will pay for your airfare, hotel,
and per diem. The event is at 11 a.m. on the 25th, so if
you could come in on the 23rd to meet with the caterer
and be sure that is all set, then you would have the rest of
the time to play in D.C.!

Anyhoo, I hope you are available. Give me a call and
let me know. It would be so great to catch up!

Yours,
Rachel (Klein) Morris
202-424-3776

Holy shit. Over two grand for one weekend. It would be so great to have a little bit of a cushion back since the great condo assessment debacle. Twenty-five hundred dollars would pay off a quarter of the loan I took from the association, meaning I could pay that off in just under eight months instead of a year, and nearly halve the amount of interest I would have to pay on what I borrowed. But it would also mean four days away from the store. I haven't missed a single day since we opened, and can't imagine what it would be like to be gone, or how I would manage it. But I also haven't had a vacation since I started culinary school, and the idea of a few days in D.C., especially on someone else's dime, is enormously tempting.

"Whassup? You look funny," Nadia says, floating back into the living room, having changed into a pair of shorts made out of vintage men's pajamas and a T-shirt with a picture of Cookie Monster on the front. Her calico hair is pulled up in a messy bun, and she looks about sixteen.

I hand her the letter. She reads carefully, chewing the inside of her lip and swaying from foot to foot. Then her face breaks out into a grin, her dancing eyebrows jumping straight into the air.

"That is AWESOME!!! Holy fuck-balls, that is like ridonculous money! You must be so psyched." She throws her wiry arms around my neck, and hops up and down. Then she stops. "Why are you not whooping? This is hugetastic. You should be whooping! Whoop, my elderly roomie, whoop!!!" She grabs my hands and starts to swing me around.

I have no idea what to do with this girl, but her energy is infectious, and before I can even think that I look completely stupid, or that it is totally unbecoming of a woman my age, I start, indeed, to whoop.

CHICKEN SOUP

Chicken soup was the only thing I ever remember my dad cooking. When my mom was pregnant with Gillian, Dad's chicken soup, from his great-grandmother's recipe, was the only thing Mom could keep down for the first six months. Sometimes with rice, sometimes with noodles, sometimes with matzo balls, clear golden elixir that sustained my mother and burgeoning sister. He was a big believer in Jewish Penicillin, and used to joke that the baby would be a rabbi and single-handedly bring our family into devout Judaism and away from our heathen, unobservant ways. My mother would try to laugh around her omnipresent nausea, saying that she would happily, officially convert if the baby would just give her some relief from endless puking and heartburn. I didn't really understand much about their banter, but I knew that there was something special about the way they talked to

*each other, something completely safe about being in the aura
of their love.*

It's a miracle I made the plane. All my travel instincts seem to
have left me, so by the time I finished giving Kai and Delia all
the instructions for the store, and Nadia every possible piece
of information about the condo, Wilbur had been waiting for
me for nearly a half an hour.

"Melanie, if we don't get a move on, you're going to miss
this flight. I can't fly over the traffic you know!" Wilbur has
been taking me to and from the airport for more than twenty
years. He was recommended to my mom by a friend, and he
used to come pick me up at the airport when I came home
from college. When I moved back, Andrew and I would hire
him for both business travel and vacations. He is ageless,
except for the white that has infiltrated his tight curls, has
a voice made for radio, and an amazing laugh. He's always
either just returned from Vegas, or planning his next visit,
and nothing makes you feel more home after a long trip than
seeing his smiling face as the town car pulls up.

Wilbur did manage to avoid most of the traffic on the way
to O'Hare, despite eternal construction on the Edens Express-
way, and a small accident near the exit to the airport. But I
forgot in the long time since I traveled how tedious the process can be. I had preprinted my boarding pass at home, and
checked my luggage at the curb, so at least I didn't have to deal
with that, but the security lines were interminable. Everyone
in front of me seemed to be first-time travelers, not wanting to
remove shoes, not knowing about packing liquids in a Ziploc

bag, juggling laptops and endless small children. By the time I got through security, I had less than thirty minutes till my flight, and of course was in the farthest possible gate. I walked at top speed through the terminal, arriving at the gate just as they were calling my group number, and got on the plane.

Settling in, I realized something sort of exciting. I was sitting in coach, and the armrests weren't digging into my hips or trying to ride up, and I didn't need a seat belt extender, and when I came down the aisle I never felt like everyone was looking at me thinking, "Not here, not next to me," or desperately not making eye contact, as if pretending someone isn't there will prevent her from sitting next to you and invading your personal space with her bulk.

But this time, people saw me, and didn't look away, and one man, a sort of cute guy who reminded me in a weird way of a professor in college I once had a crush on, even smiled at me. I was so shocked I almost dropped my carry-on. I had walked at a trot from security to the other end of the airport, but I wasn't breathing heavy or sweating. I think about how many times I spent the first thirty minutes of a flight waiting for my heart rate to slow, waiting for the perspiration to stop. I remember having twin bruises on both hips from long flights with unforgiving armrests, spending flights leaning half into the aisle to avoid encroaching on the person in the next seat, being clipped in the shoulder every time the cart came past. I have to remember to tell Carey about this the next time we chat.

You'd think with all the excitement and adrenaline and nervousness, I'd have a long, tedious trip, but blissfully, sleep came shortly after takeoff, and didn't leave me till we were landing. My idea of a perfect flight.

Rachel had sent a car for me, and after retrieving my luggage, we went to the Four Seasons. Apparently one of the JUF board members is friends with the general manager and gets great deals. Frankly, I couldn't care less why I'm at the Four Seasons, and instead am just totally ecstatic to be here. I used to take luxury hotels for granted when Andrew and I traveled. Actually, I used to take luxury in general for granted, but no more. You'd think it was my first time the way I run my hands over the little bottles of products in the bathroom, open the minibar and take inventory. I'm meeting Rachel for dinner later tonight, so for now, I unpack, run a hot bath, strip out of my travel clothes, get into the thick robe, and slide my feet into the monogrammed slippers.

I think I would like never to leave this room. Audrey Hepburn can have breakfast at Tiffany's, and think nothing bad can happen to you there, but for my money, I'd rather have breakfast at the Four Seasons where there are thick robes that finally fit me, free slippers, five-hundred-thread-count sheets and a brunch buffet with a guy frying up mini doughnuts and dipping them in the icing flavor of your choice. Because if something bad can happen to you at the Four Seasons, I can't for the life of me think what it could be, except having to leave.

I look at the bath. I think about the store. I turn off the water, and pick up my phone.

"Dining by Design."

"Nadia, it's Melanie. How is everything there?"

"Hey, Mel, can I call you back when the firemen leave?"

"WHAT?! What's on fire?"

Nadia laughs. "Nothing, silly. The local firehouse just

finished a job that interrupted their lunch, which apparently won't still be edible when they get back, so they are here picking up a replacement meal. I'll call you right back."

My heart eases itself back out of my throat and into its rightful place behind my rib cage.

I sit on the side of the tub, and in a couple of minutes my phone vibrates in my hand.

"Hey."

"Hey. Sorry about the heart attack. But they bought half the case, so we are having a good day!"

"Glad to hear it. Everything else going well?"

"No problems. Kai and Delia are bickering, I'm working the counter, and we're getting some good random early spring weather, so the snow is melting away. How was the trip?"

"Fine. Uneventful. So you'll call if anything . . ."

"Melanie, it isn't brain surgery. It's food. We're fine. Don't think about us. Just have a great weekend!"

I close my eyes and take a deep breath. "Okay, thanks, Nadia, I'll talk to you later."

"Bye, roomie!"

I let the robe slide off my body to the floor and gingerly get into the tub. My throat is tight, and my eyes sting. I'm not sure why I'm upset. You'd think I'd be relieved that everything is going so well back home, that I'd be proud of my merry band for keeping the home fires burning (and not actually setting anything on fire). But something about being here and clearly not being needed back there is disconcerting, and makes me sad. I let my body completely submerge, feeling the hot water seep into the follicles of my hair, try to get into my eyes. I float underwater, feeling the amniotic sense of being totally surrounded by warmth and wetness, and try to make my brain unclench.

"MELANIE!!!!" Rachel yells out the open window of her enormous SUV. I wave to acknowledge that I see her, and walk slowly toward the car. I hoist myself up into the passenger seat, and turn to face her. Her round, smiling face is haloed in wild dark curls, blue eyes shining with excitement. I'm immediately transported back to college and indeed vividly remember sitting in the back of a lecture hall, studying *Sir Gawain and the Green Knight*, and passing bags of candy back and forth with this cherubic woman.

"Hi, Rachel. Thanks so much for inviting me to come, it is such an honor."

"Pish, forget all that! Holy shit, you look AMAZING! I'd never recognize you. It must be so great to be thin."

I think about this, careful in my wording. "I feel really good, healthy." Since I began my program, my mantra has been health and not size. I was never trying to get thin, it was never about how I looked, and so when people compliment me on how good I look, I always remind myself why I did this by replying with how I feel.

"Well, I don't know about healthy, but you look hot! I'm jealous as hell." She pulls the car into traffic. "I'm taking you to my favorite place for dinner. Hope you're hungry! I can't tell you how nice it is to have a girls' night out. I just told Scott, he's my hubby, you take these monsters of ours to McDonald's like a good puppy, and frankly, I don't care if they get baths, just as long as they are sleeping by the time I get home! I'm going to have a nice dinner and a cocktail and pretend that I don't have crow's-feet that start at my neck and three Tasmanian devils under the age of five that are going to wake me up at six in the morning."

Now I REALLY remember Rachel, the bright personality, the constant stream of words, the sharing of thoughts and stories and opinions. I remember liking that she carried the conversation so I never had to. It's a little overwhelming at first, but comes from such a genuine place, not that self-centered talking at you of a narcissist, but more a gush of information she wants to share to bring you into her world. She chats about her husband, a wonderful guy who showed up right when she had given up on men, about her kids, two planned and one, oops, whom she clearly dotes upon. She had been in marketing research before the first baby, and is now a stay-at-home mom, which she likes better than she imagined.

We get to the restaurant, a little hole-in-the-wall place that feels like someone's living room, with a limited authentic Italian menu. We order a bottle of prosecco, antipasto to share, a small pasta course, and then a whole roasted black bass to split.

Over a shared dessert of zabaglione and fresh berries, and glasses of sweet Vin Santo, she asks about Andrew.

"It's my biggest fear," she says, taking a small dainty sip of her wine, and patting her mouth with her napkin. Fatties like us are usually very careful in public about manners, not shoveling food in, gently cutting bites, and chewing thoughtfully. True or not, when eating in front of other people, we feel watched, judged, and while we may overeat, we sure as hell aren't going to be slovenly about it.

"What's that?"

"That if I lose the weight, Scott will lose interest. He never dated a fat girl before; all his exes are these skinny little pickety-twicks, with tiny boobs and long legs, and the kind of arms that cry out for tank tops and perfect fucking clavicles to wear with their strapless dresses. And then he met me, and was like, HELLO! Curves and boobs and butt, oh my! Not getting poked by hipbones. Cuddling that feels like cuddling and not like snuggling up to a bag of kindling. He keeps saying he loves me, whatever size, but that he does want me around as long as possible, so obviously I'm doing this for my health, but there is that little voice in the back of my head that says he might lose interest."

I take the last swig of my wine. "I wouldn't worry. Scott sounds like a great guy, and ultimately, Andrew was a shit. We were always so busy with work, most of our conversations were about work and the house and where we wanted to go on vacation. I never noticed until things started going wrong, because the sex was always so good, and it was easy to live together. But really, we didn't have what I imagined we had. I had no family to speak of, and he hated his family, and we weren't going to have one of our own. So we just blithely lived our lives like two enormous babies, all id, food and sex and sleep and work and indulgent vacations and a really nice house that we filled with stuff. We never had a wide circle of friends, rarely entertained except as necessary for business, and what few hours a day we had together were spent eating and fucking and sleeping. When I was in it, it felt like the best relationship ever, in part because he was the first man who made me feel totally comfortable with my body, totally sexy and irresistible and powerful. The first guy I dated who brought home chocolates and cupcakes and never once asked if I shouldn't maybe watch what I was eating or put less butter on my bread or exercise more. And I thought that meant he loved me. But it didn't. It just meant that his sexual preference was for a larger woman, and once I started getting smaller there wasn't anything left to keep us together. You and Scott sound great, and he sounds like a real man, and I'm sure that he will love you just as much if there were less of you or more of you, regardless. You're really lucky."

I haven't really articulated this before. I mean, I've thought it, in pieces and flashes, touched on it here and there with Carey, as it related to my eating issues, but never so succinctly, never with such resignation. I had a shitty nonmarriage, from the very beginning, and I was too blind to realize it. Or too scared.

"Well, it just means the universe owes you a good one!" Rachel says.

"You're not kidding!" I laugh, surprised at how much fun I'm having.

Rachel signs the check, and we leave, getting back into her monolithic vehicle. She winds her way back through the gorgeous city, taking the long way around so that I can see the monuments lit up. She pulls up in front of the hotel. "Do you need anything else for Friday? I'll pick you up here at nine thirty."

"I think I'm in good shape. I spoke extensively with Sunny at the caterer's, and she was great. I e-mailed her my recipes, and she made some substitutions based on what is available locally, and it all sounds great. And I think I'm okay with the speech part, although I'm cheating a bit, relying heavily on Q and A to fill half the time!"

"You'll be great. What are you doing tomorrow?"

"Holocaust Museum. I've never been, and my dad's folks both lost a lot of family in the camps."

"It's amazing. Give yourself plenty of time; you won't want to rush it. Call if you need anything, otherwise have a great day tomorrow and I'll see you bright and early Friday!"

"Good night, Rachel. Thanks so much for a great night and for bringing me out here. I really appreciate it!"

"My pleasure. Us Penn girls have to stick together. See you later!"

She drives off and I head inside, ready to indulge in an in-room movie and blissful sleep.

It is the most amazing museum I have ever been inside of. I thought I would hate it, but it felt like an important thing to do, even for a half-breed nonpracticing semi-Jew like me, but no question, it started as something like an obligation. The place you should go, the place it would be good for you to see, but not exactly something fun to do. I remember sitting with Grandma and Grandpa Hoffman, looking at an ancient photo album, and having them point out the ancestors. This is Zaide and Bubbe Hoffman, they went to Treblinka. This is Aunt Rivka and Uncle Avrom and their four boys, they went to Auschwitz. Strange names, sepia photos with serious faces, picture after picture of relatives who perished, relatives who died in the marches, who went to the ovens.

Grandpa Hoffman had come to Chicago as a baby, his

father determined to get out of the ghettos in Poland. Grandma Hoffman had been twelve when her family came from Germany, the slight accent only apparent when she got agitated. Both families lost nearly everyone they left behind, generations of cousins, brothers, and sisters, close family friends, wiped out. The last trip my grandparents took together was to Washington, D.C., for the opening of the museum in 1993. Shortly after they returned, Grandma had a stroke and the two of them moved to an assisted living facility. She continued to have ministrokes almost daily, and passed away within the year. Grandpa was only six months behind her. But they both spoke about the museum as reverently as if it had been a temple, and referred to it as a holy place, right up there with the Wailing Wall, and made me promise to come. So finally being here, even though it is more than fifteen years since I made that promise, feels like a necessary familial pilgrimage.

The one thing that is true of the museum is that you can feel the care that was taken in presenting the complete picture of the war in a way that affects deeply, but does its best not to overwhelm. I have read that when they designed the physical space and the exhibits that they consulted everyone from physiologists to psychiatrists to ensure that a visitor could handle the place physically and emotionally. So as you wander, seeing the artifacts, reading the large panels, just as you think you cannot handle one more horror, there is a room devoted to a successful uprising, or a story about children who got out, or a piece about the heroism of a Gentile who helped Jews escape. Just as your feet start to hurt and your lower back starts to ache, there is a room where you are supposed to sit and watch a film for fifteen to twenty minutes, refreshing you physically. They take you to the brink of what you can stand, and then give you relief, and the ability to go forward.

I move through the exhibits, wanting to absorb everything, to read every word, to watch every minute of footage. I walk through the rail car, touching the walls marred by scratchings, imagining more than a hundred people trapped inside. I walk through the rooms completely filled with eyeglasses, with shoes, with suitcases. I sit and watch survivors tell their stories, the young girl who married the handsome GI who liberated her, the soldier who invited the man he carried out of the camp to come home and live with him and his family, the Jewish GI who rescued a distant cousin. I walk through the room devoted to the non-Jews targeted by the Nazis, the mentally challenged, the Gypsies, the Jehovah's Witnesses, the homosexuals. The stories of the African American soldiers who laid their lives down abroad in a war against oppression and discrimination and racism, only to return home to face those same evils. I look at the replicated wooden sleeping structure, imagining the faces from my grandparents' photo album packed in three or four to a bunk.

As I exit the main exhibit, I realize that I have been here more than six hours. I cross the wide lobby to the room of remembrance, a circular marble room with large simple monuments to each of the camps, and to the larger death marches. There are candles around the room and an eternal flame. I stand in front of the black granite wall with its simple lettering, AUSCHWITZ, and remember that one of the reasons I am so utterly bereft of family is because of that word. I am more than an orphan. I have lost so much more than just my parents, and the enormity of the experience overwhelms me.

I have had moments in the past few hours when I had a lump in my throat or tears swam in my eyes, but now, in this simple, silent place, the weeping comes unbidden. The tears are hot on my cheeks, flowing with a volume and speed that surprises me, my whole body shaking.

And suddenly there is a hand in mine. A strong, large hand has taken my hand, and is squeezing. I turn to see who it is, wondering if this place even has docents assigned to comforting people, but my eyes are so filled with tears that all I can make out is that it is a man in a blue shirt, and that he is pulling me into his arms, and without even thinking I am buried in a strong chest that smells of lime and spice, and I am being held tightly, with hands rubbing my back, swaying slightly, and that even as I sob in the embrace of this stranger, he is weeping too, his cheek on my head, his breath ragged.

It might have been a minute, or ten, but eventually our breathing slows, the sorrow is tempered, and I come back into my brain to realize that some strange man is holding me in the middle of a museum, and despite the fact that I haven't been held in more than a year, and that every fiber of my body craves this contact, nevertheless, it is disconcerting and I pull back.

"Hi," he says.

"Hi," I say.

He lets me go and I stand under my own power, wiping the wetness from my cheeks.

"I ruined your shirt," I say, looking at the large wet spot I have made in the middle of his chest.

"Not ruined. It'll dry. I don't even think it's a natural fabric. I think it's made of old tires or something. My mother would be horrified, probably."

I laugh. He hands me a handkerchief, and I blow my nose. Then I don't know what to do with it, since it is bad enough that I have wept all over his shirt, and I'm hard-pressed to hand him a handkerchief full of hot snot.

"I'm Nathan. Nathan Gershowitz."

"Melanie. Hoffman."

"Nice to meet you, Melanie. Us Chicagoans have to support each other." I look into his face and realize suddenly that he is the guy who smiled at me on the plane.

"You're from the plane," is all I can say.

"Actually, I'm from Evanston originally, and now I live in the Gold Coast, but I was *on* the plane." He smiles again.

"Thank you . . ." I gesture around helplessly, as if that indicates what I am grateful for.

"Thank you. I was okay in the exhibits, but this room really knocked me out, and I just didn't want to experience it alone, if that makes sense."

"Completely. I didn't even know that I felt alone until you . . ."

"Yeah, I mean, I hope you don't think I go around molesting women in museums. I just . . . well you were crying and I was crying and . . ."

"I know, and I didn't even think I was . . ."

"Me either. But then I saw you and you were from the plane."

"From Chicago, but *on* the plane . . ." I grin. He laughs.

"Right, *on* the plane, and for some reason I thought, well . . ."

"Well . . ."

"Well. Can I ask you something that may sound really

insensitive to our location?" He looks like he is truly afraid to offend me.

"Sure."

"Are you hungry? Because I'm suddenly starving, and I know a good place near here, they make chicken soup almost as good as my grandmother's, and if you're hungry too, I thought maybe you'd like to join me for a late lunch, since right now, as good company as I usually am for myself, I'd sort of rather not be eating alone. Which sounds really needy and a little effeminate, but there it is."

I look at him, the gentle rejection ready on the tip of my tongue. I can't imagine going anywhere or doing anything with this guy, and then my stomach growls louder and longer than it has ever growled before, reverberating off the stone walls. I can feel my face flush red, and he laughs.

"Well, that is an answer if I ever heard one!" And before I can utter a sound, he cups my elbow in his hand, and guides me out into the sunlight.

TURKEY TETRAZZINI

The first meal I cooked for Andrew was on our fourth date. On our third date he took me to a movie, held my hand, and then kissed me passionately on my doorstep. Before he left, he made me promise that our next date could be a quiet night in, and the look in his eyes, the tone in his voice, everything about that little phrase told me that what he really meant by a quiet night in was sex, and probably lots of it. It made me melt. He looked at me the way I look at a really nice dessert buffet, as if it all looks too good to even know where to begin, and once you start, you don't know if you'll ever be able to stop. I dated a reasonable amount for a girl my size, tending toward quiet, bookish types who read me poetry in bed, majored in missionary, and were always both shocked and deeply grateful when I gave them head. But I had never been with someone who targeted me as an object of lust,

who wooed me, who looked at me the way most guys look at Pamela Anderson. For that first dinner I made a simple green salad with homemade creamy vinaigrette, a classic turkey Tetrazzini casserole, buttered asparagus, and chocolate cupcakes with vanilla frosting for dessert.

"So then what happened?" Nadia asks, bouncing up and down. She is in her pajamas, sitting on the couch hugging a throw pillow, as I tell her about my weekend. My suitcase is in the middle of the floor, and I haven't checked my messages or gone through the mail. Nadia tackled me as soon as I came through the door, and frankly, I'm so swept up with telling her about my adventure that I couldn't care less about anything else. I can't remember the last time I had a good girlfriend dish session, especially where I was the one with the dish, but even though I feel like a weird episode of *Sex and the City*, it is elating.

"So we went to this little Jewish deli and ordered big bowls of mishmash chicken soup . . ."

"What is mishmash?"

"Everything in it . . . matzo ball, noodle, rice, kasha, and kreplach."

"Okay, whatever."

"Exactly. It was soup. It was good. We talked about life and everything under the sun. He's a documentary filmmaker, based in Chicago, but takes jobs all over the world. He just finished a film on the Maasai tribe, and is working on the editing and postproduction for the next few months while figuring out his next project. He was in D.C. for a cousin's kid's bar mitzvah. He has a huge family, very close, grew up in Evanston, lives downtown, never married but lived with a woman for six years. Never wanted kids. Sox fan, since his dad grew up on the South Side."

"What does he look like?" Nadia's eyebrows are doing a jig.

"Tall, probably like six two or six three. Broad shoulders. Big guy, but not heavy, just physically very present. Dark hair with a little gray here and there, more wavy than curly, thinning a little on top with a slightly receding hairline, but in a nice way. Olive skin, hazel eyes. Handsome face, but not pretty, lived in, in a good way. Laugh lines. Sort of a younger Jewish Harrison Ford."

"Nice. So then what happened?"

"He had to leave to go to a family dinner, but asked if he could meet me for a nightcap, and I said yes. I went back to the hotel and took a nap, and then met him in the bar, and we had a bottle of wine and talked some more. He asked if I would consider being his date to the bar mitzvah party, and I said that it would be awkward and uncomfortable, and as lovely as it was for him to invite me, I couldn't possibly be a last-minute addition to such a major event. So then he asked if he could see me when we were home, and I said yes. And then I went back to my room."

"You didn't invite him up?"

"I'm not, to use your vernacular, some skank ho."

"Skank ho or no, I wouldn't have let a free room at the Four Seasons go to waste."

"I couldn't even think of such a thing. I went up and did some last-minute mental prep for the lunch the next day, and got some sleep. Rachel picked me up, I went over the food with Sunny and she did a great job. Everyone was very nice and appreciative and I think my speech went over well, and a lot of people took Carey's flier that I brought with me, and promised to send their Chicago friends to the store, so that was good, and then Rachel took me back to the hotel."

"I'm glad it was good. I would never have been able to concentrate, I would have just been thinking about the guy the whole time."

I had, in fact, spent most of the day with my thoughts turning back to his laugh, the way his eyes sparkled, the strong forearms resting on the table. "I'm perfectly able to live my life and not obsess about a boy, Nadia. I'm not twelve."

"Well, you're a better woman than me."

"So what happened after your thing?"

"I got back to the hotel and there was a message."

"From Nathan." She nods knowingly.

I shake my head. "Nope."

It had been his mother.

"Ms. Hoffman?" she had said. "This is Ellie Gershowitz, Nathan's mother. I hope you don't mind my calling, but when Nathan mentioned that you declined his invitation to our little party, I thought I'd just check in with you to be sure you aren't available. I know it is very last-minute, but the truth is, my darling son is seated at a table with three other couples, and no date, poor thing! And we've had some people cancel last-minute, but the catering is already paid for, so the family would take it as a personal favor if you would come to the party and keep him company, and prevent him from pouting. I'm hoping to meet you; Nathan says you're a darling girl.

His number is 312-555-6732, just give him a call if you can make it."

Oh. My. God. I had reached for my phone.

"Hello?"

"No fair siccing your mother on me."

Nathan's laugh had been deep and genuine. "She stole your number off my phone while I was in the bathroom, I swear."

"I'm not sure that I believe you. But I can't disappoint her, so I'd be delighted to be of assistance with the prepaid catering."

"She didn't tell you the catering was already paid for."

"Oh yes, she most certainly did."

"I'm so, so very sorry about that. But I'm glad you can come."

"Yeah. Me too."

"His MOTHER?" Nadia exclaims.

"Yep."

"So what did you do?"

"What could I do? I called Rachel and begged off our plans for me to come over to hang out with her family. Then I ran out to Macy's, bought a dress and shoes and purse and industrial-strength Spanx, assaulted a teenage boy and embarrassed him in front of his friends by asking what he would want for a present, went to the recommended games store and bought a gift certificate, ran back to the hotel and got ready."

"It is sooooo romantic." Nadia sighs.

"It was the craziest thing I've ever done. I kept waiting to wake up."

"It's like a total fairy tale." She sighs dramatically.

"Yeah, I guess it sort of is." It has been a very long time since the attention of a man made me feel like this.

"I'm so proud of you for saying yes!"

"Yeah." I blush a little, wondering why it is that I like the sound of this child being proud of me, but it makes me feel sort of cool.

"C'mon, keep going, I want the good stuff!"

"He picked me up in a cab, we went to the party, I met his entire family, all of whom were so genuine and warm and happy I was there, and we played Jewish geography and found out that his uncle did some business with my grandfather, and one of his cousins actually went to high school with my dad, so that was really cool to hear some stories about my dad in high school. We were at a table with his first cousins and their spouses, who were very nice people, the food was typical bar mitzvah food, and there were the usual speeches and we all laughed about how the boys were shorter than most of the girls, and how much we remember those first boy-girl dances, and wondered if there is a school where DJs learn their insipid patter. We danced the horah. We sat out 'YMCA' and 'Celebration.' His family seemed to think it was really great how we met, his ninety-three-year-old grandmother called it *b'shert*, which means fated, and none of them seemed at all surprised that he would want to bring a total stranger to such a private party. By the time we left, they all hugged and kissed me like I was part of the family, and the bar mitzvah boy told me very seriously that Nathan is his favorite cousin, and he was really glad I was there with him."

"You didn't freak out, did you?"

"Freak out?"

"You know how you are about the whole touchy-feely thing. I mean, all those strangers mauling you and kissing you and hugging you and being affectionate . . ." She smirks.

"Are you making fun of me?"

"Only if it doesn't put my employment or residence status in jeopardy."

"It does not."

"Then yeah, I'm totally giving you shit."

"Fired."

"HEY!"

"Evicted."

"CUT THAT OUT!"

"Kidding. No I did not freak out, it was perfectly lovely. I've never seen anything like it. I've never been to that kind of family event before. It was really sort of amazing."

"And then you jumped him."

"I did no such thing. He took me back to the hotel, we had a drink, we made plans for this coming weekend, and then he left."

Nadia sighs deeply, shaking her head. "How old is he?" she asks.

"Forty-seven."

Nadia looks somewhat stricken, as if I have told her that he was nearing death. "Oh," she says.

I laugh at her. "Honey, I know that's nearly twice your age, but I'm going to be forty next month, he is really very age-appropriate for me."

"You're going to be forty?"

"Yes. And someday, so will you."

"Wow. What are we going to do?"

"Pick up some Depends and sign me up for AARP and put a deposit down at the home, apparently."

She hits me with the pillow. "I meant we have to have a party or something." She grins. "You can bring your new boyfriend!"

"We'll see."

"So this weekend?"

"Yes. We have plans for dinner Sunday night."

"Cool."

"I hope so."

"Your boy story is so much better than my boy story."

"What is your boy story?"

"You know I used to go to Janey's eleven a.m. class, right?"

"Right."

"But with you gone, I have been going to the evening class instead, after work."

"Gotcha."

"So there is this guy in the back of the room at the first class, I don't really even notice him until we are leaving, but I dropped my mat and he picked it up and smiled at me and then ran away."

"Interesting. Cute?" I feel sort of like an idiot, and hate myself for not being terribly interested. I wanted so much to share my weekend with Nadia, to let her know how amazing it was, to validate that I should be excited about meeting Nathan and our strange adventure, but now that the story is told and she has been duly appreciative, I want to unpack and get into comfy clothes, and check my e-mail just on the off chance Nathan has written me. I want to care about Nadia's new boy, I want to be a real friend to her, and so, following the old adage of "fake it till you make it," I put my best face on, and try to appear engaged.

She chews thoughtfully on a strand of lavender hair. It must be new; I haven't noticed it before, but it complements the pink pretty well. "He's not cute. At least I don't think so. He is ultra skinny, not in a manorexic way, just in that way that some boys get when they forget to eat. And he has terrible glasses that don't seem to fit his face, and shaggy hair that falls in his eyes. He is short, just a couple inches taller than me, and he isn't very good at the yoga. He keeps falling over during the poses, or his glasses fall off during downward-facing dog."

"But he likes you." I smile, remembering all the times in my youth that the guy I never would have thought was attractive became irresistible the moment I found out he was attracted to me. Adoration is very sexy.

Nadia smiles. "I think so. The second night he moved up to the middle of the class, and the third night to the row right behind me, and tonight he put his mat next to mine. His name is Daniel Holst, and he does something with computers, and his clothes neither match nor fit him properly, and he seems to have a four-sentence limit on conversation, and then runs away."

"So you like him."

She sighs deeply and flops backward on the couch. "I feel like I should try to like him. He isn't a musician or an artist or married. He isn't tattooed or pierced or scarred, at least not the parts I have seen. He's probably just normal, and I've never dated anyone normal, so maybe I should try to like him."

"You should allow yourself the possibility of liking him and let nature take care of the rest."

"But he is so nervous, and never talks, I feel like he is scared of me, so I don't want to freak him out. He's like some woodland creature, and I'm trying to coax him out of his lair."

I laugh. There is no angst like twenty-four-year-old boy angst. "Then do what you would do with a woodland creature to tame them."

"What's that?"

"Feed him. You say he is skinny, probably forgets to eat. Next class bring him something . . . tell him you cooked too much and thought he might want the extra."

"That is SUCH a good idea." Nadia launches herself into my arms. Then she pulls back and tilts her head to the side.

"What should I make him?"

I smile, and take her face in my hands the way my mom used to do. "I have just the thing."

BANANA CAKE
WITH CHOCOLATE FROSTING

Every birthday it would appear: my mom's signature banana cake with chocolate frosting. She had gotten the recipe from Susan, a sorority sister at the University of Michigan, and it was really the only cake she ever baked. Mom was more of a cookie baker, with dozens of recipes, and Christmastime at our house was all about cookies for what seemed to be weeks, much to my delight, since I could steal the broken ones and hoard them in my room to snack on in secret late at night. She made a decent key lime pie, her brownies were terrible, cakey and not really sweet enough, and every St. Patrick's Day she produced truly inedible Irish soda bread. But her banana cake with chocolate frosting was, in a word, sublime. Every year on our birthdays my family would wake the birthday person up with a cake, singing "Happy Birthday," and we would eat it for breakfast. If it was a school day, we'd get a piece in our

lunchbox. We'd eat it again as an after-school snack with tall glasses of cold milk, and finish it off for dinner. Banana cake never lasted to a second day in our house. And when I got old enough to bake them myself, they still never made it to the second day, even if I was the only one home.

"That was delicious, thank you." Nathan wipes his mouth on his napkin, and leans back contentedly. "I have to say, I was a little worried, but this was amazing!"

We are sitting at my tiny dining table. It is officially our third Chicago date, and I invited him over for a late supper after I got off of work. Since tomorrow is Monday, and my day off, I figured I would be more relaxed, not thinking about the store, or what needed to get done there. But I'm not relaxed. Because this is our third date, and Nadia is at Janey's having a sleepover, and Nathan and I have had two passionate clothes-on make-out sessions, and I know from watching *Sex and the City* about the third-date rule that I'm supposed to sleep with him, and I know he knows it, and I know I want to, and I'm scared out of my wits. I try to focus on conversation.

"Why were you worried?"

"Well, I know you kept telling me gourmet, delicious, good-for-you food, but in general I tend to find that people who eat ultrahealthy tend to say things are delicious when in fact they taste like lawn clippings and sawdust."

I laugh. "I know! I can't tell you how many times over the years people tried to give me soy cheese and tempeh fake-meat, and other ickiness and pass it off as yummy. I'm sorry but no, you cannot make vegetable protein taste like bacon, no matter how much salt and liquid smoke you put in it! I wanted to celebrate good food, prepared in ways that make it good for you, which is surprisingly easy to do if you know the basics. If you use exceptional products that have inherent natural goodness, you don't need to swamp them in butter or cream to make them taste good." For dinner we'd had grilled skirt steaks, spicy Thai sesame noodles from my friend Doug's recipe, braised cauliflower, and for dessert, poached pears and Greek yogurt with lavender flowers and black sage honey. Filling, balanced, nutritionally sound.

"Well, you've made me a believer. If you hadn't told me this was a healthy good-for-you meal, I wouldn't have guessed."

"That is the best compliment you could pay me!" I clear the dishes and put them in the sink. Nathan comes up behind me, slides his arms around my waist and kisses the back of my neck.

"I think a better compliment is that you are as delicious as your food."

I'm melting into a little puddle in my kitchen. Nathan gently spins me in his arms with a gentle tug on my shoulder, and kisses me. He is the best kisser. An even better kisser than Andrew, who I always thought was a pretty spectacular kisser. But where Andrew devoured me, Nathan savors. He starts gently, lips full and warm against mine, strong. His lips part slightly, so that we are sharing breath, and then just the tip of his tongue, lightly exploring. He guides me out of the kitchen to the living room, and sits me on the couch.

"So, how has your week been?" I ask, trying to catch my breath.

"My week was fine, it was mostly just something to get

through so I could be here with you." He leans in and is kissing me again. And my heart is racing with excitement and fear. I am thick with desire, everything is electric, and yet, I can't relax into it, can't imagine actually going to the next level, despite my deep longing to do so. Nathan is kissing me, kissing my neck, his hands in my hair, his body pressed against mine. I can feel his erection against my leg, his heartbeat thudding, and I want him so much, but when I feel his hand start to go up my shirt, reflexively I sit up and move away.

Nathan looks puzzled. "I'm sorry, is everything . . . Did I do something wrong, or . . . ?"

"No, you're great, you're amazing, I . . . um . . . just, I'm not really . . ."

He smiles and strokes my cheek tenderly. "You're not ready."

I look down at my hands, and try not to feel the lump in my throat, and try not to feel so stupid and broken.

"Hey, hey, stop that." Nathan gathers me in his arms, and I melt into the embrace. He speaks softly into my hair. "You have been through a lot this past year, and you were betrayed by a man you trusted completely. You've learned total self-sufficiency, and I can only imagine how scary it would be to even be considering opening up to someone new, especially someone you barely know." He cups my chin in his hands. "I really like you, Melanie Hoffman. I like the way you think and the way you tell stories, and the way you cook. You are a beautiful, smart, sexy, spectacular woman, and I'm more than happy to let you set the pace. Because as much as I want you, I only want to be with you when you are sure. You take whatever time you need, and you let me know." He squeezes me tight, lifts my face, and kisses me softly. "Am I still your date for your birthday party next week?"

"Of course."

"I'll call you tomorrow. Maybe we can get together again one night this week?"

"I would love that."

He grabs his coat, and walks to the door.

"I'm sorry, Nate, I . . ." He stops me with a kiss.

"Don't you ever dare apologize for being you, or for being honest. Thank you for a lovely evening, and a wonderful meal. I will talk to you tomorrow."

And then he is gone.

I busy myself, cleaning the dishes, straightening the kitchen. Then I go into my bedroom, get undressed, and put on my robe. I run a hot bath for myself, and while it fills, I let the robe drop to the floor and look at myself in the mirror. I have a good face, not beautiful, at least not to me, but reasonably attractively put together, handsome. But my body bears the scars of a lifetime of obesity. White stretch marks line the front of my stomach, my thighs, striate my breasts, which were once a lush 42DDD and are now a 36D, hanging deflated, defeated. The skin of my upper arms, my inner thighs, and over my abdomen is loose, and while there is excellent muscle tone underneath, the skin, which once was taut over soft pillows of fat, now slides in waves over the space I worked so hard for so long to create. There is my appendix scar, from when I was fourteen. The four little scars from my gallbladder removal. My butt, which once loomed in a massive shelf jutting out from my lower back like the stern of a proud sailing vessel, has somehow dropped into a sad double teardrop. In clothes, I'm a fit and healthy size 6 or 8. With the right bra, I have a great rack. But naked, naked I look like a newborn bird without feathers; something is not quite finished about me. I never wanted to get the excess skin removal surgery; it is costly and debilitating. But I also never really thought about being here. In this place. Alone and wanting a man and thinking that he would be disgusted.

I never felt like that when I was fat. Because when you are fat, really fat, everyone knows it, and any guy who goes to bed with you knows he is going to bed with a fat girl, so I never thought about it. And Andrew loved my fat, apparently that was really all he loved, so I was free and easy in bed with him. I have a large sexual appetite, as with all my appetites, and all I can think about is Nathan, his tall strong body, how good it feels to be in his arms, how much I want him inside me. But I feel like a fraud. Because however good I look dressed, however normal I appear to be in public, once you strip me down, I have essentially the body of an old woman. And what man wants that in his bed?

I turn off the bathwater and pull the drain, too tired to think about getting in. I leave my robe on the floor, slide into my bed, and turn off the light. Lying down, I let my hands roam my body, my breasts splayed to each side, my skin mobile and elastic. My hand crawls between my legs, exploring the wetness still there from my earlier exhilaration. I remember Nathan's kisses, the weight of him on me, his hardness pressed against me, and quickly, furtively, bring myself to a shuddering, empty orgasm. The tears are hot on my cheeks, sliding into my ears, and I bring my hand to my mouth, grateful for a small taste of something.

The next day, the phone rings just as I am putting the last of the platters into the case. I grab the counter extension.

"Dining by Design."

"Hello, beautiful."

Sigh. "Hello, Nathan."

"How are you this fine morning?"

"Fine. Just getting ready to open the doors." I pause. "How are you?" I'm completely ready for him to break up with me. Last night has been replaying in my mind on an endless loop. I slept fitfully, and this morning at the gym all I could think about was sending him home and wondering how many more times I would be able to do that before he bailed on me.

"I'm great. I wanted to thank you for a spectacular evening last night. Really wonderful."

It doesn't sound forced or fake, but his words cut me to the quick. His kindness is salt in the wound. "Well, thank you for coming, it was really good to see you."

"I was wondering if you were free tonight? Late supper?"

My stomach turns. It's one thing to space out the dates, limit the time together to postpone the inevitable, but the more time we spend together, the sooner I'm going to have to either decide to sleep with him, or to end the relationship.

"I, um, tonight's not so good, I have some stuff I should take care of, and . . ."

"Okay, no big deal. How about tomorrow?"

"Yeah, um, well, maybe, I, um . . . Can I call you? This is

just sort of a crazy week, and I get so exhausted by the end of the day I'm not terribly good company . . ." Why am I making a million excuses to not see a man I love spending time with? What the fuck is wrong with me?

"I know your workday must be a bear. I'm just thinking maybe something quiet . . . You could come over for a little nosh and we could watch a DVD or something."

I take a very deep breath. "Okay, tomorrow will probably work for that. Why don't we do it at my place? I'll just bring stuff home from the store for us to eat so we don't have to cook. You can bring a movie." I'm not ready to be with him in his apartment, on his turf. At least at my house I can use Nadia as an excuse.

"That sounds terrific. Any movie requests?"

"I'm easy, I haven't seen a movie in ages. Whatever you want to see will be great, I'm sure."

"Okay, then. Nine?"

"Should be fine. I'll call you when I'm done at the store."

"See you tomorrow, beautiful. Have a great day."

"You too."

"Psst. Mel . . ." I can feel the kiss on the top of my head, and I open one eye. I'm on my couch, wrapped in Nathan's arms, and the credits are rolling on the screen.

"I missed the end."

Nathan's laugh rumbles in his chest. "You missed the middle."

I stretch out of his arms, and turn to him. "I told you I get tired on weeknights. Was it a good movie?"

He reaches forward to pull me into his arms for a long kiss. "I would watch test patterns if it meant I could have you in my arms."

I melt against him. My heart beats with equal fear and desire. He lays me back on the couch and I will myself to let him, but I can't. I sit up.

"Nathan, I . . ."

"Shhh." He kisses me again, and stands. He reaches out a hand and pulls me off the couch. "You go get in bed before you wake up too much to get back to sleep. I'll talk to you tomorrow."

Before I slip back into sleep, I wonder if he left to protect my need for weeknight rest, or to avoid my asking him to go. And wondering if I will ever be able to choose him, to choose happiness.

After a fitful night of bad dreams, dreams of falling not flying, trying to run with leaden feet, trying to scream but no sound coming out, I drag myself out of bed and to the gym for a lackluster workout. I shower and head for the store, hoping that work will clear my head a bit. I'm checking yesterday's receipts, trying not to think about last night, when the phone rings, and I grab it absentmindedly. "Dining by Design."

"Happy birthday, Mel."

My heart stops. Andrew.

"Um, thanks."

"How are you?"

Why the fuck is he calling me? "Fine. How are you?"

"We're fine. Thanks for asking."

We. We're fine. Hey there, birthday girl? Have a wound? Here's some salt!

"Was there something you wanted?"

"There's no need to take that tone, Melanie. I was just calling to wish you a happy birthday. To see how you were holding up."

"Oh, I see, you assumed that I'd be, what? Falling apart? That the idea of turning a year older without you would put me into the pit of despair? I'm fine, Andrew. Better than fine. I love my life. I love my friends and my work and my *new boyfriend*, and I think this may be the best birthday I have ever had."

I hate the venom shrillness in my voice. I hate that by saying these things I am revealing how much I still hurt, how tender my emotions still are. My mom once said that there are certain things that you cannot respond to when people accuse you, because every proof you offer that they are wrong makes it sound more and more like they are right.

"Jesus, Mel, it doesn't have to be like this. I was just calling to wish you a happy birthday. To reach out. You were a very important part of my life for a very long time, I know that I hurt you, and you have every right to be angry, but this isn't some agenda. I really did hope that we could be friends again someday. I know that I would really like that." He pauses, and I can feel myself softening. "I know that Charlene would really like that." *Whoosh*, so much for soft.

"Andrew, you were a very important part of my past. I appreciate your reaching out to wish me a happy birthday, but frankly, what makes it most happy right now is your profound absence. I don't know if I will ever not feel that way, but I assure you that if I do decide I am ready to be friends with you, I'll let you know."

Andrew sighs deeply, the sound of an adult accommodating a petulant child. "All right, Mel. Whatever you want. I wish you all happiness, I do."

"Good-bye, Andrew."

"Good-bye."

I let the phone slide out of my hand into the cradle. I take a deep breath and wait for the tightening in my chest to subside.

The noise is deafening. "Happy Birthdaaaaaaaaaaaaayyy Deeeeeeeeeeeeeeeeear Melllllllanieeeeeeeeeeeeeeee. Happy Biiiiii-irthhhhhhhhhhhhhday tooooooooo youuuuuuuuuuuuuuuuuuu!"

I lean over the enormous confection, ablaze with candles, and look around. My friends are looking at me expectantly, Nathan is smiling, and suddenly I realize that I really don't have much left to wish for. I close my eyes. Some success for the business, just enough to give me some financial breathing room. And the continuation of this small window of happiness. I fill my lungs, and blow. All forty candles obligingly go out, and the assembly applauds.

We are at Kai and Phil's, and they have outdone themselves. Kai enlisted the help of some culinary students for prep work and serving, and pulled out all the stops for this party, skipping the sit-down dinner in favor of endless little nibbles, sort of like tapas or a wonderful tasting menu. Champagne laced with Pineau des Charentes, a light cognac with hints of apple that essentially puts a velvet smoking jacket around the dry sparkling wine. Perfect scallops, crispy on the outside, succulent and sweet within, with a vanilla aioli. Tiny two-bite Kobe sliders on little pretzel rolls with caramelized onions, horseradish cream, and melted fontina. Seared tuna in a spicy soy glaze, ingenious one-bite caprese salads made by hollowing out cherry tomatoes, dropping some olive oil and balsamic vinegar inside, and stuffing with a mozzarella ball wrapped in fresh basil. Espresso cups of chunky roasted tomato soup with grilled cheese croutons.

The food is delicious and never-ending, supplemented with little bowls of nuts, olives, raw veggies, and homemade potato chips with lemon and rosemary. Nathan is at ease, flattering Delia and asking for her recipe for sweet potato pie, flirting with Kai and Phil just enough to prove his comfort, stopping well short of being creepy or obsequious. He chats with Nadia about her jewelry, with Janey about whether taking yoga would help with some of his joint pain. He checks in with me consistently, everything from meaningful eye contact across the room, to bringing me refills on my drink.

Kai slices the cake, his version of the banana cake I have always talked about. He has made a vanilla sponge cake, soaked in vanilla simple syrup, and layered with sliced fresh bananas and custard. There is a central layer of dark chocolate ganache with bits of crispy pecans and toffee, and the whole thing is covered in chocolate buttercream, with extravagant curls of chocolate and chocolate-dipped banana slices piled in the middle. I accept a thin slice, savoring the flavors, both of the cake, and of simple joy.

Nathan escorts me out to his car, a battered Land Rover that must be at least twenty years old, carrying my booty, since despite the fact that I was specific about not wanting gifts, my friends have ignored me completely, and there are gaily colored bags and beribboned boxes. I'm flushed with food and wine, a little bit tipsy.

"Did you like your party, birthday girl?" Nathan asks as he pulls out of the parking space and heads for his place.

"It was perfect." I sigh contentedly and lean back in the seat. "Thanks for being my date."

"Thanks for letting me be your date. It was a wonderful night, and your friends are really amazing people. I had a great time."

"Well, they all seem to approve of you as well. A rousing success all around. Pity it took being this OLD to make it possible." I'm actually not really bothered by getting older. It just seems the thing to say.

"You still seem to have some miles left in you, from where I sit," Nathan jokes. "I mean, SLOW miles, but miles nonetheless!"

I laugh. "Getting slower every day!"

"Hey, are you exhausted, or can we go have a drink at my place?"

"I could probably have one drink." My heart jumps.

"Great."

We sit in companionable silence the rest of the ride. We pull into his parking lot, and take the elevator up to his condo.

His place is exactly what I imagine, an extension of him: warm woods, leather furniture with great patina, film equipment and work materials. A huge old farmhouse table covered in papers with mismatched chairs. I hang my coat on the back of one of the chairs, and Nathan takes my hand to give me the tour. It is sort of a semi-loft, open-concept living room/dining room/kitchen, and then two bedrooms in the back. I try not to look at the rumpled king-size bed, to imagine myself in it with him. He leads me back to the living room and gestures for me to sit on the couch, and then heads off to fetch drinks. I can hear Nathan futzing around in the kitchen. I kick off my shoes, my feet unused to heels after so much time in clogs and Crocs. Nathan appears from the kitchen with two snifters of Armagnac, and curls up beside me on the couch. We sip the warming liquid as he massages my shoulder gently.

"So are you stuffed to the gills?" he asks.

"I'm sated, but not stuffed. It is the key to life, recognizing that nothing is forbidden, but that nothing is your last meal either, so you taste everything once, but don't gorge as if you are getting ready to hibernate. Actually it is really nice to leave a party and not feel uncomfortably full for a change!"

"Good to know. Stay here." He gets up off the couch, and heads back to the kitchen. I shift to a cross-legged position and massage my aching feet. Nathan reappears with a plate, upon which is a lopsided mass of brown.

"I stole the recipe from your recipe box when I was over the other day. It seems to have sunk in the middle, and the frosting is lumpier than I planned, and it is probably inedible, certainly no match for that gorgeous thing Kai made, but I didn't want you to not have this on your birthday."

I look at the plate, the cake almost a replica of the very first one I made as a kid, leaning to one side and concave in the center, frosting chunky in places, with crumbs peeking out.

"It's perfect," I say. And it is.

"Good morning." Nathan is propped up on one elbow, looking down at me.

"Good morning. Are you watching me sleep?"

"I am indeed."

"How's that working out for you?"

He leans over and kisses me. "Very well indeed. Tea?"

"Yes, please."

"Coming right up." He gets out of bed, and I watch him go, still in the jeans he wore last night, button-down shirt untucked and wrinkled.

I stretch and stand up myself, trying to pull the wrinkles out of my dress. I catch a look in the large floor mirror propped against Nathan's bedroom wall and shake my head. I am forty years old. And last night a wonderful man actually baked me a cake, which despite being sort of homely, was really delicious. We talked and talked and he kissed me, and when I started to pull away he asked me to stay. To let him hold me. Said he wanted to wake up to me.

And I spent the night mentally fitful, afraid to fall too deeply asleep, afraid that if I gave myself over to sleep I might give myself over to other things and hating how much that frightens me.

"Breakfast, milady," Nathan says behind me. I turn and see him standing with a tray, two mugs, and two pieces of cake.

I smile at him. "Breakfast of champions."

"This is either a treat or a punishment, but if you really liked the cake, then it will be good, and if you didn't, it'll teach you to never lie to me about my cooking!"

"I know better than that! My grandmother always used to tell this story about my dad. . . . When he was little he used to go to Decatur to visit a friend of his, and the family had this great housekeeper who cooked for them. Anyway, apparently the first time he went to visit, she made a big coconut cake for dessert. And to be polite he said he loved it, even though he really doesn't like coconut at all."

"Let me guess . . . every time he went to visit?"

"Yep, coconut cake."

Nathan laughs. "So this?"

I reach my hand out. "Definitely not coconut cake."

He hands me a plate. I ignore every part of me that tells me that cake for breakfast is a slippery slope, and take what is offered me. It seems the least I can do.

BRISKET

When we did braising in culinary school, the chef instructor asked us each to bring in family recipes connected to our culture, so that we could discuss this ancient technique for tenderizing tough cuts of meat. There were recipes for pot roast and coq au vin and osso bucco and lamb shanks and stews. Kai brought in a recipe for short ribs in sweet soy that he got from his Japanese grandmother. And I brought in the family recipe for brisket, which got rolled out every Jewish holiday, the rich meat falling apart, soaking in tomato gravy, better on the third day than most meals are on the first.

"Close the damn oven, Teensy, you're messing with the mojo." Kai snaps the oven door shut with his foot, and then smacks my butt with a spatula.

"No respect for the boss around here, I swear to God!"

Kai looks over at me and makes the universal sign of the drama violin. "Look, you were the top of the braising class, as you are quick to point out to me at the drop of a hat. And you were the top because of that there brisket, so for the love of all that is holy, stop fussing and let it do its magic. You still have to do the orecchiette salad, the sweet-and-sour slaw, and the butternut squash is almost ready to come out of the other oven. The party isn't even for two more days!"

"Okay, first of all, it isn't a party, it's a Passover Seder. Second of all, it's a big deal, because I haven't seen Nate's family since D.C., and while that was a strange fluke sort of meeting, this is a real 'meet the family' girlfriend sort of thing. The fact that his mom even trusts me to make the main dish is MAJOR. And every family has their own style of Jew food. Some make their brisket sweet and sour and tomatoey, some make it salty and oniony. Some people make matzo kugel and some make potato kugel. And everyone wants THEIR version. It's like Thanksgiving. No matter how good the food is at anyone else's house, it isn't really your Thanksgiving unless the food is the same thing you grew up with."

"Are you people having the Thanksgiving argument again?" Delia asks as she floats into the kitchen, tying a pristine white apron around her wide hips as she moves. Delia has been coming in earlier and earlier these days, watching more carefully, asking more questions. I don't know if she even realizes how much she is getting herself ready to leave us. She claims she is coming in early because there is a new woman in the shelter with four kids under the age of three, all of whom are constantly crying. But I know that every minute she spends in the kitchen with me and Kai takes us one minute closer to the time when she moves up and out. I'm at once grateful for her company and sad at what it hearkens.

"We aren't having the Thanksgiving argument," I say.

"She is never going to let me live down that stupid Thanksgiving," Kai says.

I can't help but take the bait. "You made prime rib!"

"It was delicious," Kai says, shrugging.

"IT WAS BEEF! You can't have beef on Thanksgiving, except for appetizers like meatballs or something. You have TURKEY on Thanksgiving." Last Thanksgiving I spent with Phil and Kai, since I was orphaned and separated and Gilly couldn't make it in from London. Everything was delicious, but it was like a dinner party and not Thanksgiving. The prime rib wasn't the only anomaly. No mashed potatoes or stuffing or sweet potatoes with marshmallows or green bean casserole. He had acorn squash with cippolini onions and balsamic glaze. Asparagus almondine. Corn custard with oyster mushrooms. Wild rice with currants and pistachios and mint. All amazing and perfectly cooked and balanced, and not remotely what I wanted for Thanksgiving. When I refused to take leftovers, his feelings were hurt, and when he got to the store two days later, he let me know.

"Look," Kai says with infinite patience. "For a week we prepped for the Thanksgiving pickups." He ticks off on his fingers the classic menu we developed together for the customers who wanted a traditional meal without the guilt. "Herb-brined turkey breasts with apricot glaze and roasted shallot jus. Stuffing muffins with sage and pumpkin seeds. Cranberry sauce with dried cherries and port. Pumpkin soup, and healthy mashed potatoes, and glazed sweet potatoes with orange and thyme, and green beans with wild mushroom ragu, and roasted brussels sprouts, and pumpkin mousse and apple cake. We cooked Thanksgiving and tasted Thanksgiving and took Thanksgiving leftovers home at the end of the day. I just thought you would be SICK OF TURKEY!"

The three of us collapse into laughter, Delia wiping her eyes at Kai's fake indignation.

"You two. There is no cure for you two," she says. "What can I do?"

"You can shred the cabbage if you want; I'm doing sweet-and-sour slaw," I say, catching my breath.

"Oh, good, that's a new one I don't know," she says, washing her hands at the prep sink.

I guide Delia through the slaw: green cabbage with fennel and green apple and a light dressing of rice wine vinegar, sugar, lime juice, canola oil, and caraway seeds. Kai mashes the butternut squash with applesauce, nutmeg, grains of paradise, and cinnamon. I work on a light pasta salad that I have been playing with, orecchiette pasta with white beans, chopped celery, green peas, and feta in red wine vinaigrette with fresh oregano. The case gets filled, Kai takes off, the doors get opened, and we begin to serve customers. While Delia takes a phone order, I head into the kitchen and take the brisket out of the oven. It is mahogany brown and juicy, and perfumes the kitchen immediately, the scent wafting out into the store.

"What is that smell?" Delia says, eyes closing, inhaling deeply.

"That, is hope," I say.

* * *

"Ellie, close your ears," Nathan's dad, Mike, says to his wife. She feigns placing her hands over the sides of her head. "That is the best brisket I have ever tasted." On his other side, his mother, a woman whose name I don't know since she insists that I call her Mawmaw like the rest of the family, smacks his arm playfully. He winces. "Sorry, Mom, of course, not as good as yours." Ellie smacks his other arm. "Nate, want to help with the dishes before these women kill me? You too, Josh. We'll let you lovely ladies relax." Mike stands up, grabs an armload of dishes, and Nathan follows suit obligingly. Josh, Nathan's brother-in-law, kisses Jeannie, Nathan's sister, on the forehead and also heads for the kitchen. Ellie motions for us to all follow her to the living room while the guys work on clearing the table. When we are out of earshot and comfortably settled on the couches, Ellie turns to me.

"He's right, you know, it's much better than mine."

"Mine too." Mawmaw sighs. "Sort of like my mother used to make. And tender enough for even me to chew!" She grins, clacking her clearly fake teeth together joyfully.

"I'm never going to have a version," Jeannie says dramatically. "Alternating between Jewish holidays here and at Josh's, there's no need for me to bother to learn to cook."

I pause, not sure how to broach this. "Josh's family is Jewish?" Joshua Rodriguez is, by his own admission, a melting pot, with a Mexican father and a mother who is part African American, part Native American, and part Cuban. I assumed that he had converted when he married Jeannie.

Jeannie laughs. "Yep! There is actually a large Jewish

population in Mexico City, where Josh's dad was raised, people who were trying to immigrate to the States and got rerouted for visa problems. And his mom was adopted by a Jewish family as an infant. Isn't it awesome? I got all the shock value of bringing home a mixed-race guy, but still got to marry a Jew!"

Ellie smacks her daughter with a throw pillow, and Mawmaw mutters in Yiddish under her breath. Ellie turns to me. "We aren't that kind of family, and frankly, we have always liked Josh a little bit more than our daughter." Jeannie smacks her mother back with the pillow, and Mawmaw shrugs her shoulders and says, "Meshugge," which I think means "These women are nuts."

I love these people. I knew I liked Nate's parents and Mawmaw in D.C. Jeannie and Josh had a conflicting engagement, so they weren't there. But having spent this lovely evening with them, I think I am falling almost as in love with them as I am with Nate. They are funny and smart and they all like each other so much, not just family love, which is obviously there, but genuine *liking*. Sometimes when you go to someone else's house for a family event, you feel on the outside, you don't know any of the stories, you don't understand the private jokes, but these people have taken such care to tell the whole story for my benefit, to let me into the inner circle, to draw me out and find out about my life and my family. And the nervousness I usually feel in these situations, the desire to withdraw and just observe, all of that fell away the moment I got here, and I have been more present than I have ever been in such a new situation. I'm oddly proud of myself.

"Jeannie," I say. "You can learn to cook this stuff and then offer to bring it with you like I did!"

"Well, my mother-in-law would no more let me bring food to her house than she would let me harbor a fugitive in her guest room." She pauses, and looks at me meaningfully. "And clearly, you're going to be schlepping food in here from now on!"

I can feel my face flushing, both embarrassed and thrilled at the implication.

Ellie smiles at me and pats my hand. "At least we hope so."

"He'll never get married," Mawmaw says to no one in particular.

"MAWMAW!" Ellie says.

"What? He's forty-seven years old. He's a vagabond. If he was going to get married he would have done it by now." She has the righteous indignation of the elderly, the people who have lived long enough to speak their minds and share their opinions, tactful or not. And despite the fact that there is a twinge of sadness to hear the implication of her thought, I somehow want to bail her out.

"Mawmaw, I've already been married once, and I'm in no rush to do it again. And Nathan and I have only known each other about a month. A great month, but still a very short time. I don't think either of us are thinking much past next week, and I think that is appropriate at this stage."

Ellie smiles at me, grateful for my diffusing the situation. "Well, next year, if the two of you aren't together, you can come here and Nate can go with Jeannie to Josh's family!"

We all laugh, and settle in as the men return from the kitchen, sleeves rolled up, to see what is so funny.

"Well, it's official," Nate says, pulling up to my condo.

"What's that?"

"My family likes you more than they like me."

"What can I say? I make a damn good brisket."

"So you do." He leans over and kisses me. "Any chance of coming upstairs?"

"I'd love you to, really, but Nadia is home, and I do have work in the morning."

He sighs. "Okay, then. I'm editing tomorrow, may get caught up, but if I don't talk to you tomorrow, I'll call day after, we'll make plans for the weekend?"

"Of course. And Nate . . ."

"Yeah?"

"Thank you for inviting me to your Seder. I had a really wonderful time."

"You're welcome. Thanks for coming." He leans over again and we kiss deeply. Then I get out of his car and head upstairs.

Nadia isn't home, and I knew she wouldn't be. The lie hangs on me. I know that I'm going to have to deal with the physical part of my relationship with Nathan soon, his disappointment tonight was tangible, and I'm pretty sure his patience and good intentions about letting me set the pace are beginning to wear thin. I may lose him if I'm not careful, and I hate the part of myself that wonders if it might not be easier to lose him than to sleep with him.

I turn on my laptop and check my e-mail.

Mel—

Happy Passover! Went to a Seder tonight at a friend's house, I miss our Seders with Grandma and Grandpa. Everything else seems weird and fake. Wish I could have been with you.

Hope yours was fab!
G

Gilly—

Sorry your Seder was lacking. I also went to a friend's house, it was actually really lovely. Of course, they let me bring the brisket. ☺

Miss you.
Mel

I haven't really told Gilly about Nathan. She knows about the meeting, the whole museum thing, and that we were supposed to get together once we were home. But I don't yet have the words to tell her about how the relationship is progressing. She'll ask first thing how the sex is, and lord knows if I'm not ready to deal with myself on that issue, I'm sure not ready to deal with her.

I open the fridge, and see the container of brisket I brought home with me. I slide the lid off and grab a piece with my fingers. Salty and sweet and meaty. I wrap my hand around the container and lift it out. I settle into the couch to watch Keith Olbermann, and by the time he gets to number three on his countdown, the brisket is gone.

PEANUT BUTTER

When I was a little girl my mom would make us peanut butter and jelly sandwiches for lunch at least three times a week, crusts cut off, sliced twice on the bias for triangles for me, and into long fingers for Gilly. I eventually moved from smooth peanut butter and grape jelly to chunky peanut butter and strawberry preserves to fresh natural peanut butter with homemade damson plum jam or peach coriander confiture. The snack bar at college used to sell PB&J sandwiches for a dollar, with literally an inch-thick layer of peanut butter and a smear of jelly that tasted more of sweet than of fruit, and I'd often eat two of them in a day, a quick snack between classes.

I ring the bell, and wait. Heart in my throat. I hear footsteps within, and soon the door opens. Nathan is wearing a pair of baggy sweatpants, and a T-shirt so old it seems to be made mostly of holes with some fabric holding them together. His hair is rumpled, and there is salt-and-pepper stubble on his cheeks.

And yet, while any rational person would be pissed off to be woken at six thirty in the morning by an unexpected, uninvited guest, Nathan's face breaks into a wide grin. "Well, this is a lovely surprise!" He steps aside to let me in.

"I made muffins," I say, handing him the basket of still-warm peanut butter muffins with dried cherries. "My famous Mea Culpa Muffins."

"Well, I'm not sure what you are mea culpa–ing about, but I never say no to muffins." He puts an arm around my shoulders and squeezes.

"There's more . . ."

Nathan looks around to see if I am carrying something else.

"Not more food, more, um, something I have to say."

He gestures to the couch, and we sit.

"This is all probably going to come out wrong, so you are going to have to forgive me, but I've been up half the night, and I woke my friend Carey at like two in the morning, and I feel like if I don't say this, then I'm a coward and a liar and I'll never be able to really be with you."

Nathan nods, and doesn't interrupt.

I take a picture out of my purse and hand it to him.

"That was me three and a half years ago. I weighed 290 pounds, give or take. I know I told you that I lost a bunch of weight, but what I lost was a whole person. A whole person about the same size I am now. I carried her around for my entire adult life, and she didn't go easily. I have never, and I mean never in my whole life, dated anyone as a normal-size person. Ever. I was a fat teenager, not as big as that, but not small. I was not much smaller than that when I met my ex-husband. And whatever size I am, I'm always going to be a fat girl. It's like being an alcoholic. It doesn't matter if you can't see the fat, it is still here on the inside. Losing that much weight is good for your heart and liver and kidneys. It's good for your muscles and joints. But you don't ever look the same when it is gone."

I take a deep breath. I stop looking at my hands and look into Nathan's face. I think about everything Carey said to me in the wee hours this morning when I woke and couldn't get back to sleep for all the self-loathing I was mired in. And I follow her instructions completely.

"Nathan, I like you very much, and I'm very attracted to you. But underneath these clothes is a body I have put through hell, and it has all the battle scars. My skin is loose, from being stretched to hell all those years, I have more stretch marks than I have regular skin, and my boobs are attempting to introduce themselves to my knees. I wanted to sleep with you the other night. Hell, I wanted to sleep with you in D.C. I probably would have made love to you on the dance floor at your cousin's bar mitzvah, except I'm so afraid that once you see my body as it is now, you won't want me. I keep pushing you away *because* I like you so much, and because I'm so scared that you will be turned off by me."

Nathan stands up, kisses the top of my head, and says, "Stay here for one minute."

He walks away, and I'm shaking. Literally trembling. I can't believe I got it all out. I can't believe I actually said the words. And frankly, I can't believe he hasn't asked me to leave. Because even as I was saying it, the speech I practiced over and over while I baked the muffins in the middle of the night, recited like a mantra in the car on the way here, I never realized in the rehearsal how it would sound here in his apartment. How belittling it was to this kind man to assume he would be repulsed. How little faith I showed him. I'm tempted to run away, but then I hear a noise.

"Turn around," he says behind me. And I do. And he is standing there, totally naked. My breath stops.

He points at a large, pebbly-looking scar on his upper shoulder. "Motorcycle accident when I was in college." He points at his abdomen, a slight paunch. "Too many beers and not enough sit-ups." He points and describes over his whole body. "My pubic hair is going gray, which makes me feel like a grandfather. My balls have dropped, and I'm daily afraid that they will eventually plop into the toilet water. I have acne on my back, and hair on my butt. I also have hair growing out of my nose and ears at an alarming rate, but not nearly as alarming as the rate with which it is leaving my head. My eyelids are getting saggy, and the bags underneath them make me look like Droopy Dawg the second I get tired. My neck has begun to wrinkle and I'm sure a wattle is imminent. I have bad knees from long hours kneeling with a camera. I get breakouts of eczema in the winter, nasty scaly patches on my arms and lower legs. My left big toenail has some sort of fungus that I can't get rid of, which totally grosses me out. I sweat for at least thirty minutes after I get out of a hot shower, to the point that I can't get dressed until it stops. I have an irate colon, intolerable flatulence if I eat the wrong food, and when I drink coffee, my breath could kill at forty paces."

He walks across the room, leans over and takes my hand and pulls me off the couch. He kisses me.

"We aren't twenty, lovely Melanie. I'm so glad you did the work you did, because it means that you will be healthy and around a good long time, and I want to know you for a good long time. If I was looking for some sort of physical specimen of perfection, I'd be one of those Viagra Triangle guys trying to find some lithe thing to have on my arm. But I like that you have lived and I have lived and we have bodies that have gotten us through. And whenever you are ready to make love, I will be ready, because whatever you are, that is what I am attracted to, and anything you see as a flaw, I see as proof of how exceptional and strong you are."

I let my arms slide around his waist, feeling his skin beneath my hands, and then lean back. Because when I looked at the naked length of him in front of me, in the harsh early-morning light, I didn't see any of the flaws he was pointing out, I only saw a man I am very attracted to, and every place on the body he described in such negative terms was simply a place I wanted to place a hand, to kiss, to caress, to know.

"Take me to bed?" I ask.

And then Nathan Gershowitz does something that no man has ever done, or frankly, been able to do. He leans down, and in one swift move, scoops me up in his arms and carries me into his bedroom. And the minute I feel myself lifted into the air, all my fears fly away.

It has been a little crazy since our early-morning confessional the other day. We have spent every night together at his apartment, talking and making love and sleeping and getting to know each other and making love some more. Nathan is a kind and attentive lover, nothing excites him more than my excitement, and I feel like I have made up for my long months of celibacy in just these few days.

Tonight, we had Kai and Phil over to his place for dinner. An easy and fun foursome we made. I roasted a gorgeous chicken, and served it with a light carrot salad in a red wine and thyme vinaigrette, and a wild rice pilaf with pistachios and currants and fresh mint. Kai and Phil brought a gorgeous Gâteau de semoule for dessert, sort of a crème caramel with semolina. We ate heartily, laughed deeply, and played a rousing tournament of Rummikub for a penny a point. I won three dollars and seventy-four cents.

"Look at them. They're in love," Kai whispers, an arm easy about my waist. We look over at Nate and Phil, who are watching rugby clips, of all things, on Nate's laptop.

"Well, who could blame them, adorable as they are."

"You seem happy, Bitty. Are you happy?"

"I am." And it feels true.

"Good. He seems like a good one."

"So he does."

"And if he turns out to not be a good one, I'm totally going all Mrs. Lovett on his ass and we can sell the Nate pies in the store."

I laugh at the gruesome *Sweeney Todd* reference. "We will do no such thing. He'd be very high in fat and cholesterol."

"What are you hens cackling about over there?" Phil calls over.

"We're talking about whether we should meet up with our

younger, more attentive boyfriends later, since the two of you seem so intent on whatever that crap is," Kai calls back.

"That's my cue," Phil says, and wanders over. Nate follows dutifully behind and we make our good nights, with a plan to do it at their place next week.

We barely get the leftovers into his fridge before falling into each other's arms. Nathan strips my sweater off and drops it on the floor, pushing me against the refrigerator and kissing down the length of my body. He pulls my skirt up, and pulls my panties down, burying his face between my legs, his tongue insistent, his hands gripping my ass and pulling me toward him. I claw at his shoulders, dizzy, and come in a flood, knees buckling. Nathan catches me in my swoon, guiding me gently to the floor, cradling me in his arms. I look up at him, and he is smiling down at me.

I smile back. "I love when you look at me like that," I say.

"Like what?"

"With affectionate pride of ownership."

"You think I look at you like I own you?" He looks puzzled.

"No. More like, you know I'm your girl and the fact of that tickles you."

He leans down and kisses me deeply, and I can taste myself on his lips. "So you're my girl, huh?"

I reach up and cup his cheek in my hand. "I'm your girl."

He looks at me very seriously. "I love you, Mel."

I smile, even as the tears prick my eyes. "I love you too, Nate."

He grins. I grin. Pretty soon we are laughing and hugging, and kissing, and we drag off the rest of each other's clothes and make love there on the kitchen floor.

I wake up early and sneak out of Nathan's bed. I pad naked to the bathroom, pee for what feels like ten minutes, wash my hands and face and then head to the kitchen. I pass up my bedraggled dress in favor of Nate's shirt, realizing that I'm finally at a size where I can actually fit into my boyfriend's shirt, another new experience, and I prance a little bit in the kitchen. I see my cell phone light blinking, and pick it up to check my messages.

"Mel, it's Nadia. It's about midnight. I guess you are staying at Nate's tonight. I wish you had let me know that you were sleeping out. I thought you were supposed to come home, so I sent Daniel back to his place after dinner. It would be great if you could give me a heads-up next time. See you tomorrow, I guess."

She sounds hurt and disappointed, and I feel at once ashamed that I didn't think to call her when I realized I wasn't coming home, and irritated that this child who I am allowing to live with me is so presumptuous as to try to make me feel guilty for living my life like a grown-up.

I put on the teapot for myself, and flip the switch on the coffeemaker for Nate, since he set it up last night before we went to bed. I look in the fridge for breakfast fixings, and spot a white paper butcher's package. I look at the label. Thick-cut maple bacon from Gepperth's. They smoke their own, and it is the food of the gods. And while I tend to shy away from bacon, which is my nemesis, I figure on a morning such as this, I've earned it. I'll work out later.

I lay the bacon on a sheet pan and pop it in the oven, while I scramble some eggs with chives, and toast a couple of bagels. Nathan appears, drawn out of bed by the scent of coffee and bacon, and looks me up and down.

"Now that is a happy sight."

He crosses the room, puts his arms around me and kisses me deeply. "Good morning, woman I love."

I blush. "Good morning, man that I love."

"You do know I'm going to have to ravish you again as soon as I get some coffee and breakfast in me."

"Why do you think I got up early to get it ready?"

I look over at my phone, thinking that I should call Nadia to let her know I probably won't be back until later, but she's probably asleep. I'll call her later, at a more human hour. I push all thoughts of guilt out of my head, and focus on breakfast, because I know what is coming after.

I let myself into the apartment in the early afternoon, having spent a gloriously luxurious morning with Nathan. In the kitchen I can see that Nadia must have had a peanut butter sandwich; the jar is still on the counter, open. I open the fridge to grab a bottle of water, and when I close the door I jump at the sight of Nadia, who is standing behind it. The bottle drops and rolls away. She bends and picks it up and hands it to me.

"Sorry. Didn't mean to startle you."

"It's okay, but damn you are quiet!" I accept the proffered bottle and crack it open, taking a long draught. All that sex and bacon is very dehydrating.

"Yeah," she says, opening the fridge and grabbing a bottle

of murky-looking green juice. "My grandma always threatened to put a bell on me."

I try not to look at the crumbs on the counter, the knife, coated with peanut butter, resting on the side of the sink. I reach over and put the lid on the peanut butter jar, noticing that there is jam on the lip of the jar, and I take a deep breath, willing myself not to go mental over something as small as using the same knife in the peanut butter as she used in the jelly.

She pointedly ignores my cleaning up her mess, wanders over into the living room, plops on the couch, and picks up a magazine. Her whole body language is of someone who has been stewing on something. And I hate that I feel so guilty, so resentful. Who the hell is she to give me guilt about anything? This interloper in my house, here out of the goodness of my heart. Even though I know that as generous as I like to think I am being, I'm also benefitting from her being here. It isn't pure philanthropy that places me in this situation. But I refuse to let the joy of this wonderful night and morning be marred by a whole bunch of hurt feelings and resentments on either end.

"Hey, Nadia, I'm really sorry I didn't call. I just got caught up, and didn't think. I'm not used to having someone to be responsible to, so I have to remember to take you into consideration."

"It's okay. No big deal." And even though everything about her says that this is a lie, I'm in no mood and have no inclination to do anything other than pretend that she means it.

"Well, good."

The silence is fraught with the things unsaid. She flips pages and drinks her bilious concoction.

"I'm going to do some laundry, do you have anything you want me to throw in?" A small peace offering.

"Nah, thanks. Daniel and I are meeting at the Laundromat later tonight to do it."

"Wow, that's great!"

"Yeah, I guess."

I'm not going to do this. I'm not going to play this game. She isn't my kid; I don't have to placate and smooth her ruffled feathers and cajole her into telling me what's wrong. If she wants to share her feelings like a grown-up, she can reach out. I've done what I can.

"Okay, well, I'm going to get some stuff organized, and then maybe go to the gym."

"Okay."

I head back to my bedroom, feeling dismissed, and rapidly losing the elation that I felt before coming home. I hate all that passive-aggressive crap. I take a deep breath and close the door behind me, knowing that I'm hiding, and refusing to care.

SPAGHETTI AND MEATBALLS

Once or twice a month my mom would come home and tell us to get ourselves ready. We didn't go out for dinner that often, but when we did, we almost always went to Rosebud in Little Italy. Dad had met the owner, Alex, at the little luncheonette he had opened downtown near Dad's office, and they became friends. When the new place opened in Little Italy, going there seemed like a way to keep Dad alive for us. Alex greeted us like family, brought my mom special reserve glasses of Chianti, sent extra nibbles of things. Once we were there and Frank Sinatra came in and had dinner and Alex introduced us. Every time we went, Gillian and I always got spaghetti and meatballs, even as we got older and our palates got more sophisticated. If we went to other Italian restaurants we might get veal piccata or braciole or risotto. But to this day, if I go to Rosebud, I get spaghetti and meatballs.

And to this day, if Alex happens to be there, he always sends me a glass of reserve Chianti and something extra to taste.

"Sounds like it is going fantastic!" Carey says. "I'm so thrilled for you. I think this is all so wonderful and romantic."

"Thanks. I'm trying to live in the moment and not overthink or look too far ahead. I was just a little worried about how lax I've been about exercising and being careful about my eating."

"Look, it sounds like you're getting plenty of extra exercise, missing a few sessions on the treadmill isn't going to kill you. And while you should pay attention to eating when you aren't hungry, indulging a little here and there isn't going to derail you in any meaningful way."

"I know, and I don't think I've gained any significant weight, maybe a couple of pounds. It just makes me nervous. We go out for late dinners after I get off of work, he wakes me with fresh croissants in bed, his fridge is full of great cheeses and olives and BACON, for chrissakes."

"Moderation, and honesty. You know how to order in a restaurant, and you know how to eat a sensible portion of any food under the sun. If you're spending that much time at his place, bring some stuff from the store to leave in his fridge. And mostly, don't get too much in your head."

"Will do."

"Good for you. We'll chat in a couple weeks?"

"Yeah. Thanks, Carey!"

"I'm proud of you, keep up the good work!"

I hang up the phone in my little office and head back into the store kitchen. Delia is mixing something in a large bowl.

"What's going on with Strawberry Shortcake?" she asks, using her nickname for Nadia, who reminds her of the cartoon due to her age and the shades of pink in her hair. "She seems to be in some sort of mood lately."

I sigh. It's true that Nadia has been withdrawn of late, not sullen, exactly, but not her usual bubbly self. "I'm not really sure. Everything seems to be going fine for her, she and that guy Daniel have been, to use her vernacular, hanging out, and I think she likes him even though he's a little bit strange and not her usual flavor. And she's certainly doing well here, the customers love her. But I haven't really seen her that much lately. I've been spending most of my time outside the store with Nate."

"Perhaps she feels a little abandoned?" Delia asks, tasting her concoction and adding a pinch of salt and a grind of pepper and stirring some more.

"I'm not her mother; I'm her boss and roommate. If she thought that by moving in with me I was going to be responsible for spending all my time with her, she was mistaken."

Delia's head snaps up. "That was a little harsh and a lot defensive." Not an accusation, just an observation, and I feel instantly chided and guilty.

"You're right. I guess it is a little bit of what scared me about having her move in. She's a great kid, but I don't really know her. She doesn't talk much about her past. All I really know is that she grew up somewhere in Indiana, was raised by her grandmother, was bulimic in high school, and has horrible taste in men. Janey met her a few years ago at some wellness seminar in Indianapolis and they hit it off, but she seems unclear as to why Nadia was there."

"What does her past have to do with anything?" Delia tastes again, and reaches for a handful of chopped parsley.

"It's how you get to know someone; you share your past, you tell your stories, and you let someone know where you came from. All I know about Nadia is from the last couple of months before I met her. It's weird."

"Some people would rather leave the past in the past. It doesn't mean anything bad necessarily." Delia hands over the bowl. Inside is a salad and I grab a tasting spoon. There are black beans, shredded pork tenderloin, corn, red peppers, celery, scallions, and toasted pine nuts in a vinaigrette that tastes of lime and cumin and has some back-of-the-throat heat to it.

"D, this is delicious."

She smiles sheepishly. "We had those few slices left of the pork from yesterday and I thought I could stretch it. I only used a quarter cup of oil."

"It's wonderful. Be sure to write down the recipe and let's put it in the case today. Thank you."

She beams, and starts to mound the salad on the white rectangular platters we use for selling. "Mel, if I may . . . I know your life hasn't been a bowl of cherries, but there is nothing in your history that is particularly shameful. There is nothing in your history that you might think would prevent someone from liking or respecting you or being your friend. We all aren't so lucky. I don't know where Shortcake came from, and I don't care. She's a good kid, a little weird, but sweet and a nice addition to our strange little group, and I think something is going on here. You might not have wanted to be too involved with her, but she's here now, and she's hurting a little bit, and I don't think you'll lose your handsome new boyfriend if you're a little sensitive to her. Maybe tell her to bring her boy around so you can meet him. Have a double date. Reach out to her to let her know you aren't the kind of friend who disappears when you have a man in your life. Free advice, and worth what you pay for it." She floats out of the kitchen to add her salad to the case, and I think about Nadia. Does it really matter if I don't know who she was as long as I feel like I know who she is? And I'm not sure I know the answer to that. But I do know that Delia is right. I have taken her on, and in light of that, I need to figure out the best way to help mend this small rift.

"This is going to be so much fun, thanks Mel!" Nadia says, coming out of the bathroom twisting her chameleon hair into a loose bun with tendrils hanging down.

I reach over and tug a loose strand of deep magenta. "This new?"

She smiles. "Something I'm trying out. Too much?"

I laugh. "It's all in the same pink family, I think it looks good." I'll never understand Nadia's obsession with coloring her hair, but I have to admit it looks good and almost natural on her in a strangely unaffected way. As if it was supposed to be four shades of pink. Most kids I see with the punk hair colors always seem as if they are trying to scream some statement at me, political or otherwise, but Nadia just seems to need some pink in her hair, and it's between her and her head as to what it means.

"You look great, Mel. I love that dress."

I'm in one of my favorite things, a pale, sage green wrap dress that hides all my flaws and accentuates all my good spots, and is as comfortable as pajamas. It is made of some magical jersey material that moves with me, never clings, and never wrinkles. Plus it makes my eyes look almost olive green. "Thanks, sweetie. What time is Daniel expected?"

She checks her watch. "Seven." She pauses, looking sheepish. "He might be a little late. He isn't very good about timing."

"That's all right. The great thing about this meal is that the only thing that can get overcooked you don't even make till the last minute, and everything else is all ready." I've made one of my favorite salads, celery, green apple and shaved Parmesan, which will get a squirt of fresh lemon and a drizzle of olive oil at the last minute. Homemade tomato sauce is simmering lightly on the stove, and tiny veal meatballs have already been browned. The precooked meatballs are so small that they will heat through in the sauce in the time it takes for the pasta to cook. Nadia helped me make a thin-as-paper apple galette with fig glaze, which is cooling on a rack.

"I never knew spaghetti and meatballs could be so fancy! But I'm glad you suggested it. Daniel has sort of a limited palate. Very boring meat-and-potatoes kind of guy. The other night I wanted to go to this Chinese place and he ordered a hamburger! I didn't even know they had it on the menu!"

"Not everyone is a foodie, or has to be. But I'm glad you think this dinner will meet with his approval. And I'm glad things are going well between you."

"Well, I think they are." Nadia pauses, eyebrows furrowing. "We haven't, I mean he hasn't, there isn't exactly . . ." She trails off.

"No sex yet?" Poor thing. She seems a little bit stricken. "But I thought you've spent a couple nights together, when I was at Nate's?"

"EXACTLY! We have. But we just SLEPT together, we haven't done anything. Nothing. I mean, not totally nothing, we've kissed, you know, but that's it. When we spent the night, we just cuddled." She runs her hands through her hair. "I've never been in this situation. All the guys I've ever dated have, like, totally pounced on me the moment they got a chance. And I'm not so good at the whole taking-it-slow thing, I just feel like, sex, you know, it's so natural and something our bodies were meant to do, and if it isn't good, then you aren't going to last anyway, so you might as well find out. . . ."

"I suppose that's one way to look at it. But didn't you ever think that maybe waiting, getting to know someone a little bit, letting the anticipation build, that might make the sex better?"

She looks at me as if I have offered up Einstein's theory of relativity. In Mandarin. "I guess I never much thought about that. Usually I figured that if a guy wanted to sleep with me, my best shot at him hanging out with me again was to do it."

My heart breaks for her. I was that girl. The one who assumed that if a guy was even momentarily attracted to a fat girl, she had better jump on that opportunity and hope it was good enough to keep him coming back for more. Luckily for me, more often than not, it was, and most of my boyfriends began as either a hookup at a party, or a late-night study session turned make-out session. I think it's why I didn't even know Andrew and I were dating at first; I'd never had that normal progression of someone asking you to do something and not making it immediately sexual.

"Nadia, there's obviously nothing wrong with sex; I personally am a big advocate for sex. But there's also nothing wrong with waiting. Do you feel like the relationship with Daniel is just building slowly, or do you feel like the chemistry isn't there?"

She bites her lower lip gently. "I feel like when we first started hanging out, that he was totally into me, and I wasn't that interested, but felt like I should try and break my bad-boy pattern for a change. And I liked the way he looked at me, the way I felt powerful around him, like, you know, that old saying, it is better to be the person in the relationship who is loved more than they are in love, or something like that, you know . . . like he looked at me as if I were some amazing thing, and that made me feel good, and even though I wasn't totally, you know, hot for him, I thought it would be nice to be with someone who might just be nice to me for a change." She shakes her head. "But the more we hang out, suddenly I feel all powerless again, and he doesn't seem to really be that interested in me, you know, physically, and that makes me wonder what is wrong with me, that this total geeky guy, who is like, no one's idea of a prize, isn't at least attempting to get into my pants, even when we spend the night together!"

"Nadia, do you like him, or do you just want him to like you? Because if you don't really like him, it isn't very nice to . . ."

"I LOVE HIM!" She throws her arms into the air, and drops her chin on her chest. "I mean, I think I might want to love him, or something. He is so smart and weird and none of his clothes match, and he looks like he needs a haircut, even when he just had a haircut, and one of his eyes is hazel and the other one is blue, like three-D glasses, and when he smiles, which isn't a lot, he has these tiny little baby teeth, perfectly white and even, like a row of corn kernels, small, but not gross small, just like, different. And he has beautiful hands and he only listens to music on actual records, like big black plastic records, and he's from Nebraska!"

This all comes out in a rush, as if any of it would make sense to me, as if she were giving a woman's usual litany of the ideal guy. But where most of us would say that he was smart and funny and kind and cute with a great butt and a good relationship with his mother, Nadia has offered up a series of qualities that I think only she can understand.

"Well," I say, sort of at a loss. "If he's from NEBRASKA . . . that is, um, something."

Nadia looks at me. And then she smiles, crooked teeth winking, eyes wide. "I guess that all sounded totally bizarre, huh?"

"Yeah, little bit."

"What do I do?"

"Tell you what; I'll see if I can spend the night tonight at Nate's. There is a really nice old cognac in the bar. Ask him to stay for a nightcap, look him in the eyes and tell him that you like him, that you are attracted to him, and while you don't want to pressure him, if he was thinking it might be time to take it to the next level, you are feeling ready for that. My guess is, he's probably just a real gentleman and wants to be sure that you are ready. Tell him you want him. I bet the night gets passionate very quickly."

"You're right. I have to let him know. Thanks, Mel!" She grabs me in one of her attack hugs, rocking me back and forth, and then disappears into her room to keep getting ready.

I call Nate.

"Hey!" he says. "I'm just jumping in the shower, and I'll be over within the hour."

"Hey, yourself. Wish I were there to help with the rub-a-dub."

Nate laughs. "Me too. What's up? Do you need me to bring anything besides the wine?"

"Nope, just wanted to know if it would be okay for me to come crash at your place tonight."

"Of course. You know I'd never turn down your company. I thought we weren't sleeping over tonight since you have to be at the store early tomorrow?"

"We weren't but I want to give Nadia home-court advantage with her boy tonight, making myself scarce."

"You are a good woman. That is a very sweet thing to do. And that makes me extra lucky! Something to really look forward to. I'll see you soon, kitten."

"See you soon."

I head back to my bathroom. If I'm going to be staying at Nate's tonight, there is some extra primping to be done.

This is the longest meal I've ever suffered through, and if Nathan Gershowitz pinches my thigh one more time under the table, or nudges me with his foot, or goes into the kitchen to get something and raises his eyebrows at me over Nadia's and Daniel's heads, I'm going to fucking punch him in the throat.

Daniel arrived forty minutes late, by which time the tenor of the evening had already slid downhill. Nate, thinking he was helping me out with my curiosity problem, basically spent those uncomfortable forty minutes interrogating Nadia with all of his investigative skills. She deftly answered all his questions about family and background and history without actually giving away any information. And since he is a documentarian, he couldn't let it go. The more she dodged sharing real info, the more he pressed. "What did your dad do for a living?" "What did you do for Christmas?" "Where do your siblings live?" He was relentless, and Nadia, who had been sitting straight and feeling confident, and ready to take on confronting her guy, sank into the couch, her shoulders dropped, her eyes unsparkled. I grabbed Nate and asked him to help in the kitchen, and whispered for him to knock it off, but I didn't really do it in a very nice way, so he narrowed his eyes at me and clearly was irritated. By the time Daniel finally arrived, we were all grateful for what we assumed would be the relief of a new person.

Not to be.

Nadia was now really nervous, and Nate made no less than three snarky jokes about Daniel being late, including one where he implied that her boyfriend was so excited to see her he clearly forgot where she lived. Daniel is as quirky as one would expect, based on Nadia's description, and has alternated between not participating at all in the conversation and giving long, incomprehensible monologues related to the inner workings of computers and his admiration of some guy he calls The Woz. He picked all the apples out of his salad, and left the rest. "Celery. No. No food with strings." He separated the meatballs on one side of his plate, and the pasta on the other, ate the pasta one strand at a time, and waited till it was gone to eat the meatballs. "Don't really like to mix my foods."

He also brought every other bite to his nose and sniffed deeply before eating.

On the one hand, I'm sort of grateful for his peculiarities, since Nate seems now more interested in poking at me to indicate some sort of amazement at this kid's oddities than in being irritated at me for chiding him. On the other, I'm watching Nadia practically disappear she is getting so small, and she is inhaling everything in sight, taking huge second and third helpings, which makes me very concerned, since bulimia, like any eating disorder, never goes away, never leaves your psyche, and this bingeing behavior might lead to a relapse.

I take advantage of the current lull in conversation to ask if everyone has finished with the main course. "Nadia, why don't you and I clear, and we'll bring dessert to the living room. Nate? Daniel? Tea or coffee?"

Daniel pats his mouth delicately, and then drops my grandmother's linen napkin directly onto his plate, where I can see it soaking up the remains of the tomato sauce. I cringe inwardly and suppress all desire to jump across the table and pluck his eyes out with the salad tongs. "Not for me," he says blithely. "Can't drink brown liquids."

Nate rolls his eyes. "I'd probably prefer bourbon."

Nadia and I clear the plates. She grabs the napkin off Daniel's plate as soon as we get into the kitchen, and begins running it under cold water, scrubbing it together, adding the dish soap in a frantic attempt to prevent the damage we both know is already beyond help. Her shoulders are shaking.

I put down the plates, touch her back, and she flinches. I pull her around and into my arms, and stroke her hair. "Guess this wasn't such a good idea I had, huh?"

Good Enough to Eat 147

She laughs and sniffles. "This is a disaster."

"I'm so sorry, sweetie, I really thought we could all just have a good night and get to know each other better."

"I know. And I don't know what happened. Daniel isn't usually THIS strange, I mean, you know, he's an odd little rabbit, but tonight, this is really the most ridiculous behavior, I just don't know where it came from, and your napkin . . ." She trails off.

"It's a napkin. I have a full set, it's one of twelve. And I can only fit six people at that table anyway. He couldn't know."

She whispers at me violently, "He's thirty! He could know that you don't drop a fabric napkin on your plate! He could know that you show up to a dinner party on time! He could know that you don't have to give some weird explanation for not wanting to eat or drink something, you can just politely decline. HE COULD KNOW TO JUST FUCKING LEAVE THE MEATBALLS IN THE PASTA WHEN YOU EAT SOMETHING SOMEONE HAS MADE FOR YOU!"

We laugh. "Guess you're not asking him to stay over tonight, huh?"

"Not a chance."

I think for a minute. I think about what I would do in her place. If it had been me who suffered what she has suffered tonight, I would have waited till everyone was gone, and then eaten every bite of the leftovers. I would have made a huge bowl of popcorn drizzled with butter and polished it off in front of the television. I think about how truly tempting it will be for her, all alone, to binge more and then purge, to have some control over something. And I make a decision. "How about we have some dessert and something to drink and then kick these retarded boys out and watch girl movies all night?"

She looks up at me, eyes wide. "Really?"

"Really. Frankly, I think neither of them deserve our company tonight."

She smiles wide, and hugs me. "Thanks, Mel."

I hug her back. "C'mon. Let's get the dessert out there. The sooner we serve them the sooner they'll go."

I slice squares of the apple galette, and put them on plates with forks. Nadia pours Nate a neat bourbon, and we head out to the living room.

Nate and Daniel are talking in low voices, and stop when we enter the room. They accept their plates, and the four of us sit in awkward silence as we eat the light, crisp galette, the crust buttery and shattering, a whisper of apple melting on top, the light fig glaze providing a caramel depth.

"This is really good," Daniel says softly.

"Delicious," Nate says, taking a deep draught of his bourbon.

We finish our morsels, and I motion Nate into the kitchen with me.

"I'm going to stay here tonight after all," I say.

"Yeah. I sort of figured." He runs his hands through his hair.

"For what it's worth, I'm sorry. Sorry for putting you in this situation, sorry for snapping at you before, sorry for bailing on you . . ."

He leans forward and kisses me gently. "Me too."

"Thank you. I love you."

"I love you too. Want me to get that idiot out of here so you and Nadia can talk about how dumb men are?"

I laugh. "Please."

He kisses me again. "Done and done. I'll call you tomorrow. Maybe we can grab a late bite or something when you get off work tomorrow night?"

"Sure, sounds good."

We head to the living room.

Nate claps Daniel on the shoulder. "So, buddy, what do you say, should we thank these gorgeous women for dinner and get out of their hair?" He says it in a way that doesn't really make it a question, but more of a proclamation. Daniel looks flustered, but gets up anyway.

"Thank you for dinner, Melanie. It was very nice." He puts out his hand and I give him mine in return. His hand is surprisingly soft. His sleeves are frayed around the cuffs, and there is something about this that suddenly seems sort of dear. He smiles, somewhat pained, and lets go of my hand to hug Nadia. He whispers something in her ear that makes her smile sheepishly.

Nate comes over and holds me tight, kissing the top of my head. "See you tomorrow, beautiful. Love you."

I look up into his face. "Love you."

They leave together, and Nadia and I look at each other.

"Thanks for trying," she offers, shrugging.

"Yeah. Let's never do this again." We laugh. "We'll leave the kitchen for tomorrow. Pajamas in ten minutes?"

She grins. "You bet."

She heads down the hallway, and I go to my room to change. The evening was a disaster, and I have to worry about my fragile roommate, who has suffered more than anyone ought to for the sake of a nice evening at home, and who, despite her best efforts to the contrary, needs me. And I, despite my best efforts to the contrary, sort of like it.

CHILI

Andrew and I, while we didn't entertain much at home, were famous for our Super Bowl parties. The festivities eventually got sort of legendary. Our last Super Bowl party was also the last time Andrew and I made love. He hadn't touched me in months, claiming everything from exhaustion to strained muscles from racquetball to sinus headache. I'd actually wondered if we would bother with the party, now that I wasn't at the firm anymore, but when our Bears actually made it to the big game, the party became essential. We pulled out all the stops, had T-shirts made with the official Super Bowl logo, bought Bears caps for everyone. Things had been so tense between us, our first real rough patch, I thought. We'd been so disconnected, but at the party, we were our old selves, hosting and laughing and our hearts breaking when the Colts beat us. We stayed up late with our friends, commiserating over

chili and beer, and when we went to bed, Andrew reached
for me and we fell into each other as we always did. Differ-
ent, quieter, gentler. He touched me with tenderness, as if I
were fragile, as if I were some delicate flower he didn't want
to damage. A couple of months later, he left. I haven't made
chili since.

"Today, Miss Nadia, we are making chili." An assignment
from Carey. Food does not have power, not over us, not over
our emotions, not over our lives. The only food you should
ban from your life is food that you dislike for its own inherent
qualities, not for the qualities you imbue it with. I've purged
phrases from my vocabulary like "chocolate pudding is the
devil" and "Cheetos are out to get me." I've tried to stop
thinking about food as "bad" or "good," and only to think
about it as fuel for my actions, sustenance for my body, pleasure for my soul. Carey was talking about a new chili recipe
she had tried that she loved, a low-fat ground chicken version
with green chilies and white beans and offered to send me the
recipe. When I admitted that I hadn't eaten chili, one of my
former favorite foods, in more than a year and told her why,
she told me to get the fuck over it, reclaim and disempower
it, and remember it only as a source of joy. And protein. Ever
dutiful, I've got Carey's recipe in my bag, have made some
initial changes to it, and am actually looking forward to cooking it today.

"Cool. I love chili."

"I used to love it. I'm hopeful that I will love it again."

"Excellent. So, um, Mel, I, um, have an idea for the

business," Nadia says quietly beside me in the car on the way to work.

Things have been pretty good between us since the dinner party debacle. I think she really appreciated my choosing her over Nate, and while she's still vague about her past, she is more open about her thoughts and feelings, seems to be more relaxed at the store, more comfortable at home. Every time I think about trying to get more information out of her, I remember what Delia said about some people needing to keep their past in the past, and suppress the urge to press her. She and Daniel are still hanging out, and she confided that they have indeed consummated their relationship, and that it was better than she anticipated. She is referring to him as her boyfriend, and while I don't particularly understand the attraction to him as a person, I am proud of her attraction to him as an idea, someone stable and unlikely to con her, cheat on her, or leave her in emotional ruin. I can't say that I hope they survive, but I hope they hang in there long enough for her to realize that she deserves someone to be nice to her, that she doesn't have to give more than she receives, that love shouldn't be a source of pain. She's also been slowly getting more involved at the store, chatting with customers, asking Kai to show her some basic knife skills, giving Delia neck and backrubs when she gets tired and sore from lots of chopping and stirring and schlepping bags of produce.

"You do, huh? What's that?"

Her voice is low, almost sheepish. "Well, you know that Sacramento Sloane business? The low-cal food delivery service?"

"I do." One year, relatively early in our marriage, Andrew

got handed a big case that was being run out of the Los Angeles office, and had to go out there for six weeks. I thought I'd take the opportunity to maybe drop a few pounds, and signed up for the service. It was exorbitantly expensive, and the food was inedible. I'd eat the miniscule portions, add a salad, a piece of fruit, and then an hour later I'd be face-first into a bag of chips, or on the phone ordering real food.

"Well, you know Janey thinks they killed her mom?"

I almost slam on the brakes. "What?!?"

Nadia laughs. "Yeah. A couple of years ago, Janey's mom, who had been subsisting entirely on fast-food takeout and things fried in bacon grease her entire life, decided that she would try and lose some weight. She was pretty heavy, and was having some cardiac issues, so she signed herself up for Sacramento Sloane. They made her first delivery on Monday afternoon. She ate her first meal for dinner Monday night. By Tuesday she was dead."

"Food poisoning?"

"Heart attack. But still. Anytime anyone says Sacramento Sloane, Janey says, 'She killed my mom, you know.' It's pretty silly. Anyway, I was just thinking, people spend a lot of money on that stuff and it isn't very good. What if you started a delivery business yourself? I mean, wouldn't it just mean making more of what you already make for the store and packing it up? You could charge for delivery or people could pick it up at the store . . . you know . . . I've just been thinking about it lately."

I'm stunned. It's a brilliant idea, and a logical one, and something that never in a million years would have occurred to me. It would be a big undertaking, but is such a natural offshoot of what I'm already doing, I can't believe I haven't thought of it myself.

Nadia takes my stunned silence for disapproval, and jumps back in. "I'm sure you probably don't want to deal with it, and just want people to come to the store, never mind . . ."

"It's brilliant."

"What?"

"It's brilliant. You're brilliant. I never thought of it, but you're a genius!"

Nadia looks at her lap, and grins. "You really think it's a good idea?"

I pull the car into the parking space behind the store and turn off the engine, turning to face her. "Honey, it's fucking AMAZING. And I love you for thinking of it, and if you're interested, and it works, I'd be able to have you on full-time to run it."

"Really? You'd let me do that?" She seems shocked.

"It's your idea, why don't you do some research into what other services are available in Chicago, what they provide and what they charge. I'll pay you an extra few hours to track down the info, and then we'll see if this is something that makes sense for us. If it does, we'll see what we need to do to make it happen, and if we get the business, then it can be your baby. You handle the customers and orders and I'll handle the food. Deal?"

She smiles at me, eyebrows dancing madly. "Deal."

"C'mon. Let's go to work."

She hops out of the car, somehow looking taller, older. And suddenly, I feel very lucky to know her.

We head inside and begin getting things organized. We've

barely started when Kai flies in. He crosses the room and grabs me in a powerful hug for someone so small.

"Oh, Ittly Bittly, poor, poor little Mellie Mel, I couldn't believe it myself. Is it a shock? Did you know? You couldn't have known and not told me! The balls! And the gall! The unmitigated gall balls! Do you want me to cover you today? I can get you in with my masseuse. . . ." Kai is rubbing my shoulder, his brow furrowed, deep concern for my well-being pouring off him like feverish heat. And I haven't the faintest idea what he is referring to.

"Kai, honey, I'm not sure exactly what you are talking about here. I'm fine. Why on earth do you think I have reason to not be fine?"

Kai puts on a soothing voice, similar to the tone you would use when speaking to a small child or someone of limited intelligence. "Melanie, princess, don't you read the paper?"

"Like, the newspaper?"

He shakes his head. "No, the Pickwick Papers. YES, the newspaper!"

"Sometimes I do the crossword . . ."

Kai reaches into his bag and pulls out a section of the *Chicago Tribune*. "Sit, honey. Nadia, make some tea."

Now I'm concerned. I sit down on one of the stools in the kitchen and Kai hands me the paper. Engagement announcements. Pictures of happy young couples, posed so you can see the engagement rings, son of so and so, daughter of so and . . . my heart stops.

Andrew. Andrew and Charlene. Andrew Lezak and Charlene Lindsay announce their upcoming nuptials to take place this June in Majorca. Andrew is grinning in the fake toothsome way he always does in pictures. Charlene, in all her enormous glory, is flashing a ring the size of a fucking doorknob. They are getting married next month, in goddamned Majorca, which was supposed to be where Andrew and I were going to go this year for our tenth anniversary. I feel sick. I feel hurt. I want to cry. Or maybe throw up. Or maybe throw up and then cry. Nadia puts a cup of tea in front of me, and sees what I'm staring at.

"Oh, Mel. That's so awful."

I take a deep breath. I am not going to lose it. They aren't worth it. "Well, they've been together for nearly three years, why shouldn't they get married?"

"He could have called you, given you some warning. . . ." Kai says.

"Why? He didn't bother to tell me that they were fucking each other behind my back, why would he tell me that they are engaged?"

Nadia and Kai look at each other, unsure of what to do.

"I'm fine, guys, I'm fine. It's a surprise, unexpected, but ultimately none of my business."

They look at me blankly. My shoulders drop. "Not buying it, huh?"

They shake their heads in unison.

I think about it. I fight every urge to put on a brave face and muscle through this day. "Kai, if you can take care of things here today, that would be great. I'm going to leave. Nadia, if I go out I'll leave you a note at home or send you a text or something. Thanks, guys."

I grab my bag and keys and head out to my car. And somehow, I don't really want to go home. As I pull out of the alley, I dial Nathan.

"Good morning, beautiful." His voice is gruff, and I know I have woken him up. "Why aren't you here?"

"Do you want me to be there?"

"Of course. I always want you here."

"Then unlock your door and tell the doorman I'm coming and go back to bed. I'll be there soon."

I wind the car through the Chicago streets, the calm of the early morning always surprising in such a big city. I'm feeling numb. I don't know why it should shake me so; it isn't like I would want him back even if he wanted to come back. And frankly, I've always felt sorry for Charlene as much as I was angry with her. Charlene had little experience with men, one of those self-loathing heavy women who allow their size to distance themselves from people, to prevent them from seeking out romance. In the time we knew each other she often said that she didn't have time to worry about dating, and I got the impression she didn't feel worthy of love, or that she was someone who could be an object of desire. I'm sure that when Andrew began paying her attention it was intoxicating, and while I can't condone her behavior, I have always understood how it happened. Hate that it happened, but I get it. I've always gotten it. And when I realized that Andrew is at his very core simply only physically attracted to larger women, and Charlene, for all her moral turpitude, is very much what I was—smart, driven, successful, and most important, substantial—the two of them made perfect sense to me.

But married. And married in a place that Andrew and I had researched endlessly, talked about, planned on. It is such a slap in the face. And to put the announcement in the paper, it is insult to injury. Everyone must know. Everyone from my old life, our old colleagues, our old friends, they all must know that he was cheating, that I was being made a fool of, that I was one of those pathetic wives who didn't suspect or chose to overlook the blatant infidelity. I'm mortified. As much as those people are no longer in my life, it feels awful to know what they must be whispering, what they must be thinking of me.

I find a parking space in front of Nate's building. His doorman tips his hat and buzzes me in, and I take the elevator upstairs. The door is unlocked and I let myself in, drop my coat and bag on the couch, and go to the bedroom, shedding my clothes as I go. Nate is lying on his back, arm thrown over his head. Naked, I slip under the covers and slide up against the length of him. He turns and pulls me close into his arms, running his hands over my body, bringing his lips to mine and kissing me deeply. I melt into his embrace and give my thoughts over to his deft touches until nothing else in the world exists except for me and this man and the pleasure we can give each other.

"So, to what do I owe this unexpected visit?" Nate asks me around a mouthful of French toast.

"I decided to take an extra day off."

"You never take an extra day off. You barely take your regular day off, off. What gives?"

"Andrew is getting married." On our second date I told Nate about Andrew's affair, about the double betrayal, about finding out that my marriage, which I always thought was so great, was just a sham. "Kai brought in the paper today and there in the announcements, Andrew and Charlene and their engagement and her ring and their happiness and I just had to get out of there. Instant extra day off."

Nate puts down his fork and takes a swig of coffee. "So you came here."

I smile. "Sanctuary."

His face is impassive. "You'll have to forgive me if it takes some of the shine off the morning."

"What do you mean?"

Nate pauses, thinking carefully. "I mean, I thought that you just woke up this morning and missed me. I thought you had a flash where you suddenly wanted me so badly you couldn't stay away, had to suppress all your work ethic and run to my arms. I thought this morning was about you and me, not about you and your ex."

I can't believe he is actually upset that I came to him. "You're kidding, right? I was shocked, yes, thrown for a loop, certainly, a little hurt and angry, to be expected, but I came here to feel better, because I wanted to remind myself why I shouldn't care what the hell Andrew and his slamhound get up to. I came here because I love you, and I would have thought that you would want to comfort me."

"Ah, but there's the rub. You didn't come to me and tell me you were upset and in need of comfort. You didn't come to me and say that you had this big shock and that you wanted me to know that my love makes it all better. You didn't say anything at all, you just called and invited yourself over, sidled into my bed, and worked out whatever your personal demons are."

My hands are shaking. "So, what, you feel, I dunno, used? Like I just came here to pounce on you, lure you into sex for my own insidious purposes?"

"Don't get overly dramatic, I'm just telling you how I feel. Not used, exactly, but not included either. It isn't that I don't understand why this would bother you a bit, I just wish you had been honest with me about your motivation for coming over."

"Sorry to be such a manipulative drama queen, and such a disappointment to you." I get up and grab my bag and coat off the couch where I dropped them earlier.

"Don't do that; don't run out on this like some child."

"NOW I'M A CHILD!" Of all the insensitive, stupid things he could say to me. Whatever anger and betrayal I felt earlier about Andrew and Charlene is now focusing full attention on Nate. "You know what, Nate? In a relationship the point is to support each other, to help each other, to be there for each other. I'm sorry if I offended your delicate sensibilities by not telling you everything that happened before I got here. Frankly, you didn't give me much of a chance. You didn't bother to ask why I was coming over, and when I got into bed you kissed first. I guess I should have thought to stop you and say 'Gee, honey, before we get all hot and bothered, I just want to have full disclosure of my mental state,' but at the time I was just so happy to be here with you that it didn't occur to me to give the news bulletin. Not to worry, it certainly won't happen again."

I cross the room to the door and move through it. It catches behind me, and shaking, I press the elevator button. And to my enormous and devastating disappointment, the elevator comes and Nate's door remains closed. He isn't coming for me. I get in, and watch as the elevator doors slide shut, and wonder if this is a place I'll ever visit again.

It takes me about twenty minutes to get home, fuming and

alternately trying not to cry and muttering, "fuck fuck fuck asshole fuck" under my breath, and I have no idea if I am referring to Nate or to Andrew, which in a weird way makes me wonder if Nate wasn't the teensiest bit right, and that is the worst feeling in the world. Because the most basic human impulse, the most core desire of any person, is to be right. And on a day like today I need it; I need to be the one in the plus column, I need to be infallibly right, and even if I'm not, I needed Nate to pretend that I was.

I go upstairs and let myself in, wanting a long hot shower, hating that I can still smell Nate on my skin, that I can still feel his touch, the evidence of him throughout my body.

Going to the fridge to grab a bottle of water, I notice a container from the store with a note on the shelf. I take it out.

Mel—

I'm really sorry about your ex and that whole thing, it totally sux and I hope you are having a good day and doing something fun. In case you needed it, I wanted to bring this home for you . . . I told Kai about your plan for the day and he and I worked this up. I think it is awesome, and hope you do too. See you at some point, if I'm asleep when you get home, feel free to wake me if you need to vent or anything.

Nadia

I open the container.
Chili. Perfect.

Without even thinking I turn and in one fell swoop throw the thing against the backsplash over the sink with all the force in my body. The container explodes, making a splotch on the wall that reminds me in a sick way of movie special effects when someone shoots himself in the head. The smell of the spicy, meaty stew as it slowly oozes down the wall turns my stomach, and I leave the kitchen, head for the bedroom, and close the door. I open the nightstand and grab my Ambien, a prescription my doctor gave me for occasional insomnia. I take a little white pill. Crawling into my bed still dressed, I leave all of my messes behind and fall into dreamless sleep.

When I wake up, it's dark outside and the clock reads nine forty-five. I've been asleep almost eleven hours, and my body aches, and my head is groggy. I reach for the water bottle on the nightstand and drain it in one go. I get up and realize I'm still in my clothes, and take them off, grabbing my pajamas and slipping into my robe. I head for the bathroom and run the shower, letting the needles of hot water bore into my muscles, and soak my hair. I scrub myself from top to bottom, and, feeling refreshed, get into my pajamas and head for the kitchen, suddenly starving, and also remembering that I have some truly nasty cleaning to do.

But my kitchen is spotless. There is no evidence of my earlier apelike behavior.

"Hey," a voice says softly behind me. Nadia is sitting on the couch, a book in her lap.

"Hey."

"You okay?"

"Not really. Thank you for cleaning up, that was very unnecessary . . ."

"Don't even think about it. I was sort of proud of you, actually. Kind of glad I got to see it."

"Why?"

"You're so together, and calm all the time and I guess, I mean sometimes I want to throw things and yell and hit something, and I feel like a freak, but if you can be pushed to, like, attack your own house with food, then I'm probably more normal than I thought."

There is an odd logic here that makes me smile. "Well. I'm glad that my tantrum is a source of comfort for you."

"Was the chili that bad?"

"No. Chili is not bad. Men are bad. Chili is an innocent bystander."

She looks confused, but I don't have the energy to explain.

"Is there anything I can do?" she asks, letting my inane chili commentary go without question.

"Not tonight, honey. Thanks, though. I just had a shitty day, and all I want is to eat something and go back to bed and start over tomorrow."

"Can I make you something? When I was blue as a kid my mom would always make me buttered noodles. I know I'm not a great cook, but I could do that, if you wanted."

She is so sincere, so sweet, and buttered noodles sound pretty good to me right now, soft and soothing and totally benign. "I'd love some buttered noodles, actually, that would be great. Try to go easy on the butter, though, okay?"

She bounces off the couch, glad for a job. "You sit over here and watch TV, and I'll bring it to you. Light on the butter, I promise. I think you have a thousand episodes of *Cold Case* on your TiVo."

"Perfect." I sit on the couch, and Nadia actually tucks the throw blanket around me and hands me the remote before heading for the kitchen. I turn it on and settle in to watch a strong, smart woman solve the problem.

APPLE PIE

There are dog people and cat people. Coke people and Pepsi people. Night people and morning people. And there are cake people and pie people. I'm a cake person. Always was. Not, obviously, to the exclusion of pie. I'm still me after all, so if someone puts pie in front of me, with the exception of mince-meat, I'm going to eat it, probably to excess. But if you hand me a dessert menu, the cake options have to be pretty bad for me to pick pie instead. While I'm not a pie person, even I have to admit that Gilly's signature apple pie is spectacular. There was never rhyme or reason to when she would make it, Gilly isn't predictable, so it wasn't a holiday pie or a birth-day pie or anything like that. It was usually a Tuesday pie, or an "I had a nice day" pie, or, in a house of three women, PMS pie. You'd come home and there it would be, brown and fragrant, cooling on a rack. Once, when we were in high

school, Mom took us out to Quig's Orchard to pick our own apples. We laughed and picked three bushels and ate cider doughnuts, and came home and made applesauce and apple butter, and Gilly made four perfect pies. Gillian always does her own thing, follows her own rules, is independent often to the exclusion of making deep connections, but when she makes you her apple pie, you have to forgive her.

"Wait, wait," Gilly says, sounding surprisingly close for someone an ocean away. "Andrew is marrying that heifer and you are mad at your boyfriend. Andrew and she can have each other and good riddance, but when did I miss the boyfriend part?"

I sigh. "Well, remember when I went to D.C. for that event, and met that guy in the museum?"

"Yeah, I remember that. Now he's your boyfriend?"

"I think so, yes, but I'm not sure for how long."

"Honey, why didn't you tell me? That's so great for you to be seeing someone. I mean, obviously not if he's a schmuck. But still, good for you! Why the secrecy?"

"Gill, c'mon, we talk so rarely, and by the time I get home from the store I just want to collapse, sending long e-mails about boys seems like the last thing on my mind."

"I know, I know, mea culpa. I'm a terrible sister, I never write, I never call, I don't make you a priority, but I love you and of course I want to know that there is a boy. Yay you. So now fill me in, bullet point it for me."

Gilly and I have gotten good at bullet points, both in e-mail and on the phone. Actually our relationship has always been, in many ways, bullet pointed—small concise bits of time, specific tasks or events, everything at its most fundamental and unadorned. We aren't excessive with each other, but our love is strong. We don't need each other generally, but when we do, the need is deep and the response is instantaneous. "We started dating, it's been great, met his family and love them, sex is fantastic, makes me laugh, makes me feel like me, but we are having our first real fight, and I don't know if it is something minor or something we're not going to come back from."

"I see. So congrats, and I'm sorry."

"Thanks, kiddo."

"Blue-ish alert level?"

"I'm at cornflower. I was azure yesterday, and midnight on Tuesday, but I'm hoping to downgrade to sky later tonight when I see him for dinner."

"Okay, so I don't need to hop a plane to kick his ass and make you pie?"

And this is what I love about Gillian. Because if I said yes, she would pay through the nose for the next flight out, and be here before the day is through. And somehow, for whatever else our relationship is, this is what makes it special and important. "I'm okay. We're grownups, we've had time to cool off. He called yesterday to apologize and sent a lovely bunch of flowers, and I'm assuming that tonight we will both have a chance to express ourselves in a less emotional way and figure out why we both ended up so hurt and upset. I'd always rather you make plans for a real visit, when I'm in a good mood and we can do fun stuff."

"I know, me too. Tell you what, why don't I come for Fakesgiving?"

When Gillian first moved abroad, I always wanted her to come home for Thanksgiving, but it is such an awful time to travel anywhere for any reason, and it isn't like she got the days off from her job in London, so we invented Fakesgiving; we'd pick a weekend when flights are cheap, and I'd make a full Thanksgiving dinner, and we'd watch our DVD of the 1985 Super Bowl when the Monsters of the Midway routed the Patriots, just to have some football on the television while we napped after dinner. We haven't done it in the last couple of years, and I miss it. I think about all the people I now have in my life, and think about how much fun it would be to do a Fakesgiving with all of them included.

"I would love that. You pick the weekend and I'll make sure to keep it clear for you."

"I'll check my calendar tomorrow with my assistant, and send you some dates. In the meantime, for what it's worth, I'm sorry your ex is such a complete and total butt munch, and I'm sorry that your boyfriend is behaving badly, and I'm really sorry that I'm not there to get you drunk."

"Thanks, little girl."

"Love you, sis. And please, keep me in the loop, I really do want to know everything that's going on with you, 'kay?"

"Promise. And don't forget to send me those dates. I want them in red ink on both our calendars."

"Promise. Bye, honey."

"Bye."

Nate is picking me up from the store, and I've arranged for Nadia to take my car home. I'm nervous, stomach fluttering, more nervous than I was on our first date, even more nervous than I was the first time we made love. I have very little vocabulary for relationship problems. With my dad gone, my mother took the attitude that she had already had "her husband," that she had no time or inclination for dating, that me and Gilly and her friends were enough company for her. So I never saw her dating, never watched her work through any sort of relationship difficulties. My own dating life, pre-Andrew, was placid, the men I chose were mild in every way, and I was quick to have the "let's just be friends" conversation at the slightest sign of potential problems.

Andrew and I never fought. We didn't bicker, we didn't rail, we didn't disagree. I know it seems amazing to think of, people who lived together for nearly eight years before marrying, and stayed married for another nine, but frankly, there was never really much to argue about.

We both made plenty of money and carried no debt beyond car payments and our mortgage, and we lived within our ample means, so there wasn't any financial tension. We had the same politics, liked the same music, wanted to see the same movies, and we both loved food and sex more than anything. With no real family to speak of, there wasn't any need for either one of us to get defensive about the behavior of our kin, no need to bicker about how to split up the holidays. We were both neatniks, slightly anal about keeping the house tidy. And though we certainly both had interests the other didn't share, it never caused tension. Andrew was an avid art collector and I never really understood what moved him about pieces, but he never brought anything home I thought was ugly. And I collected DVDs nearly obsessively, especially classic black-and-whites from the thirties and forties. But while Andrew didn't know why I had to own them, he liked to watch them with me, and even had special shelves built in the library to house them.

Of course we had the occasional cranky moments, when someone would snap at someone for forgetting to do something or agreeing to a social engagement without checking in with the other one first. He hated the way I drove, aggressive and impatient, and I hated how poky and conservative he was on the road, so any time in the car could be a little bit tense. Occasionally one of us might say something unintentionally hurtful, but when called on it, we both were quick to apologize, to forgive, and to get naked to make it go away. But really, I can't remember a single major fight, neither of us ever raised a voice to the other or said something mean until the day he told me he was leaving me and confessed to the affair, at which point I unleashed on him all of the fury I possessed.

I have no mental framework for dealing with a problem like this. Today was spent in endless discussion. I had filled in Kai and Nadia and Delia about the fight, and the vote was split. All three agreed that Nate handled the situation badly, considering, and thought he should have saved his ire for later when emotions weren't so high, especially since he would have had to know I hadn't intended for him to be hurt. But while Kai and Nadia were both of the mind that he had no reason to be upset, Delia insisted that she fully understood where he was coming from, and thought that even if he dealt with it badly, there was a lot of validity to his feelings.

Then they tried to make me call in to an advice radio show at lunchtime, to talk to a couple of sisters that Nadia says "are like TOTAL relationship gurus," Kai deems "fierce,"

and Delia calls "very Oprah-like, for a couple of white girls."
I've heard of them, they are local celebs, and getting some
national attention now that they have a television show in the
works, and I know that they are very well respected, but I
thought that hiding in the office to ask advice from strangers
on the radio during the lunch rush seemed silly at best, and
if, at forty years old, I can't find a way to talk openly with my
boyfriend about my feelings, then what use am I?

I get ready in the tiny back bathroom, letting my hair out of
the tight bun I keep it in when I'm working so that I don't have
to deal with it or worry about it falling in the food, changing out
of my chef's coat and black pants and into the skirt and blouse
I've brought with me. I throw some mascara on, a little con-
cealer, some blush and lip gloss and figure that if it's possible I'm
headed to a breakup dinner, I'm not getting overly fancy for it.

When I come out of the bathroom, Delia and Nadia are
waiting for me.

"You look great!" Nadia says as I hand her my car keys.

"Very lovely." Delia nods approvingly.

"Thank you both very much for your hard work today,
and for all the advice."

"I'll hope to not see you at home later," Nadia says lascivi-
ously.

"Oh, child, really? Is that necessary?" Delia shakes her
head, believing that any entendre is unnecessary and vulgar
for a woman.

Nadia laughs at Delia's discomfit, and grabs her in one of
her patented attack hugs. "Oh, Mama Bear, loosen up. If they
have to have a fight, then at least I can hope that they make up
in such a way that requires long hours of the night!"

I didn't know that it was possible for an African American to blush, but Delia's color deepens noticeably as she gives herself over to laughing at this elfin child purring like Mae West, her eyebrows performing tricks above eyes that sparkle a little too knowingly. Delia smacks her on the bottom, making her jump.

"Don't think I won't take you over my knee for sass, little miss. Get over there and close out that register before you work my last nerve!" Delia winks at me. Nadia feigns subservience, and heads over to run the credit card report.

Delia turns to me and her mouth goes straight. "If he is a good man, then he is worth having, but only you know if he is a good man. Sometimes no man is better than the wrong man. I know you been hurt, I know this is new and hard for you, and I know that now that this man is in your heart it is so easy to just go along to get along. But if he wants you to change, then you might want to think about whether you worked this hard to be who you are just to let some man tell you that who you worked to be isn't good enough for him. I'm not saying, I'm just saying."

I look at her impassive face, no different from if she had told me that the beets I ordered were moldy, or that she thinks she has an idea for a black-eyed-pea dish. I look into her eyes, which show the wisdom that only comes from knowing the worst that man is capable of, and all I can do is nod. She smiles softly.

"You are enough for any man, and any man that doesn't see that, doesn't really see you."

I hear a knock at the front door and see Nate's face in the window.

She pats my shoulder and I head out to meet the man I love, but don't fully trust.

"So," Nate says.

"So."

"I thought it was a good meal. That apple dessert was amazing!"

"Yeah, they do a wonderful job." We are in the car leaving Prosecco, a fine-dining Italian restaurant where I know the sommelier, and where I am always able to get a delicious and relatively healthy meal.

"I liked your friend. I usually don't pay that much attention to wine, but everything he picked really enhanced the food, I thought."

"He's very talented." The meal was good, conversation focused on work for both of us, some family updates on his end, current events. Light and easy, but with the obvious underlying tension of what we have been through. I don't want to bring it up, but as much as I've been dreading having to have the conversation, I'm suddenly eager for it to begin, even if it is just to get it over with.

"Did you want to come over?"

"Did you want me to come over?"

Nate sighs. "I'm not good at this, Mel, never have been. There are many reasons I've never been married, and even my ego isn't so huge as to not be able to recognize that at least a part of that is related to how I deal with communications. In my work I'm either alone, or with a skeleton crew, and their job is to take direction from me. I like to think I'm collaborative, but ultimately, it's my vision they are there to support, and my opinion counts more. It's hard to shut that off. I'm sorry about how I handled things the other day, as I said on the phone yesterday, and I know that just apologizing doesn't fully take care of anything, because obviously you and I have very different perceptions of what happened between us. But I love you, and I have heard your side and shared my side, and I hope we can try to understand each other better. So yes, I want you to come over, and I hope that we can have a drink, and talk, and then I hope that you'll stay over and that tomorrow we will wake up together in a better place. But I also know that this whole thing between us is still in the early stages, and maybe you might feel like it's too soon to be having deep relationship conversations, and that you might just want a little space to ease back into things. It's your call."

"I'd like to come over. But you're right, I don't want to make more of this than necessary. It was a strange situation, a unique set of circumstances, and I'd like us to recognize that and not belabor it too long, if that makes sense. I think we're both independent, wary of needing anyone, reluctant to trust, I know I am. But I also know that if we focus too much on it, it becomes bigger than it needs to be, and we have every chance of getting into another tiff over it. I love you, and I'm sorry that I hurt your feelings."

"I love you too. And I'm sorry I was insensitive to you and upset you."

"Then take me home."

And I think that we'll be okay, that this isn't going to be some long, horrible thing, that for all my worrying, it isn't going to go the way I feared.

We get back to Nate's place, share a brandy, and go to bed. But for the first time, we seem somehow out of sync, bumping teeth when we kiss, knocking noses. I can't relax enough to come, and Nate's erection waxes and wanes, until finally he mutters something about not being as young as he used to be and that he shouldn't have had the brandy on top of all the wine. He kisses my forehead and pulls me close, but after a few minutes he rolls over and settles into sleep, leaving me in a lonely space next to him, trying not to doubt myself, trying not to think that the fight has made me less attractive to him. I try to hang on to Delia's statement: I am enough.

But what if I'm not?

TOMATO SOUP
AND GRILLED CHEESE

Some things are universal. I have tried, but I can't find anyone who doesn't like the smell of freshly cut grass, who hates puppies, who thinks a fire in the winter is a bad idea. I'm sure there are exceptions to every rule, but in my world, everyone loves the feeling of clean, hot towels just out of the dryer, waking up to find you have three more hours to sleep, and tomato soup and grilled cheese when you are sick. Not stomach-bug, puking sick; if you're nauseous the idea of acidic tomatoes or gooey cheese will make you ralph for certain. But if you are NyQuil sick, sniffly-sneezy-achy-stuffy-head-fever-sore-throat kind of sick, then cream of tomato soup with a grilled cheese sandwich is just the ticket.

Everything hurts.

My eyelashes ache. The little bits of skin between my fingers are sore. The tendons in my knees are tight. My earlobes are sad and tender. I have a sore throat that has lodged itself at the very top of my sinuses, feeling like it is right at the internal base of my nose. My eyes are puffy and bloated feeling. My head is stuffy, but when I blow my nose, nothing comes.

I'm fucked.

In most jobs, although it isn't encouraged, you can usually fudge if you have a cold. If you aren't barfing, then it's just about suffering through your day in a haze of cold medicine and hot tea with honey and trying not to breathe on people. You can buy some of that sanitizing gel and wash your hands a lot and get through your day.

But in the food business, you can't go to work when you are sick. In fact, you're supposed to leave work the moment you feel the tiniest symptom coming on. Because kitchens are tiny places where you share air and touch one another constantly and any contagious sickness can spread like Ebola if you aren't careful, taking down a whole staff. And what is worse, you can pass something on to a customer. As careful as we have to be with general sanitation to prevent food-borne illness, we have to be equally vigilant about colds and the flu. I thought the headache I had when I came home last night was just the result of a long day at the store, but I appear to be wrong.

I roll over and pick up the phone.

"Weensie! Whassup?" I have no idea how Kai can be so chipper at five thirty in the morning.

I put on my saddest, most nasal Edith Ann voice. "I'm sick. I habe a code in by node."

"Oh, no no no no no. Poor thing, you sound peevish and peaked and you must STAY THE HELL AWAY FROM ME!

Phil and I are going up to Door County this weekend, and I will NOT spend my mini vaca languishing in bed with the sniffles, DO YOU HEAR ME? Go back to bed. I'll call Delectable and see if she can come in early. But before you go back to sleep, go wake the little pink-haired pixie and tell her to come on down and help. Suggest she go stay with that boyfriend of hers for a couple of days so she doesn't catch the plague from you. I'll call you later."

"Danks, Kai. I readdy appreciade id."

"Get some rest. It's only Wednesday. Hopefully if you take care of yourself today and tomorrow you'll be right as rain by Friday."

"Oday. Dalk to you lader."

I drag myself out of bed, feeling like I weigh a million pounds. I knock on Nadia's door, hear a muffled noise and open it.

"AAAAAAAAAAAAAAAAAGGGGGGGGGGGGGGGGH-HHHHHH!" A naked Nadia rolls off the side of the pull-out bed.

"Oh, I, um, I, hi . . ." An equally naked Daniel reaches down to the foot of the bed to retrieve the rumpled sheet, which he pulls to his chest like a timid bride.

"Oh, crap. I'm so sorry, I, um . . . I didn't dow . . ." I back out of the room and close the door. I stand in the hallway, stunned. I can hear rumblings and stumblings and mutterings behind the door. Suddenly the door flies open, and Daniel, red-faced and with his shirt on inside out, exits.

"Sorry, Melanie. I, um, it was very nice to see you again." And he runs up the hallway, and I can hear the door click as he leaves. Nadia stands in front of me in her bathrobe.

"Jesus, Mel, you scared the ever-loving craparoonie out of me. What's going on?"

"I'm sick. I habe a code. I can'd go to work. Kai is going to open the store and see if Delia can come in early, but he asked me to check to see if you could come id as well to hep him oud. I didn't know you had company. I'm sorry I walked in od you."

"Oh you poor thing, you sound TERRIBLE! I'll jump in the shower and go down to the store to meet Kai. Is there anything you need, anything I can do for you before I leave?"

"Pack a bag."

She looks stricken. "What? You want me to leave? Just because Daniel slept over without asking you? He brought me home late, we had a nightcap, we fell asleep watching TV, I didn't think it was . . ."

It takes my fuzzy head a minute to realize she thinks I'm kicking her out. "No, no, no, stop. I'm dot mad. I'm a little embarrassed, and we should probably habe a system for warning someone about things like dis, but I meant that you should go spend a couple nights at Daniel's place so you don't catch my code. I don't want to make you sick."

She laughs. "Paranoid much, Nadia? I'm sorry, Mel, it's early, and I didn't sleep much, and the look on your face when you came through the door. You're really not mad?"

"I'm too stuffy and shitty to be mad. I'm just glad you can go help Kai. But serioudly. Dis id a really icky code, I don't want you to ged id. So tell Daniel his punishdment for violating the sancdidy of my house id to pud you up for a couple nights till I ged bedder."

"Will do. Go back to bed. I'll call later to see how you are doing, and you can let me know if you want me to get anything for you."

"Thanks, kiddo."

I slump back into my bedroom, crawl under the covers, and fall back into the dead dreamless sleep of the afflicted.

I wake in a pool of sweat, my fever having broken while I was asleep, making the sheets uncomfortably sticky. I throw off the covers and get out of bed, still leaden and aching. I go to the bathroom and run a hot shower, find an old mentholated bath disk under the sink and put it on the floor of the shower, hoping the eucalyptus vapors will cut through the cotton in my head a little bit. I put on a shower cap, deciding that wet hair is going to be a bad idea, and knowing I have neither the strength nor inclination to use the hair dryer. The hot water scalds a bit at first, my skin still clammy from the fever sweat. But gradually it stops stinging and starts soothing, and by the time I get done, I feel a little better.

I get dried off and get into my cashmere lounging pajamas, a birthday gift from Gilly, and a luxury I thought was ridiculous until now. I head out to the kitchen, and put on the kettle for tea when there is a gentle knocking at the door. I walk over and open it up.

"Hey, beautiful!" Nathan says.

I slam the door in his face. "Go away!" I yell at the closed door.

"I will not. Open up."

"Dot a chance. I'll make you sick."

"I'll take that risk. Open this door."

"You can'd make me. I habe a miserable code, I feel like crap, I look like crap, I'm nod up for company. And I don'd wand you to get id. Go away and lub me from afar."

"I am going to love you from anear, and I've had my flu shot this year, and I think you look lovely, and I am going to come in there and take care of you. Now open this door."

"No, no, no, no, no. I will nod and you cannod make me."

"You leave me no choice." Suddenly I hear a key in the lock, and the doorknob turns, and the door is open.

He grins, dangling the key at me. "Nadia called and told me you were under the weather, and she loaned me her key in case you were sleeping when I came over." He is carrying a big bag from Treasure Island. He leans over and kisses my forehead. "No fever, that's a good sign. Go get yourself settled on the couch and I'll get this stuff put away and bring you a cup of tea, how's that?"

"The kettle is on. Thanks, Nate, readdy, I . . ."

He puts a gentle finger on my lips. "Go get comfy, sweetheart. I'll be in with your tea shortly. Have you eaten anything yet today?"

"Not yet."

"Think you can manage something, or is your stomach wonky?"

"It isn't a stomach bug, just a bad head and chest code."

"Excellent. Then I'll bring you something to eat as well. Now scoot."

I head into the living room, and curl up in the chaise section of the couch, pulling the throw blanket over me. I bought it in Christchurch when Andrew and I were in New Zealand for our fifth anniversary. It is a pale blue leaning toward teal, heathered with brown, and made of a combination of merino wool and Chinese possum fur. It is the coziest thing I own next to these pajamas. I can hear Nathan puttering around in the kitchen, and suddenly I start to cry.

Alone isn't bad, mostly. I'm independent; I don't need constant company or socialization. I was always okay eating alone, going to movies solo, keeping my own counsel. The time I've had since Andrew and I split hasn't been easy, but it isn't the alone part that was tough; it was the betrayal and feeling of being such an idiot that made things hard. But the one time that being alone really sucks is when you're sick. Having to take care of yourself, make your own food and clean up, having to get yourself dressed enough to go to the drugstore for Kleenex and cough syrup.

The last time I got a cold like this was about a month after I moved into this place, and I was amazed at how truly depressed I got having to take care of myself. But now, as shitty as I feel, I'm so grateful to have this man in my kitchen, making me tea and breakfast, here to take care of me.

Nate comes in with a tray, and I quickly blow my nose and wipe my eyes before he sees that I'm emotional. Lucky for me, he is paying very close attention to not spilling what's on the tray, which he puts down on the coffee table in front of me.

"Tea with honey and a little bit of lemon. Toast with some of that apricot jam you like. And a sliced banana."

"Thank you, Nate, it's all wonderful. Now can I please ged you to leave? I'm serious, it's a nasty bid of business, dis, and I'm going to feel so bad if I give id to you, especially since, unless you ged id on a Monday, I can'd redurn the Florence Nighdingale favor."

"I once did a film about doctors, and you know what I found out? The common cold is at its most contagious in the three days before the symptoms appear. By the time you get sick, you are really unlikely to make anyone else sick unless you are swapping spit or coming into contact with mucus and the like. So, while I will refrain from juggling your snotty tissues, making out with you, or eating off your fork for the time being, it's likely that I'll be safe. And since I haven't seen you in four days, I should be reasonably out of danger."

"Id dat true?"

"Yep. So stop trying to get me to leave, and let me take care of you, okay?"

"Okay." He goes to the kitchen to tidy up, and I drink my tea and eat the toast and banana. It makes me feel better. He returns with a glass of water for himself and a bag from Walgreens, which he hands to me.

I open the bag and find daytime cold medicine and night-time cold medicine, cough drops, little Kleenex packets, and a stack of silly tabloid celebrity magazines.

He smiles at me. "Figured while you were getting better you might want to catch up on all your Britney Spears gossip and find out how many more kids Brangelina are planning on adopting."

I laugh. "You think ob everything."

"I try."

I yawn deeply, the hot shower and tea and food hitting me all at once.

"Why don't you see if you can nap for a little while, rest is the best thing for you."

"And what are you going to do while I'm sleeping?"

"I brought a book and the crossword, and who knows,

I may even grab some winks myself. Don't worry about me, just settle in." He gets up and tucks the blanket more carefully around me, putting a small throw pillow behind my head. Then he kisses the top of my head, picks up my empty tray and heads back for the kitchen. I'm asleep before he returns.

When I wake I'm groggy with the discomfit that comes with oversleep. The room isn't dark exactly, but it is clear that I've lost a large percentage of the day. I stretch, feeling the tightness in my muscles that comes with too long a sleep in an odd position.

"Well, look who's up!" Nate says from across the room. He's sitting in a chair, small reading glasses perched on the tip of his nose, his feet crossed on the coffee table, a book facedown across his stomach.

"Hey." My voice is rough, my mouth dry and foul tasting to me.

Nate gets up and crosses to the couch, sitting next to me and stroking my face. "I think your fever came back a little, how do you feel?"

"Stiff, out of it. And parched."

"Let me get you something to drink."

He heads for the kitchen and I get up off the couch and go to the bathroom. I pee, wash my face, brush my teeth. I look awful. My skin is pasty and gray. My hair is matted with sweat and sleep, my eyes dull. I head back to the living room, where Nate has brought me a large glass of ice water, and another cup of hot tea. I drain the water in one draught, feeling the coolness run down my throat and settle in my belly.

"What time is it?"

"Nearly five."

"Good lord, I've been asleep all day! You must have been bored out of your skull."

"Nah. Not at all. I did the whole crossword, read my book, did some work, took a little snooze myself. It's been a very peaceful day. Plus you're very cute when you sleep."

"You are a very nice liar."

He laughs. "Hungry?"

I check in with myself. "Starving, actually."

"Good. I'll whip something up. Sit tight."

He gets up, and I reach for one of the magazines he brought, and start flipping through it, shocked at how purely enjoyable it is to read gossip about famous people, even if most of the people on the pages are young enough to be my children, and I have no idea who they are or why they are famous. Whatever *High School Musical* is, it must be very popular. Ditto something called *The Hills*.

I'm comparing snippy comments about the "What Were They Thinking" outfits on the back page, when Nate reappears with the tray. This time it's cream of tomato soup and a grilled cheese sandwich. I can't remember the last time I had this, but I can't think of anything in the world that I would be as happy to see as this simple meal.

"Campbell's?" I ask him.

"Yep."

I pick up a triangular half of the sandwich, seeing the perfectly golden brown exterior, the way the cheese oozes, just short of dripping. "Kraft?"

"On Wonder bread."

"I lub you bery, bery much."

"I love you back. Eat your soup."

I dunk the sandwich in the soup, slurp my spoon, lick the crumbs off my fingers, scrape the last bits of plastic-y cheese off the plate.

"Goodness, I'm in love with a Hoover!"

I look up, having totally abandoned myself to the joy of this childhood favorite, forgetting that Nate was even in the room. "Sorry," I say, sheepish.

"Don't be! Appetite is a good sign. I believe you will mend. So much for starving a cold."

"Thank you for taking such good care of me."

"You're welcome. Now, how do we feel about sherbet?"

"Perfect."

"Orange or lime?"

"Orange."

"I'll fetch it."

Nate clears my tray, and brings two bowls of sherbet, and we cuddle up on the couch. Kai and Nadia both call to check in, and insist on my taking tomorrow off as well to rest up. Nate raids my DVD collection, and we end up watching *Capricorn One*, a very supercheesy seventies sci-fi extravaganza, that makes us both weep with laughter at the predictable dialogue, obvious special effects, and brilliant casting of Telly Savalas as a crop duster of all things. Nate runs me a hot bath, telling me that it will help calm me down before sleep. Despite my continued protests, he stays, holding me close, not caring that my fever makes me sweat on him, and for all my sense of personal empowerment, I'm very grateful to give over the care of myself to him.

After another day of rest, this one spent mostly playing Scrabble with Nate, who continued to cook me the invalid food of my childhood: Cream of Wheat with brown sugar, Spaghet-tiOs with crumbled Ritz Crackers on top, ginger ale with a scoop of lime sherbet in it, little Jell-O cups. For dinner we ordered in Japanese, huge bowls of broth and slippery noodles with tender slices of pure white chicken. We spent another night spooned together in my big soft bed, and in the morning, I suddenly found that I was feeling better. Much better. Better enough to adequately show Nate how grateful I was for his care of me.

We shower together, soaping each other with mounds of suds, Nate washing my hair, standing behind me so that I can half-lean into his body, giving myself over to the feeling of his strong hands on my scalp. Clean and pink, we dress compan-ionably, and I call Kai, letting him know that I will be able to make it in to the store today, that if he can get things started, I'll be in within an hour or so.

"Glad to have you back in the world, beautiful."

"Glad to be back in the world. You can tend to my health anytime."

"And so I shall. Do you have time for breakfast, or do you need to get to the store right away?"

"I have time for some quick breakfast here. You can have toast and fruit, and I can probably whip up some eggs."

"Toast and fruit is fine. I have a lunch meeting at Hugo's with some of those money guys who think you should eat a side of beef at lunchtime."

"Fun. Toast and fruit coming up."

I put on the kettle, and set up the coffee press for Nate and my little teapot for myself. We sit at my tiny little table.

"Is Nadia coming back tonight?"

"Yeah. I sent her a text message giving her the day off and telling her that it should be safe to come home."

"Do you want her to come home?"

"Of course! I mean, you know, as much as I want anyone living with me who isn't a romantic partner. She's generally a pretty good roommate. And she is fun."

"But if you had your druthers . . . you'd not have her here."

"Well, you know me; obviously in a perfect world I wouldn't need anyone here."

"Do you really need her? I mean, I know that it is a little breathing room financially, but it isn't a windfall. You would certainly be solvent without it. . . ."

"Nate, I get the impression that you are trying to get me to ask her to leave. Any particular reason?" His tone worries me, the way he is pressing.

He smiles. "Of course not. I just want to remind you that you took her in as a temporary measure. And that you are the one in charge of when that temporaryness is done. If she and that weirdo are doing this well, maybe all she needs is a little push to move in with him. . . ."

"I don't want to push her to move in with him so soon just because I would prefer to be alone, Nate. She's a troubled girl, she needs some independence, and she's been nothing but great to me and terrific for the business."

"Hey, I didn't mean to get you all riled up, honey. Forget I said anything. I should never speak without having all the information." He gets up to clear my plate, and I wonder exactly what information he is referring to.

FRIED CHICKEN

In law school Andrew and I became connoisseurs of takeout. There was just never time to go to the grocery store or make a meal. Everything was eaten with case-law books open, or legal pads full of notes, or half-asleep in front of the television. But the last Sunday of every month we would do a potluck party, just to have some sort of home cooking. One Sunday a girl from our study group, Jenny, invited us all to her mom's house in Hyde Park for a true Sunday Soul Food Dinner. Jenny's mom, Billie, a tiny woman with skin the color of café au lait, and silvery hair in a perfect chignon, laid out a soul food spread that brought a tear to the eye. Barbeque ribs, macaroni and cheese, collard greens with ham hocks, bread dressing, green beans, biscuits, candied sweet potatoes, creamed corn, and in the center of the table, a huge pile of fried chicken. I had never tasted anything like that fried chicken. The perfect

balance of crisp batter to tender juicy meat. Everything that
day was delicious, but the fried chicken was transcendent.

"Mel, I was wondering what you were doing on Monday
night?" Delia asks, bringing me platters for getting the food
ready for the case.

I think for a second. "I don't really have anything, I was
probably going to see Nathan, why?"

"We're having a party at the shelter, one of the women
who's been there for almost a year is moving out. She got a job
and saved enough to get her own place for her and her kids, and
they've been a really great family, so we wanted to make them
a small party, and they suggested that we use it as an excuse to
invite the people who are working with us to come see the facility and meet the other women. I'm doing the cooking."

"Oh, D, I'd be thrilled to come! Thank you for inviting me.
Is there anything I can bring or do?"

"Well, I was wondering if I could use the kitchen here for
some of the prep? The kitchen over there is fine for getting
dinner on the table for the residents, but it will be easier to do
some stuff here and bring it over."

"Of course! Would you like me to sous chef for you?"

Delia turns to look at me. "You'd really want to do that?"

"Are you kidding? I plan on stealing all your secrets!"

She smiles at me. "That would be wonderful."

"Let's talk later, you can fill me in on the menu and what
we need to do. It's possible we can get some stuff prepped over
the weekend so that Monday isn't so crazy."

"That sounds wonderful. Thanks, Mel."

"Of course!"

Kai flies in from the front at his usual breakneck pace. "Delectable, Teensie, did you see what happened next door?"

We're in a strip along Lincoln Avenue that has a series of small buildings, most of which have storefront space on the main level and either storage, office space, or living space above. We have the corner space, and immediately to the north of us is a small antiques store. We just have the one level, but next door, while a smaller floor plan, has an apartment upstairs. The owner of the store, a cantankerous gent named Joe, came in once the week we opened, made some denigrating comments about the food, and never came back.

"What happened next door?" Delia asks.

"There is a sign up saying everything must go, the place is for sale!"

"Wow. That's wild!" I can't really believe it; I think Joe has been running his little ramshackle shop for probably forty years.

"I wonder what will go in there?" Delia says.

"Let's all pray for something that will drive in some business! Maybe an exercise equipment store, or fitness clothing . . ." It would be nice to have something else in the block that would attract the kind of clientele that might want to shop here as well.

"Let's pray for someone nice to work next to for a change," Kai mutters.

We all laugh, thinking about Joe's pinched face, his rude behavior, the way he refuses to look at any of us when we walk by his windows.

"What's so funny?" Nadia enters the kitchen, carrying a large folder.

"We're just talking about Joe's place next door being up for sale."

"Oh. Wow. I wonder what will go in there?" She tilts her head in the direction of Joe's store.

"That's what we are all wondering," Kai says.

"So," I say, as Nadia hands me the folder, "how about a quick company meeting?"

"What's up, bosslady?" Kai asks, perching his tiny butt on a corner of the counter.

"Well, Nadia has a great idea for the business, and has been doing some research for me, and I think we have determined that it is something we might be able to take on, provided everyone is on board."

Nadia blushes, and Delia sits down on a handy stool.

I keep going. "We all know about the trend for food delivery services; people are too busy to cook for themselves, and are having all of their meals delivered, both for convenience and also for being able to really control portions and fat. Most people are doing it for weight loss, but some are also doing it purely for the ease of not having to think about it. Places like Sacramento Sloane charge an arm and a leg for food that may be healthy, but isn't particularly good."

"You know she killed Janey's mom," Kai says, and Nadia and I chuckle.

"Yes, we are aware of the unfortunate coincidence. But aside from being a deadly weapon, her food is simply not particularly tasty. And in many ways, I think that it sets people up for failure because if you love food and the food you are eating for your health isn't delicious, eventually you are going to fall right off that wagon, and binge on things that you do want to eat. But our whole mission here is to make food that is good for your body and good for your soul. Craveworthy. So Nadia has looked into how many other services there are available in Chicago, and what their prices look like, and I think that there is room for us to get into the fray. So I'm thinking about adding Delivery by Design to our business, essentially packing up meals out of the foods we make here in the store and delivering it to people."

Delia nods her head, but says nothing. Kai runs his hand through his spiky hair.

"So really, we would just be making more of what we already make and packing it up to be portable?" he asks.

"Essentially," I say. "We'll need to add some breakfast items, but none of that is terribly complicated. We already do the Morning Energy Muffins and the homemade granola and plenty of different fruit salads. And Nadia has come up with the great idea of allowing customers to always choose a 'purse option' substitute for any of the meals, in case clients know on a particular day that they will be traveling, or not near a microwave, or having to eat in the car or something. Protein bars, cheese chunks and veggies, muffins and the like. I've talked with Carey about writing up little articles and things that we can pack in with the meals, little bits of relevant info, success tips, inspirational writings and the like."

"That sounds lovely," Delia says. "I bet people will really take to it."

"I'm glad everyone likes the idea! I'm meeting with my accountant tomorrow to find out about what the whole project will entail financially, what adjustments we may need to make in terms of insurance and such, but I'm pretty excited!"

"Good for you, little dreamer Mel!" Kai says, jumping

off the counter and patting me on the back. "And clever Nadia, the idea gal. Aren't you a surprise! But we now have to open the front door or all the hungry hordes are going to head up the block to McDonald's, yes?"

Kai heads into the front of the store to unlock the doors, Delia stands up and goes back to loading the case, and Nadia and I grin at each other, and then go back to work.

Nadia wanders into the living room just as I am getting my coat on.

"Going over to Nathan's?"

"Yep. Haven't seen him all week, he's in the final push to get his film finished, so he's editing around the clock. But I suppose getting him from ten p.m. to five a.m. is better than nothing!"

"Yeah. That's the great thing about Daniel's job, no late nights. He works till six or six thirty, but then he's off the clock. And all mine!" She blushes prettily when she says this.

"So it's still good with you guys?" I'm a little worried about her, to be honest. Daniel is perfectly benign, but frankly, I feel like she could do so much better, and I hate to see her get involved so deeply with him.

Nadia flops down on the couch and twiddles her feet in the air. "Oh, Mel. It's so great. He's the best boyfriend I've ever had."

"Well, that's not exactly saying much." This comes out slightly snarkier than I mean it to be, and Nadia's face falls a bit as she sits up.

"Well, it says a lot to me. You don't have the best track record yourself, as I recall." She gets off the couch and starts to head back to her room. "Have a good night with Nate, I'll see you tomorrow."

"Nadia, I'm sorry, I didn't mean . . ."

"Yeah. Actually, I think you did. Relationships are hard, you know that. Our hearts make choices that we can't understand and aren't always good for us. It's hard to be smart all the time, Mel. And you should know better than anyone that choosing the wrong man isn't a personal character flaw."

"But, sweetie, choosing ten wrong men in a row might be an unhealthy pattern." Her eyebrows fly straight up into the air. Crap, nothing I'm saying tonight is coming out right.

Her eyes narrow. "Goodness, you are self-righteous for someone whose marriage was a façade and who has a boyfriend with obvious commitment problems."

"Wait, wait, let's just take a breath. Neither of us meant to get into a disagreement over this. I'm sorry what I said hurt your feelings."

"You know what, Mel, in my experience, people who say things that are hurtful mean to hurt, and the ability to apologize for it after just makes them think they have permission to do it."

"I don't know what I can do besides apologize."

"You can not say things to begin with. Is it that you think I don't know that I've made bad choices for boyfriends? Did you think perhaps that I need the sage wisdom of your years to tell me that the guys I have dated have been abusive and cruel and taken advantage of me? Is it that you think somehow I don't KNOW that I'm all fucked up? I'm smarter than you give me credit for, Mel, and all I can say is that considering my life, it makes more sense than you could ever understand."

"How can I consider your life when you don't share your life with me? All I know about your life consists of leaving Minneapolis with Barry to come here and then getting dumped. Where is the life before that? What have you given me to use as a basis for understanding? If you want someone to be sensitive to you, to take your history into consideration when looking at your behavior, you have to give them that history to consider. You want to be the mystery girl, hatched into the world at twenty-three, raised by no one, growing up nowhere, with no family and no past and no stories to share, fine. But then don't ask someone to understand what you've been through, because I haven't the foggiest idea what you've been through, and my ESP isn't fine-tuned enough to figure it out on my own."

"I don't want to talk about this anymore, Mel. I get that you didn't mean to pick a fight. Let's just leave it at that. Say hi to Nate for me." She turns and heads down the hall to her room and closes the door. And unsure of what else to do, I grab my bag and leave.

"So how are things at home?" Nate asks. We are luxuriating in postcoital bliss, entangled in his bed, sheets askew. I'm snuggled up against him, head on his chest, as his hand travels up my hip, across my back and shoulder and down my arm back to my hip again.

"Sort of excruciatingly polite. Friendly, but it feels like it is a little forced. Not that we aren't friends. I just think we both have very different ideas about how to communicate and what forgiveness means, and so it feels like the trust that was built is now diminished and we're working our way back to even."

"Well, you'll forgive me saying, but something is just not right about that kid. This whole having-no-past thing, it's sort of creepy. I mean, I know you like her and I know she hasn't given you any cause to be concerned about her, but something is off. I can't put my finger on it."

For some reason, despite my own frustrations with Nadia, I immediately feel the need to defend her. "She's not creepy, Nate. She's obviously been through some sort of difficult past that she doesn't want to talk about, and she's a little bit damaged. But she's been great. She's been very respectful and easygoing around the house, and terrific at the store and . . ."

"Darling, don't get overly mama lioness on me. I'm not saying I think she's dangerous in some way, I just think she's troubled, probably in deeper ways than you are even aware of."

"Probably you're right. The silly thing is, while it's none of my business, her past, I want to know, not just because I'm curious, but because I feel like it would help me be a better friend to her."

Nate kisses the top of my head. "No one could be a better friend than you."

"That is very sweet of you to say."

Nate rolls over and kisses my mouth. "I'm a very sweet guy."

"And so you are." Nate begins kissing down the length of my body, and all thoughts of Nadia are quickly extinguished.

Delia and I get the last of the food into my car with more than an hour to spare. We've spent the day cooking in exactly the opposite way of what we do every day: liberal with fat and sugar and butter. We've got a carload of food that is a nearly identical spread of what I ate at Billie's house back in law school, made with the same sense of pride and history, the same connection to family and tradition. Delia told me about her grandmother's bread dressing and her auntie Jeanine's macaroni and cheese. I learned about Daddy's corn bread, and Uncle Jimmy's pulled pork. We made her sister Ella's sweet potato pie, and her mom's greens with salt pork, and her own fried chicken. Her secret to keeping the meat moist and the outside crisp?

"Oh, honey, I never mastered actually cooking that chicken in the oil. I poach it in milk so that it's cooked through, and then pat it dry, bread it, and fry it just to heat it up and make that crust."

It's ingenious, a perfect solution to dried-out meat or burnt skin and raw meat, and I tell her so.

"Shucks, I just got tired of making shitty chicken. My grandmother used to make a milk-poached chicken for ladies' luncheons, and that meat was always so tender, the idea just came to me."

"You have the mind of a chef."

"I have the mind of a cook. All that chef business is too fancy for me."

We get in the car and head out to the shelter.

"Can I ask you something?" Delia says quietly.

"Of course, D, what is it?"

"What would you do if something you needed and wanted, something good came to you, but came from a place that was evil. Would it be bad juju to keep it?"

I think about this for a moment. "I think that if something

good comes to you, and the source is bad, but you haven't done anything bad to get it, or asked someone else to do something bad to get it for you, then you can put it back in the world as something good."

"Yeah. That's sort of what I was thinking."

"D?"

"Yeah?"

"You want to fill me in?"

Delia takes a deep breath. "Lawyer called my sister up in Louisville, looking for me. Seems that asshole I was married to is dead."

"Wow. I can't even imagine what you must be feeling."

"Honey, I don't even know what I'm feeling from minute to minute. I ain't exactly sorry he is dead, but I didn't wish it on him. He was my husband, and I did love him for a time, and he was the father of my baby boy, and I wouldn't have traded knowing that child for that brief time for anything, so I can't hate him for that. But what he did to me was the lowest thing a person can do to another person, and I surely can't forgive him for that."

"So, what did the lawyer say?"

"The lawyer said that apparently he never filed divorce papers or separation or anything, and that he didn't even tell most people I was gone. So his life insurance and his pension come to me. The house was in his family, and goes to his sister and her kids, but the money comes to me. The lawyer is sending the paperwork." Her voice is soft and steady.

"Oh, D! I think that's wonderful. Something good has come of this, and lord knows you deserve it. Is it enough money to get you out of the shelter?"

"The pension money is enough to get me out of the shelter and be able to afford my own space. The insurance is something I'm going to have to figure out, it's a large-ish chunk of money for someone like me, and I'll need to find a way to invest it for my future. Maybe I could talk to your financial guy?"

"I'll give you his number tomorrow; I know he'd be delighted to work with you." I'm so excited for her windfall, for the independence it will afford her, for that cruel bastard doing one right thing in his life. But then my heart sinks. "I would guess it's probably enough that you won't need to work with me anymore, huh?"

"Child, I don't rightly know. Nothing is going to change in the short term. It's going to take a couple of months to get the money in my hands, and I have a lot of decisions I have to make before I do anything. Frankly, my first thought is to get out of that shelter and free up the space for someone else who needs it. Having a real home to call my own again, that is my priority. What I decide to do about the job, I can't think about that part yet. But I promise I won't leave you high and dry."

"Oh, sweetie, I'm not worried. I always knew you were a gift with an expiration date. It'll be hard to see you go, but I'm so thrilled that you will have the choice! If you want to stay, you will always have a place with me, but you don't owe me anything other than your friendship, and when it is time for you to do something else, I hope you won't hesitate to go after your dreams."

"Thank you for that. For all of it."

"Thank you. Do you know, is Nadia coming tonight?"

"I think so. Are you guys okay?"

"I think so. It was a bad fight and she and I both sort of hid from each other the last couple days. She's been staying at Daniel's, and I've been staying at Nate's so we've only seen each other at work. But yesterday it seemed pretty normal, so I think we're over it. I hate that all I seemed to do was push her more toward Daniel."

"What exactly is it you got against that boy?"

I think about this for a moment. "Nadia isn't much older than I was when I met Andrew. You think you are smart and mature and a little invincible, but you're not. You think you're making great choices, but you aren't formed enough to do it. You know when you meet those couples where the woman is this amazing creature, and she's with some little nothing guy, and you wonder why on earth she would settle for him when it is clear to everyone in the world that she could do so much better? I don't want Nadia to be that girl. I don't want her to pick him just because he isn't the same kind of shithead that she's used to. Someone just treating you like a human being isn't enough, and she's amazing and she could have someone amazing in her life, and I want her to have amazing and not just safe."

"Sometimes, honey, safe is amazing."

This is something I never considered.

I pull up in front of the shelter and park the car. "Shall we feed the people?"

"Oh, yes, honey, let's get this party started!" It is the most jubilant I've ever seen her. We get out of the car, and walk around to the trunk. Delia puts her arm around me and squeezes. I squeeze back, and we each grab a tray as some people pour out of the shelter to help, and we start getting the food inside.

* * *

"Okay, so I have to say this out loud, especially because I am so ashamed for feeling it, but I have to name it and claim it."

"Go for it," Carey says.

"I'm a little bit jealous."

"Of Delia's inheritance?"

"Yeah. Isn't that awful? I mean, she went through hell with that man, physically and emotionally, she had to pack up and leave her whole life behind without a word, she's been living in that shelter for over a year, and I wouldn't trade places with her for anything. But the idea of not just a small chunk of money, but also a monthly check, I admit, I'm jealous. And it goes against every independent, feminist bone in my body, but there it is. My pride was too big to take alimony from Andrew. I figured half of the value of the house and investments was so much money! But then you buy a business and a condo and before you know it you're month to month and wondering if there will ever be anything extra, and you think about how nice a cushion it would have been. I was so pleased with myself for declining maintenance payments, and now, now I sort of wish I hadn't. Isn't that awful?"

"It's neither awful nor unusual. I had another client whose younger sister got engaged, great guy, plenty of money, a dream scenario. She got the huge ring, the nice house, the ability to stop working if she wanted. My client was so happy for her sister, truly thrilled that she had gotten so lucky, but she was also deeply envious. And like you, my client is very independent, self-assured, believes in a full, rich life without marriage, but deep down, she had to admit that there was a part of her that loved the idea of a man coming along and making everything easy and feasible."

"So I'm not a traitor to my sex?"

Carey laughs her throaty laugh. "Oh, honey. We're all programmed at the earliest stage to want Prince Charming to come sweep us off our feet and give us a life of luxury. It's normal to fantasize about it. As long as you don't make unhealthy personal life choices to chase it, you shouldn't worry."

"Good to know. I have to get back out there. Thanks for the pep talk!"

"Anytime, I'll talk to you in a couple of weeks."

I hang up and head back out to the kitchen, where Kai and Delia are talking excitedly.

"What's all this then? No work to do?"

They both turn to face me, and shut up, guilty looks on their faces.

"What's going on? You two look like I caught you with your hand in the cookie jar!"

"We can't say yet. Sort of a little secret. But we'll be able to say something soon," Kai says.

"A mystery, huh? All right, have your little whisperings. But let's keep the case full too, okay?"

"You got it, Bitsy!"

We all get back to work, and I wonder what exactly the two of them are planning. Quite a pair, they are. I hope that Delia doesn't leave me anytime soon, if only for the amusement of watching her and Kai together.

CORNED BEEF HASH

I'm not naturally a breakfast person. There are only two things in life I prefer to food, and they are sex and sleep, and the chance to have either will trump breakfast anytime. This is not to say that I don't like breakfast food. I love breakfast foods, and can happily eat them all day long, with the exception of early in the morning, when, again, I'd rather be sleeping or screwing. But take me to a diner or greasy spoon at lunch or dinnertime, and I'm far more likely to order pancakes or an omelet than I am to order more time-appropriate fare. I'm an equal-opportunity breakfast-food girl, which can be a problem, since I never know whether to get an egg-based meal or a pancake-based meal, and bacon versus sausage always feels like Sophie's Choice to me, so I'm a big fan of those enormous breakfast platters that have a little bit of

everything. But if you had to make me choose, my desert-island breakfast food is corned beef hash.

I tend not to drink to excess. I love good wines with food, a small nightcap before bed. But I very rarely get drunk. In high school, when all my classmates were experimenting with Bartles & Jaymes wine coolers acquired with fake IDs, whatever they could swipe from their parents' liquor cabinets, or get someone's older siblings to buy, I had a small circle of oddball friends, and we weren't included in those adolescent bacchanals. In college I did some of the usual frat parties, made my share of mistakes that resulted in a night over the toilet (whoever thought peach schnapps was a good idea should be shot), but I quickly learned that I neither enjoyed the loss of control that came with overindulging nor the crappy way I felt the next day.

For me, my hangovers always come almost by accident. I'm out, someone is filling my wineglass more often than I'm fully cognizant of, and before I know it, I'm giddy and then forget to stop. I don't pound shots, I never set out to get tanked, it just sort of sneaks up on me, especially with my beverage of choice, champagne. I live for sparklers, from top-of-the-line French to my new everyday tipple, a lovely bubbly from Albuquerque, of all places, called Gruet, which I stock in both full-sized bottles for company and half bottles for my own pleasure. A long day, and you are likely to find me in a hot bath with a flute in my hand. But you are unlikely to find me passed out with an empty bottle at my side.

However, now and again, something happens that makes me do the cliché thing, and turn to the bottle for solace.

Nate and I are having breakfast when Nadia gets home. "Oh, sorry, I don't want to interrupt, I just need to get my yoga stuff." Nadia has been good about staying with Daniel on Sunday nights so that Nate can stay at my place.

"Don't worry, it's fine. You have a good night?"

"Yeah, thanks, Daniel says hi. To you too, Nate."

"Tell him hi back." Nathan's voice is a little cold for my taste, but maybe it's just morning grumpiness.

She zips into her room and reappears in a flash, carrying a bag and a rolled yoga mat. "See you guys later, have a good day off."

"Bye, honey, say hi to Janey for me!"

"Will do." And she is gone in a flash of pink hair.

"I want to chat with you about her." Nathan sounds deadly serious, and I'm really not in the mood to hear his reservations.

"Again? Really, Nate, I know you don't like her, and I know I complain about her moods sometimes, but I'm not looking to kick her out, she's a good kid at heart."

"But you don't know . . ."

"I don't know a lot, but I do know she hasn't given me any reason to question her."

"I've been doing a little research. You know, with the movie done, and no new project solidified as yet, I've had some time on my hands, and all her secrecy really troubles me."

"What do you mean 'research'?"

"I've been able to find some stuff out. About her past."

"What, did you hire a private detective?"

"Of course not, nothing that dramatic. I just did a little digging, some public records, some newspaper articles, a couple of phone calls."

My stomach tightens. On the one hand, I'm furious at him for sticking his nose in. On the other, I'm horrifically curious to know what he discovered, especially since it must be somewhat unsavory based on his obvious desire for me to kick her to the curb. I'm utterly split: I want to protect her, and tell him to stick his ill-gotten info up his ass. And I want him to tell me everything.

"Look, Mel, I'm not out to get her. I think she's a sweet kid. But she's living in the home of the woman I love, she's becoming more and more involved in your business, and as protective as you are of her, I am that protective of you. I just wanted to be sure she wasn't some con woman who might run off someday with your life savings."

"Okay, first of all, if I had any life savings I probably wouldn't need a twenty-four-year-old roommate of uncertain history. If she's a con woman, she's the stupidest con woman in the world for not picking someone who had some money! She should be working the elderly and wealthy, not the middle-aged and poor."

He doesn't respond.

I drop my head, knowing that as much as I wish I were the kind of person, the kind of friend who would say that nothing matters except the kindness she has shown me, that it isn't who she was, but who she is that really counts, I'm not remotely strong enough to be that woman. "Tell me."

The tale is a sad one, and one that makes my heart break

for her more than it makes me worry about myself or my non-existent fortune. Her mother was raised Amish in Indiana, but was shunned when she became pregnant out of wedlock by Nadia's father, who wasn't Amish. It's unclear how they met, but Nadia's mother was kicked out of the clan and went to live with Nadia's paternal grandmother, who was widowed. Nadia's parents never married, as Nadia's mother was underage and did not, for obvious reasons, have parental consent. Her dad developed first a drinking problem, then a drug problem, and ended up dead in an ill-conceived convenience store robbery shoot-out. Nadia's mother decided to return to the Amish when Nadia was two, unable to handle the responsibilities of mother-hood and seclusion from the only community and life she knew. She was eighteen years old, and gave legal custody of Nadia to the grandmother, and went home to suffer her punishment and eventually be accepted back into her family.

The grandmother raised her as best she could, but in high school Nadia began to rebel: petty shoplifting, not coming home nights, school truancy, and suspensions. She started drinking and experimenting with drugs, although it appears neither really took hold of her in a meaningful or dangerous way.

Whatever self-destructive tendencies remained in Nadia seemed almost entirely relegated to her choices in men. A week after her eighteenth birthday, she ran off and married a thirty-three-year-old used-car salesman, who gave her the orange Saab as a wedding present. Three weeks later the marriage was annulled, and she returned to her grandmother. She attended local community college for three semesters, but left despite decent grades. When she was twenty, her grandmother died, leaving her the house and a small amount of money. She sold the house, the proceeds of which a family friend who was a lawyer arranged to have put into a trust that gave Nadia a small but steady monthly income, and used the cash to move to Nashville. She met a married sculptor at a local art fair and packed up and moved to Indianapolis, where she lived in his studio. Then she dated a bouncer at the bar where she was working, who used her as a mule to transport the meth he dealt on the side, but didn't bother to bail her out when she got busted. She did four months in a women's prison on the drug charge, and then moved to St. Louis, where she had a distant cousin. She left St. Louis after only a few weeks, heading to Minneapolis, where she had a friend from her brief time in college. In Minneapolis she met Barry, the shithead musician who moved her to Chicago and then dumped her.

Nate lays it all out for me, succinctly and simply. And when he is done, my heart breaks for her. Such a series of crappy details, and I suddenly know exactly what Delia meant when she said sometimes the past is the past for a reason. None of it changes the Nadia I know, except to make me even prouder of her for surviving. None of it changes my desire to keep her around me.

"It's a horrible story, Nate. But not a dangerous one. Not one that would make me at all concerned about being connected to her. Doesn't it elicit your sympathies at all? Doesn't it make you want to help her? Why do you still seem to want her to move out?"

"Look, I feel for the kid, she hasn't had much of a break. But I'm a pragmatist. Her history is to get involved with the wrong guy and then move away. Now, I know that this Daniel kid, for all his oddities, isn't some criminal mastermind. But she likes bad boys, so how long before she dumps him and latches on to some asshole who might be a danger or a threat? Who might be a thief? How long before she feels like she needs to move on, and leaves you in the middle of the night without a word? You're putting a lot of faith in someone who is flighty at best. You're giving her tremendous responsibility with the new delivery venture; I just don't want her to bail on you and leave you in a bind."

"The delivery venture was HER IDEA! How could I not let her be a part of it? Nate, she may have had some bad judgments in the past, but I believe in her. I have to trust her, because she hasn't given me reason not to." And now I hate that I know what I know. I hate that I didn't have the strength to not listen.

"Are you mad?"

"I'm disappointed. Frustrated, I guess. And trying not to be mad. I know that you did it from a place of love, at least I want to believe that, and not think that you were simply attracted to the idea of solving a mystery. But it is such a violation, and I hate that you took it upon yourself to investigate her, even if your intention was to protect me."

"I admit, when I started digging, it was pure curiosity, since she was clearly hiding something. But the first thing that popped up was the drug bust, so that made me want to find out the whole story to be sure she wasn't a danger to you. Promise. No other ulterior motives. Are you going to tell her?"

"No. She's a fragile thing, Nate, and if anything would make her run, as you fear, it would be knowing that the past she has taken such pains to conceal has come to light. No, I'm not going to tell her what I know, what I wish I didn't know, and I hope you won't tell anyone else."

"Of course not."

"I should really get going on my day, I have a ton of stuff to do."

"Yeah, I should get home. We okay?"

"Yeah, we're okay." Trust is such a big thing for me. It goes against every instinct to not just scream at him, to not let this escalate. I take a deep breath. I try to focus on what I want to believe about him. "I love that you love me enough to be worried, I just wish that you hadn't told me."

"Sorry, can't unring that bell."

"I know."

He gets up and grabs his bag. "Talk to you later?"

"Okay."

He kisses me. "Love you."

I clean up the breakfast dishes, and sit with a second cup of tea. I check my watch, it's nearly ten. In a couple of hours at most Nadia is going to come home and I'm going to have to figure out how not to alter my behavior with her, how to not just pull her into my arms and hold her and tell her it's all going to be okay.

Nadia doesn't come home. She calls to tell me she is hooking up with Daniel and staying at his place. I avoid Nate's calls all day, ignoring him in favor of errands and dealing with all the accumulated tedium of the week. I wish it made me tired, but I toss and turn under the weight of my knowledge and don't get much sleep.

Tuesday, Kai and I get in early to do our once-a-month strip-down cleaning of the kitchen and walk-in. The day is long and draining. But the worst is when Nadia comes in, happy from what has clearly been a couple of lovely nights with her strange boyfriend, and is exuberantly demonstrative in her delight, extra hugs and huge smiles. All afternoon she checks in with me, brings me cups of tea, reminds me to eat. Every ounce of her solicitude strikes straight into my heart. I know her secrets, her shame. It weighs on me.

After work, we pack up some stuff from the store, and head home for a quiet late dinner. Nadia seems to think that she has a recipe that will guarantee a good night's sleep; she is worried about the bags under my eyes. All I know is that it is warm, spicy, lemony, and sweet and apparently deeply and importantly alcoholic, because within no time at all, I'm seriously buzzed.

"So you had a good time with Daniel, huh?"

"It was awesome. We had a great time. He wants me to move in with him."

"Isn't that a little soon? It's only been a couple of months . . ."

"You've only been with Nate a couple of months; wouldn't you move in with him if he asked?"

I think about this. "Probably not. It's too soon; we don't know each other well enough."

"But you love him, right?"

"I do. But sometimes love isn't enough, sometimes love isn't right, sometimes you can love someone who won't honor that love or return it in a healthy way."

"But you still have to love. You still have to be hopeful about love."

"I think you have to be hopeful, but responsible about

love. Don't shut yourself off from it, but don't be afraid to use your head either. There's no shame in loving someone for a time, in a way, while it works. Not everything has to be a thousand percent."

"Yes it does, Mel. Or it isn't love."

"It's a recipe for disaster."

"I'm used to disaster."

"Yeah, honey, I know." Shit.

"What do you mean?"

"Well, you know. Barry and all that. I mean, you yourself say that you have bad taste in guys, I just, I want you to be careful."

"Oh."

Grasping for anything to fix it, to shift the focus, I say, "Besides, I've gotten used to having you around."

"Why am I feeling a little bit like Eliza Doolittle?"

"You didn't need me to change you; you are fine just as you are."

"Except for my taste in guys."

"Well, yeah, that."

We laugh, and I'm glad the initial danger moment has passed. I pour myself another drink.

A few things have become readily apparent to me. One, I'm going to lose her as a roommate sooner rather than later. Two, I'm going to have to figure out how to fess up about what I know at some point, because otherwise something is going to slip out. And three, I'm reasonably certain that tomorrow is going to be my first corned beef hash morning in a really long time.

CREAMED SPINACH

When we were little, our grandparents were members of a
private club called the Covenant Club. It was a Jewish club
that had been around since the early 1900s, established as a
place for Eastern European Jews to gather, since the other
downtown Jewish club, the Standard Club, was at that point
exclusively for German Jews. Grandpa went three times a
week to play racquetball and take a steam, or as he called it,
a schvitz, with his buddies. Grandma went once a week to
play bridge or mah-jongg. Once a month or so we would all
go have dinner there. The Covenant Club was the first place
I ever ate creamed spinach. I was never much for veggies,
and Mom often covered them in cheese sauces, or hid them
in casseroles to get me to eat them at home. But my grandpa
would always order the creamed spinach, and once I tasted
it, I was hooked.

*   *   *

Nathan and I walk into Chalkboard, where I'm greeted with a hug by Gil, the chef and owner. "Mel! How's business?"

"Good, thanks." I gesture around the packed restaurant. "And for you as well, I see!"

"No complaints, no complaints."

"Gil, this is Nathan, Nate, this is Gil. He's the chef."

Gil extends his hand and the two men shake firmly.

"Great to meet you. Mel has raved about your place, so I'm very excited to finally get a chance to eat here!"

"Well, Mel knows I wish she'd close up shop and come hang out in my kitchen instead! So, any special occasion tonight?"

"Nate just finished his new movie, so we're celebrating."

"Wow, that's fantastic. Congratulations."

"Thank you. It always feels weird to have something finished. I'm glad to get it off my plate and at the same time, I have the time to second guess every choice I made."

"I feel the same way about a new dish. The minute it goes on the menu and I get the kitchen up to speed, I'm tempted to change everything about it!" Gil leads us to a cozy table near the front window. Nathan pulls out my chair, and then sits next to me. Gil looks at us with a smile. "So, anyone allergic to anything?"

Nate and I shake our heads.

"Anyone have anything they hate?"

"I'm not big on shellfish," Nate says.

"Me either!" says Gil. "Okay, is it all right with you guys if I just take care of you? I'll just keep sending stuff out till you say 'uncle.'"

"That's very kind, thank you." I mentally add two more hours of exercise to my weekly schedule.

"Wow, that's terrific, thanks!" Nate says, clearly impressed that the chef is going to design a meal especially for us.

"Fantastic." Gil waves over our server. "Let's get two glasses of the Taltarni for these lovely people." He turns to us. "My new favorite sparkler from Australia. You'll love it. I'm going to go into the kitchen and play, just tell me when you want me to stop!" He disappears just as the waiter comes back with two flutes filled with a delicately pink sparkling wine, and Nate raises his glass at me.

"Cheers."

"Congrats, honey, I'm so proud of you. And the movie is beautiful." We spent the afternoon in a screening room downtown watching the final cut, and it is a spectacular film. I was very moved by the story of this nomadic African tribe, and was impressed that Nate's work was seamless and invisible. Sometimes when you watch a documentary, you can see the director's handprints all over it; their opinions, politics, and biases become clear, and you can feel them manipulating you through the story as they want you to see it. But here I just felt like a fly on the wall, the camera seemed to have been a totally objective observer, and the editing, while serving to clearly define a narrative arc for the piece, never felt heavy-handed. The production company who hired him is apparently very pleased, so whatever second-guessing he is doing now is totally just his own perfectionism.

"Thanks, that means a lot to me."

We clink glasses again, and sip the light wine. Our server

arrives with the first course and we submit to the pleasure of good food and good wine and the company of someone you love.

"Melanie, darling, how are you?"

"GILLY! My god, kiddo, it is good to hear your voice. What's going on?"

"I'm just checking in to see how you're doing, how you're hanging in there."

"I'm good."

"Mel . . ."

"What? I'm good!"

She sighs breathily into the phone. "Look, Mel, you don't have to put on the brave voice with me. I know what this week is. And I'm calling to say that I know, and that it sucks, and that if you need me, I'll come."

This is the week Andrew and Charlene are getting married. I hate that she knows it. I hate that anyone knows it. Especially me.

"Gillian, you're sweet, and yes, it sucks, but truly, I'm fine. It's a little piece of shit in the toilet that needs an extra couple flushes. I'm not thinking about it, I'm not dwelling on it; I'm just dealing with it. And I love you, and I'd love to see you, but you don't have to come to rescue me."

"Okay, then. How is everything else, how is Nathan?"

"Good. We're good, you know."

"That's not the same as great."

"I think I'm not fully ready for great, you know? It's too

soon for great, it's too hard to believe in great. I have to really think hard every day to be happy with good, to trust it. I'm working my way up to being prepared for great, you know?"

"I know, honey. And you take whatever time you need. But Mel, Andrew was a shit. An unflushable little turd, to borrow your phrase. You have to believe he is the exception that proves the rule. Not all men are shits. Yes, you should be cautious, but not to the point it kills a chance at happiness."

"I know."

"Do you?"

"I do. Swear."

"Pinky swear?"

"Pinky swear. How is everything there, how's it going being partner?"

"It's good, you know, busy busy."

"And any boys for you?"

"When I need them."

"Fair enough. You know, Gilly, we've never talked about it, but . . ."

"But?"

"If you're a lesbian, that is totally cool with me, you know."

Gilly laughs, throaty and deep. "Good lord, Mel, don't you think if I were in that way inclined I would have told you by now? Yeesh. I'm not into girls; I'm just not into relationships at the moment. I date, I get laid, I'm fine. I have a plan, and I'm on track. You know I never wanted kids, that whole thing. The work is good, I have plenty of friends to eat with and laugh with and travel with. If a guy comes along and is the right guy, I'll keep him. In the meantime, I'm good."

"Okay."

"A lesbian. Really."

"Okay, okay!"

"All right, lovely, I have to go. You're sure you're okay?"

"I am, I'm good. And thanks for calling, I really appreciate it."

"Love you, sis."

"Love you back."

Kai is waiting for me when I get to the store.

"You're here early."

"I had Phil drop me off; I wanted to be here when you got here." Kai looks very serious. My heart drops.

"What's going on? You have a look on your face I don't like . . . Is something wrong?"

"Let's go inside, nothing's wrong, but I want to talk to you about something and I hope it is a good something, so don't be worried."

I unlock the door and let us in. Kai heads over to the stove and puts on the electric kettle, grabbing our two mini teapots and two mugs from the shelf above. "English Breakfast or Jasmine?" he asks.

"English Breakfast, please."

Kai spoons tea leaves into the little mesh baskets inside the teapots, and waits for the water to boil.

"So, I have some news," Kai begins.

"Obviously. What the hell is going on, Kai?"

"We bought next door."

I don't immediately understand. "What did you buy next door?"

Kai laughs. "Oh, Slim, we didn't buy something next door, we bought the BUILDING next door. We bought Joe's place."

"You're kidding? Why?"

"Well, a couple of reasons. First, as you know, Phil doesn't really let me pay for much, generous thing that he is, so I've saved up a few thousand dollars that I thought could use investing. And Delia had her windfall . . ."

"Wait, you and DELIA bought next door?"

"Me and Delia and Phil. Delia's insurance, and my little savings, and Phil making up the rest."

I plop down on the stool as Kai pours the now boiling water over the tea leaves. It's sort of shocking, the idea of the three of them doing this without even talking to me. Kai brings over a teapot and mug to where I am sitting and grabs the small container of skim milk out of the lowboy fridge for me.

"So, here is how things went down . . . Delia gets this chunk of dead hubby money, right? A couple of weeks ago, Phil comes by to pick me up, and Delia is here and she and he start talking about investments, and he says that real estate is the best investment, and she says maybe she should buy old Joe's place next door, and then Phil thinks about it, and says that maybe she should. But when she tells us how much money she got, we know that it isn't enough to buy the place outright, and she needs the monthly pension to pretty much cover her bills. But then Phil and I start talking, and the place is a good investment. Great location, storefront space to rent out on the first floor, we start thinking about it. For us, there is the tax break and the potential rental income, and for Delightful there is the apartment upstairs, so she will have a place to live that she owns. We went to look at it, got an independent inspection, talked to the real estate people and Joe is a pretty motivated seller, so the place is pretty reasonable, price-wise. Long story short, the three of us formed a limited partnership, and bought the building!"

My eyes are filling with tears.

"Oh, Mellie Mel, don't be mad."

"I'm not mad, you goof. I'm so happy for Delia! She is going to have her own place to live, all her own that no one can take from her. And it's right next door, so even if she quits, I'll still get to see her! I think it's WONDERFUL. But why didn't you guys tell me?"

"Well, we, um . . . We kind of thought with all your financial problems of late, that us getting all excited about buying property together might seem a little insensitive. Especially because, and maybe I'm wrong here, but I think that if you were more solvent, had a bigger nest egg, you might have thought about buying the place yourself, and it might have made you sad to think that we could do it and you couldn't."

"I appreciate the sensitivity, but I wish you'd told me. I'm excited for you guys, and for Delia, and I'm so relieved that it is you three that will be handling things! What are you going to do about the first floor?"

"That is something I want to talk to you about." Delia is standing in the doorway, having appeared silently I have no idea when.

I jump off my chair and hug her. "D, I'm so happy for you. Congratulations!"

She hugs me back. "Thank you, Melanie. I'm very glad to hear that."

"You must be so excited, a place of your own that really belongs to you! When do you close?"

Kai heads over to put on a pot of coffee for Delia. "We close at the end of June, occupancy July first."

Just a few weeks away. "Well, D, if you need any help, painting or putting up shelves or anything, I'm right next door!"

"Thank you, Mel. But there is something else."

"What's that?"

"I've been talking to Kai and Phil, and I'm thinking that maybe you and I could use the first-floor space to open another café."

"You and me? What, like expand to next door?"

"No, more like a sister store. You know I love to cook, but you also know that my true cooking passion is very different from yours. I don't know anything about running a store, I've never been to culinary school, but I know how to cook good old-fashioned comfort food that people seem to enjoy. I also know that a lot of the people who want and need the kind of food you make here, live with people who don't have the same issues . . . They have kids who can eat whatever they like or husbands or wives without weight problems. I thought, if you and I together created a second store, one that sold essentially the opposite of what you sell, they would complement each other. A woman who is trying to be healthy can come by and pick up dinner for herself here, but head next door to get ribs for her husband with the fast metabolism or macaroni and cheese for her kids. You know the business and mechanics of the thing, and I could just be in the kitchen."

"ISN'T IT BRILLIANT?" Kai jumps in. "When I told Phil, he flipped out. I mean, it's total genius! And then we are all partners together! I'm going to work here with you in the morning, and then afternoons with Delia, so I get the best of both worlds!"

My heart sinks. "Okay, first of all, D, it's a great idea and I know you will be a success and I'm going to be so proud when you open your place. And Kai, you and Phil couldn't have a better person to back. But as you said earlier, I have no means at the moment to invest, and as much as I would love to be a part of what you guys are doing, and of course I'll help however I can, I won't be able to be a partner." I hate this. I hate that an opportunity like this could fall into my lap and I would be totally unable to take advantage of it.

"We will figure something out, Mel," Kai says.

"I'm sure there is something . . ." Delia pipes in.

I raise my hand to stop them. "Guys, it's okay. I know you want me involved, and I promise I'll help however I can. I'm so glad you'll be right next door, and even though I wish like mad that I could come on board with you, we all know it just isn't possible right now. But I love you, and I'm so flattered that you would want to include me, and knowing that will have to be enough for now. And just because I'm not a partner doesn't mean we can't do great cross-promotion . . . I think you're right, the two places will complement each other, and hopefully we'll both see bigger business because of our proximity."

Kai and Delia look at each other, brows furrowed.

"Hey. Guys, it's okay! This is a cause for celebration, let's not bring it down!" I reach my arms out to them, willing myself to be happy for them, willing myself to remember how blessed my life is. They both move forward to hug me, and

I can feel their love for me, but also their pity, and it nearly breaks me.

"Can we get to work?" I say. We release our embrace.

"Absolutely," Kai says, reaching for an apron.

"What are we doing today?" Delia says, heading over to the prep sink to wash her hands.

"I think today we should see if we can't adapt some good old family recipes. I know a couple of things I've been meaning to try." I need creamed spinach. A vat of it.

"Well, then," Delia says. "Let's get to it!"

CHOCOLATE CHIP COOKIES

Chocolate chip cookies are no-brainer go-to giveaway food. A Valentine. An apology. A hostess gift. What you give to a pal who is blue. It's usually one of the first things you learn to bake as a kid, often starting with just baking premade tube cookie dough, eventually moving up to mixing your own. My mom taught me how to make chocolate chip cookies as a part of the annual Christmas cookie festival, and while I've tried over the years occasionally to mess with the recipe, to be honest, the Toll House classic on the back of the Nestlé chocolate chip bag is hard to improve upon. The dough tastes great, and the finished product is that perfect blend of crispy on the outside and soft on the inside that for me is the perfect cookie. They freeze beautifully, and travel well, so you can pack them in care packages and ship them off, and keep them in the freezer for emergencies.

*   *   *

"I've gained five pounds," I say to Carey.

"How does that feel?"

"Scary. I haven't been bingeing; I don't feel out of control, I've just been the tiniest bit less diligent. I mean, it's been harder and harder the past few weeks to make time to exercise, with everything going on and trying to make time to see Nate, and I haven't been to the gym at all this week between the cold and working. I've just been too beat. And I know that I've been eating out more with Nate, and certainly ate weird when he was here with me while I was sick. I just haven't been paying attention. Delia has been coming in early to test recipes for the new place next door, so there has been some seriously yummy food lying around, and a lot of tasting and testing. But it's weird how I haven't felt like I could possibly have gotten so far off track, and yet, there it was on the scale, up five."

"What is your first instinct?"

"To eat a vat of mashed potatoes."

"Why is that?"

"Because they are delicious."

"That isn't a real answer."

"I'm tired. I'm tired of being good all the time, I'm tired of maintaining. I'm tired of feeling like my value in the world is the fact that I lost the weight, and feeling like I'm judged for it. If I keep the weight off, I'm annoying to people who are struggling. And if I put it back on, it just proves that fat people never have enough willpower or determination to not be fat. And on top of it, I picked a fight with Nathan yesterday."

"What about?"

"He brought over Homemade Pizza Company for dinner last night, and he got a large sausage pizza with fresh tomatoes and red onions, and a salad, and one of their big chocolate chip cookies. Now, he knows that sausage-onion-tomato is my favorite, right? So did I thank him for remembering my favorite pizza? No. Did I appreciate that he was diligent about making sure there was also a healthy food option around so that I didn't feel the need to overeat the pizza? Nope. Did I find it sweet that a mere two days after we made chocolate chip cookies to send to his sister and her husband to congratulate them on getting pregnant, and telling him all about what chocolate chip cookies mean to me historically, that he brought me a big cookie? Hell no. I accused him of simultaneously tempting me with the pizza and cookie, and telling me I shouldn't eat it by buying the salad, and warned him that feeding me was a dangerous game, because I could relapse at any moment, and I'm pretty sure he wouldn't want me if I were fat again."

"What did he say?"

"He asked what was really wrong with me."

"And what is really wrong with you?"

"I don't know. I weighed myself yesterday, so I know I was particularly aware that I'm off. And I know that I'm not supposed to pay attention to the scale, that I'm only supposed to look at how my clothes fit and how I feel, but it bothered me how fast, how sneaky, those five pounds were. It made me feel like if those five could come back, the other hundred and forty are right behind them. And it made me wonder if I had still been big when I was crying in that museum if Nate would have reached out to me."

"So what I'm hearing is that you are having some trust issues, with him and with yourself. You don't trust yourself to stay healthy, to manage your eating, to keep yourself active. And you don't trust Nathan to really understand your issues and be supportive of you."

"I know I have all this trust baggage because of Andrew, but Nate hasn't done anything to mitigate that. He went behind my back and did all that digging about Nadia, he keeps taking me out to restaurants and filling his fridge with tempting foods, and I just think he doesn't get how bad it makes me feel to think that if he had met me when I was fat he wouldn't have wanted me, he wouldn't have loved me, and I resent him for it, even though he hasn't done anything to show me that!"

"Do you think you are subconsciously eating extra, exercising less, so that you can gain a little weight to test him? To see if he cares about it?"

I hadn't thought of this. "I don't know. Maybe."

"Do you really think you would go all the way back to where you were?"

"I have dreams where I wake up and my old body is back. And half of me is so upset and sad, and half of me is like 'Hooray, tonight I can have a hot fudge sundae and a pile of french fries!' and I'm pretty sure that makes me a crazy person."

Carey laughs. "Oh, sweetie, you aren't crazy, you've just got a lot going on, personally and professionally. You've got the new business venture next door, you've got Nadia in your house and the pressure of everything you now know about her, you have this very new relationship, which is being tested in all sorts of ways, and unless I'm mistaken, your ex got married yesterday."

"I forgot about that."

"No, you didn't."

"No, I didn't."

"What do you need? BESIDES mashed potatoes."

"I need to forgive myself."

"For?"

"For making myself feel bad about my weight."

"Because?"

"Because my weight doesn't matter, only my health matters."

"And five pounds isn't scary because?"

"Because I can fluctuate safely within a five-pound range, which can be affected by everything from water retention to stress and because I know that my body naturally wants to be at a healthy weight and to eat things that are good for it, and as long as I pay attention to my hunger level and finding balance, my body will naturally maintain its healthy weight." The basis of our work together, the reason it was and ultimately is, successful.

"Get back to the gym, remember to eat regular meals, and for goodness sake, articulate whatever you need to express to Nathan to ensure that he is a good partner for you where food is concerned. Ask him to meet you at the gym and work out together. Ask him to check with you first before making executive decisions about meals. I'm not a couple's therapist, I can't speak to the other trust issues, but when it comes to your eating and exercising and things related to your body and your health, I can tell you that any relationship that doesn't support your process and allow you to deal effectively is not going to be successful."

"I know. Thanks, Carey."

"Do me a favor. Don't get back on the scale for at least a month. Try to get your focus back, to get back to some exercising. If in a month you check in and are feeling like the problem has become magnified, if you gain more, then we'll come up with a more specific plan. In the meantime, you're feeling a little bit adrift, so eat grounding foods. Root veggies, sweet potatoes, anything that grows with firm roots in the ground will be stabilizing. I know summer is peeking around the corner, but don't be afraid to rely on some of the foods that are a little bit autumnal. There's a reason you said mashed potatoes and not cake. You need grounding. Let the ground foods help."

"Okay, will do. Thanks, Carey."

"You are very welcome. I'll talk to you soon."

"Yep. Talk to you later." I hang up the phone and stretch my arms over my head, feeling immediately better, immediately empowered, and immediately guilty about my tiff with Nate. And what is worse, I hate that not only did I pick the fight, but I did it on the day Andrew and Charlene fucking got married. Which means that for all my defensiveness about the Andrew issue when Nate and I had our first fight, obviously it is much more deeply rooted in my psyche than I realized. And once again, I didn't tell Nate that yesterday was the wedding day, didn't give him a chance to be extra sensitive to me. I didn't even tell him that I gained some weight and that that dredges up a lot of shit for me, I just went for cranky and bitchy.

I head out of the office, and back into the kitchen, where Delia is pulling a tray of mini tins of peach cobbler out of the oven.

"Hey, D, that smells amazing."

"Thanks, Mel. It's one of my grandmother's recipes, and I think I finally have it down. I never thought about how different it is to cook for selling instead of cooking just for dinner or for a party! Trying to figure out how to portion things, to make sure they travel okay, directions for how to reheat and serve at home. It's crazy!"

"I know! I think the thing that is most difficult for me is finding consistency. When you cook at home, you add a little of this, a little of that, a pinch of whatever. But when someone comes to you to buy something they have bought before, they want it the way it was the first time, they want the identical experience. Imagine if you went to McDonald's and suddenly the fries were fat steak fries with the skin on! You'd be so disappointed! So even though I can be tempted to alter a recipe, I have to restrain myself and put that creative energy into something totally new so that my customers know I'm not going to constantly change the stuff they like. And, of course for me and this place and not so much for you, I have to be sure that I'm really diligent about ingredients when I'm cooking. I can't just add more oil if something starts to stick, because the calorie count on all my stuff is so precise. I have to measure very carefully or I will be accidentally sabotaging my clients."

"I know what you mean about changing the recipes. Lucky for me, most of the stuff I'm cooking is stuff that has been handed down for so many generations that a field of folks would be spinning in their graves if I veer from their instructions!"

"Well, good to know that all your ancestors are keeping you honest."

"It smells so yummy in here!" Nadia flies in, pink-and-blonde tresses in a messy plait flowing behind her like a tail on a kite. "Whatcha making, Mama Delia?"

"Peach cobbler, little girl. Still needs to cool fifteen minutes before you can taste."

"Excellent! Anyone want tea? D, coffee?" she asks.

"No thanks," I say.

"I'm good, sweetheart. Thanks, though."

"No problem." She makes herself a quick cup of tea, and bounces back up front.

"That child has the most ridiculous energy," Delia says, transferring the tiny cobblers to a rack to finish cooling.

I head up front to check the case, which we restocked after the lunch rush, and still looks pretty good. Nadia is straightening the bookshelves where we keep the nutrition and health books.

"Hey, kiddo?"

"Yeah?"

"Are you coming home tonight, or are you at Daniel's?"

"Daniel's working late, so I'll be home. Are you going to be at Nate's?"

"Nope."

"Girls' night!" She grins.

"Sure." I've been so uncomfortable with Nadia since Nate shared what he has discovered, that I haven't spent too much time with her. Not that I'm actively avoiding her, but I am being extraordinarily careful about what I say and how I say it. So the idea of a quiet night at home with her is nerve-wracking. Especially since it's the perfect time to come clean in a safe environment, and I haven't the foggiest idea how she'll react.

"I've been craving Thai food. Do you want to order in?"

"Yeah, that sounds great. Things look good up here. If you don't need anything, I'd better get back to the kitchen."

"Go, go, I'm fine. I'll holler if I need anything."

I pause in the tiny hall between the front of the store and the kitchen. Stuck between two places, between two mind-sets, seems to be where I'm living these days. Between wanting to be open to Nate and the possibility of the relationship, and not really trusting him and wondering if I'm ready to be so serious and committed to anyone. Wanting to be a good and honest friend to Nadia, and wanting to forget that I know what I know so that I don't have to admit to my prying nature. Being excited about the new business ventures, the opportunity of the delivery service and the café with Delia, and being scared to death that adding the extra stress and time commitment and uncertainty is too much to take on at a time in my life when I clearly need to be very careful about taking care of myself physically. Part of me is very proud of myself for embracing change at this stage of my life, and a part of me is so angry at being forced to have a coming-of-age at forty, when my life should have been settled and comfortable. I take a deep breath and take a step toward the kitchen, toward having a purpose, toward control over what can be controlled.

"Hey, can I have some of this sherbet?" Nadia calls from the kitchen, having found the leftovers from my short time as an invalid.

"Please, have as much as you want!"

"Do you want some?"

"No thanks, I'm stuffed."

Nadia reappears with a bowl, licking the back of a spoon. "Why is it that in a million years I would never think to buy sherbet, or to order it at the ice cream shop, but there is something so profoundly soothing about it, and when I eat it I am utterly delighted?"

"I have no idea. But you're right, the chances of me getting out of any ice cream store without something in the chocolate/caramel/peanut butter family is slim to none, but there is something about a bowl of sherbet that satisfies on a much deeper level."

"It's because it has sherbetude."

"Sherbosity."

"It's sherbeterrific."

"Sherbetacular."

She giggles at the silliness of it. "So, are we going to watch a movie or are you going to make me watch some Cold-Law-Without-a-Trace-of-Order-Case?"

"Are you making fun of my TiVo selections?"

"Not I. I'm too full of sherbetliciousness."

"I thought maybe we could talk."

Nadia sits bolt upright on the couch, and puts her bowl on the table. "Am I in trouble?"

"No, honey. You're fine. You're better than fine. But I might be in a little bit of trouble."

She sinks back in and fixes her rapt attention on me, her voice full of concern. "What's going on?"

"I've done something that isn't a very nice thing to do to a friend, and I've been trying to figure out how to make it right."

"Is she mad? Your friend?"

"She doesn't know, yet. I want to tell her. And I want to make amends, but ultimately I don't know if my apology will be enough."

"Well, you can only try." Nadia shrugs, playing the sage. "The rest is up to the universe."

"You're right about that. So here goes. A little while ago I had an opportunity to find out some information about your past. And even though I knew that, for whatever reason, you weren't ready to trust me with your history, and had been pretty clear in your own way that it wasn't up for discussion, and even though I knew that a good friend and a good person would not take that opportunity, I wasn't that strong, and I let my curiosity take control of my better nature. I don't know why you didn't want me to know about where you came from or what you've been through, but I do know that I should have respected your privacy, and waited for you to share yourself with me in your own time and at your own pace. So I wanted to tell you that I know, and that I'm so, so very sorry for violating your trust and invading your privacy."

She is white, her dancing eyebrows in a straight line over eyes that have gone a deep forest green. Her voice is steady, but her hands tremble. "What do you know?"

"I know about your mom, and what happened to your dad and that you were raised by your grandmother. I know about the marriage and dropping out of college and the drug bust and the jail time. I know that you lived in four or five cities in as many years."

"I see."

"I also know that none of it changes what I think of you,

or makes me respect you any less, or makes me care about you any differently."

"Really? And what is it that you think of me, exactly? Or should I guess? I'm flighty and irresponsible and have really bad taste in men and I'm easily led."

"Oh, sweetie, I think you're only twenty-four and you've been through a lot, and you are a remarkable young woman."

"I'm not so young, Mel. I've lived too much to be young. And you don't really mean young, you mean immature."

"I most certainly do not mean immature. I think you're extraordinary."

"Some charity case, some broken little girl."

"Not at all. I think you could use some stability in your life . . ."

"I see, a mother figure who isn't a religious extremist from another century or an old woman saddled with the only proof that her deadbeat crackhead son ever existed? A place to live that isn't someone's couch or the bed of a married man or a criminal? I mean, I know you clearly want a better boyfriend for me, someone who isn't weird and different and quirky. As much as you disapprove of the ones who came before, it's obvious that you think Daniel is somehow not significantly better than any of the assholes who I've been with. Maybe I just need some career direction, a bigger job under your watchful eye, more responsibility in a place you can back me up when I fall. So you can fix me."

"Nadia, I'm so sorry. I don't think those things, I really don't. I think you've had a rough time of it, I think you've been sent more than your share of difficulties, and while I'm very ashamed of how I know what I know, I'm not sorry that I know it, because it's a part of who you are, and I care about you. And you shouldn't be at all embarrassed about any of it."

"Really? So I shouldn't be embarrassed by the fact that I dropped out of college when the married professor I was sleeping with knocked me up and then made me get an abortion so he didn't lose his wife or his job? I shouldn't be embarrassed that I spent four months being a full-time personal slave and source of cruel amusement to my cunt of a cellmate so that I at least didn't have to become some other woman's unwilling sex toy? I shouldn't be embarrassed that when I went to stay with my cousin in St. Louis I got drunk at a party and was date raped by his best friend, or that I ended up with Barry because the girlfriend I was living with in Minneapolis kicked me out when she caught her husband spying on me in the shower when he thought she had left the house?" There is fire in her eyes. And tears in mine.

"Oh, Nadia, I didn't know any of that."

"Then you should ask your spy or private eye or whoever for your money back, because you only got part of the story. He should have told you that when my grandmother died I went to find my mother, who told me that I didn't exist and that I was making the whole thing up and that she had never had a child before she married her husband. He should have told you that I have two little brothers and three little sisters who don't know I'm alive and who I will never know. For someone who is poor enough to need to take in a lost wastrel like me for a pittance a month, it seems a very odd way to spend what little money you have. You'd have been better off just kicking me out on a hunch and losing the free hours of help at the store."

"Nadia, please. I know it's hurtful and that I have broken trust with you, but I swear, I didn't pay anyone, I didn't go looking, the information just presented itself and I was an asshole and accepted it."

Clarity registers on her face. "Nate, right? The ultimate researcher? What, am I going to be the subject of a film now?"

"I can't excuse his behavior. I know that your secrecy about your past concerned him, he thought that if he checked up on you he might be protecting me in some way or saving me from hurt. The first thing he found out was about the imprisonment, and that really scared him, and so he kept digging. I wish he hadn't and I wish when he told me he had found out some stuff that I had told him to not tell me, but I didn't. But mostly I wish that you had nothing to find, nothing you wanted to hide or forget. I wish that you had an idyllic childhood with a mother and father who loved you and took care of you, with siblings you got to know and love. I wish you had a life filled with nice boyfriends and safe homes and people who were good to you and friends who didn't let you down. I wish that for you now. For you to have a life from now on that helps to make up for all the crap you've been dealt. And I want to be the kind of friend who you can trust and lean on. I know you're hurt and angry and you have every right to be. But I hope that you'll give me a chance to make it up to you."

"I don't know if I can do that."

"Are you at all willing to try?"

She looks down at her hands. "I don't know if I can answer that right now."

"Tell me what you need, what I can do to start making it right?"

"I'm going to leave. I'm going to go to Daniel's for a couple of days, and I'm not going to come into work for a couple of days. I need some space, some time. I'll call you when I'm ready to talk."

She gets up off the couch and goes down the hall to her bedroom. I sit, sickened and sad, tears flowing down my cheeks, wondering what kind of person I am that I could be capable of damaging the trust of someone I care about in no less a violation than Andrew perpetrated against me.

How did I get here? How could I, who loves to think of myself as a good person, come to a place where I could hurt someone as badly as I've been hurt? What would have been worse—to spend the rest of my life harboring the secrets and pretending I didn't know, or coming clean and possibly losing her? Nadia moves at a swift pace through the living room, not looking at me, and flies through the front door.

I want Nate.

I want to eat.

I want my mother.

But I don't feel worthy of any sort of comfort, not the comfort of a man's arms around me, or the comfort of food. I need to feel this pain, I need to accept the punishment of disappointing and hurting someone I care about, I need to own my anguish. And so I sit on the couch to settle into the reality of the mess I have created for myself and the deep chasm I have opened between me and the friend I had no idea I needed so much.

BACON

There is no single food that affects people as deeply as bacon. Bacon appeals to our basest desires of meat and fat and salt. It elevates everything it touches, transforming a burger into a celebration, taking simple lettuce and tomato and making them more delicious than any salad vegetable has a right to be. Bacon is the ultimate polyamorous food, loving everyone equally, eggs and pancakes, sandwiches and salads, meats and vegetables, mains and sides, savory and sweet. Bacon on grilled cheese? Delicious. Bacon dipped in the maple syrup from your French toast? Sublime. Watch a breakfast buffet, and see where people consistently overindulge. I bet it will be the vat of bacon, which sends its smoky siren song out to everyone.

* * *

I'm numb for the first day after the big fight with Nadia. I feel completely isolated. I don't want to tell Nate, since he will probably feel bad about his part in it, and also think me dumb for telling her in the first place. I can't confide in Delia or Kai, because I can't open Nadia up for any more hurt or prying, and lucky for me the two of them are so focused on developing a menu for the new café and getting all their ducks in a row for the closing, that they don't really notice that Nadia isn't around and that I am subdued.

I called Gilly the morning of the second day, and she said that I had to forgive myself, I was only human, and if Nadia couldn't forgive me, then it was her loss. I put off getting together with Nate, claiming exhaustion and needing to work on stuff for the delivery business, which is scheduled to launch full force right after the Fourth of July, just two weeks off. I work and try to not call her, to not e-mail her, and just to let her be. The apartment is eerily quiet.

It's been three days and I'm just heartsick that perhaps I really may have lost her forever. That I'll have to eventually explain to Kai and Delia why she's gone, that I'll have to figure out how to look at Nate and not blame him for ultimately my own weakness of character. I'm closing out the register when there is a knock at the window. I look up to see Daniel waving at me. I cross the room and unlock the door for him.

"Hi, um, Mel."

"Hi, Daniel. Please, come in."

"Thank you." He comes in and I relock the door.

"Can I get you anything? Are you thirsty? Hungry?"

"No thank you, I'm fine."

There is an awkward silence. I have to break it. "Is she okay?"

"She's surprisingly good, I think."

"Does she hate me?"

"I think she is struggling with her own demons. It isn't totally about you, Mel, it's about Nadia."

"Do you think she'll forgive me?"

"Right now I'm working on getting her to forgive herself. She's frustrated, Mel, I'm not going to lie to you. You saw her as trying to hide her past. She was trying to forget her past and move forward. You see her as a product of that past, and she is trying to be a product only of her present. She wasn't trying to be dishonest or manipulative or secretive, she was trying to exert control over who she is, the face she wants to put into the world, the person she is trying to become. The past was an anchor for her that she was trying to rid herself of, and you knowing it means that when she sees you, she feels the weight of you knowing. I think she wants to get past it, but also wants to get back to a place where the past is just that. She knows you weren't actively trying to hurt her. She knows that you care about her. She also knows you don't think ill of her. I do think, however, that she will never forgive Mr. Gershowitz, and she isn't sure how that impacts your future friendship, since obviously he is very much a part of your life, and if she is also going to be a part of your life, the two of them are likely to intersect."

I had no idea he could be so articulate, and not only is it clear that he cares about Nadia, but I'm starting to understand what Nadia sees in him as well. "Daniel, what do I do? Do I have Nathan call her to apologize? How do I make it right? What does she need me to do? What did she say to tell me?"

"I'm not here on an errand. I'm here because when you get home tonight she is going to be there. I'm here because I think that you are an important and positive person for her to have in her life, and I want the two of you to make up. I'm here because I love her and want her to be happy and healthy, and I think you are a part of that right now. I can't give her everything. I can't be her only support system. She loves her job, she loves you and Delia and Kai, and she doesn't want to have to leave. But she also needs to not be smothered. When you are maternal with her, it reminds her that she never had a mother. If you are overly solicitous, she will feel that your relationship has changed. Go home, Mel. And try as much as you can to follow her lead. Try not to give into your desire to apologize all over yourself and make it up to her, as you say. Don't do special things for her to win her back. Just let her be, and try as hard as you can to be no different from how you were before you knew what you know, and it will be okay. And if possible, don't let your boyfriend come around her for a while."

I hug this strange boy, a bag of bones in my arms. "Thank you, Daniel. For loving her and taking care of her and coming here to help me."

He blushes deeply, and pushes his glasses up his nose, hair falling over his eyes.

"Do you know? The details of her past, I mean?"

"I know that when she came over the other night so upset, and told me that she had some terrible things in her past that you had found out about, in part because she was so secretive that it made you suspicious of her, she was equally worried that I might be concerned about what she had chosen not to share with me. I told her I wasn't concerned at all. She asked if there was anything I wanted to know about her. I said I only wanted to know if she loved me. She said she does. That was all I needed to know, and all I frankly want to know. I don't care who she was, who she is is plenty for me."

"You are a very good man."

"Well, then I do hope you'll try to stop telling her she can do better."

I blush. But then he laughs. And I laugh. And suddenly everything feels truly much better. And for the first time in three days, I can't wait to go home.

I turn the key in the lock, steel myself, Daniel's words ringing in my ears, and go inside. Nadia is sitting on the couch.

"Hi," I say, trying not to put too much emotion in my voice.

"Hey," she says, looking up from her magazine. "Did you eat?"

"Nope, not yet."

"I was thinking of picking up Athenian Room for dinner; want to split a Greek chicken?"

"Sure." I pause, thinking about how I can be normal, how I can assure her that things aren't different. So I say the only thing I can think of. "You fly, I'll buy."

"Deal."

"Deal."

Nadia calls in our order, and heads out to go pick it up. And when she is gone I let the tears of relief fall, and let my shoulders unclench, believing that possibly, just possibly, everything is going to be okay.

* * *

I make plans to meet Nate at Toast for breakfast Monday morning, having avoided him all week. I finally told him about the fight and reconciliation with Nadia, and while he seems to not truly understand why the whole thing was such a big deal, why I felt so bad and why she was so upset, he certainly seemed glad that we were mending the rift, and understood that it wasn't a good time for him to come around the apartment. I am trying very hard not to blame him for the rift, not to punish him for acting on his concern for me, however misbegotten an exercise it turned out to be. And I'm so relieved that Nadia and I are finding our way, that I'm trying not to imagine a time when I might have to choose between them, and what it might say about me if I don't choose him.

I grab a table for us in the window and order a tea while looking over the menu.

"Hey, beautiful," Nate says, kissing me on the top of my head and taking the seat across from me.

"Hey, you."

"You are a sight for sore eyes." He nods to the waitress when she waves the coffeepot at him.

"Back at 'cha. Crazy week."

"You aren't kidding."

We order: scrambled eggs, fruit, and an English muffin for me, and a cheese omelet, bacon, potatoes, and rye toast for Nate.

"I got an offer for a film," he says, once the waitress leaves the table.

"Great! What's the project?"

"It's fascinating really. It's about the new young professional class in Russia, the money they are making and spending, the lifestyles they are leading. The production company has found a dozen possible candidates to film, they are going to pick the best four and have four crews follow them for a year. They want me to oversee the whole project, coordinating with the different crews, and working with the editors to make sure the whole thing comes together. They want to fly me out in a couple of weeks to interview the twelve candidates and help narrow them down."

"It sounds fascinating. But what does that mean in terms of you? Would you have to be in Russia the whole time, or just checking in periodically?"

"I'd need to be there essentially the whole time."

Wow. He's talking about leaving to move to Russia for a year as if it is no big deal. "That's pretty major. Do you want to live in Russia for a year?"

"I think the project is interesting and compelling, and the company I'm working with has a great reputation. It's the first project I've done that would be qualified to be under Oscar consideration. Would I prefer it was Paris? Sure. But my family is from Russia originally, so there is a sense of history that is attractive about it."

I poke at my tea with my spoon. I'm not going to be the one who asks what this means for us. "Well, congratulations, Nate, that is amazing and I'm really happy for you."

"Thank you. Wanna come?"

I almost choke on my tea. "Come where?"

"To Russia. With love." He grins.

"To visit?"

"For the year."

"Oh, Nate, be serious."

"I am serious. The money is really good, not just documentary good, really good. Housing and living costs are covered, as is transportation."

"What the hell would I do in Russia while you are running around making a movie for a year?"

"I dunno. Take Russian cooking classes. Teach American cooking classes. Come hang out with me while I work."

I suddenly feel like this man has no idea who I am at all. "Nate. I can't just up and leave for a year. I have a business, a business that is expanding; I have a home and responsibilities. I appreciate that you have the thought of wanting me there but you have to see it just isn't feasible."

Our food arrives. Nate takes a big bite of his omelet. "Well, never let it be said I didn't ask."

"Are you upset?"

"No, honey. Not really. I just don't know what to do. I want this job, it's what I do, and it's a great project. I'm not in a position to turn it down because it's inconvenient for you and me. And I do love the idea of coming home at night to your smiling face and your home cooking. I knew it was a long shot. And I'm not upset that you don't feel you can come. But I am concerned about what it means for us."

"You mean whether we wait or not." I can't imagine that in one breath he is going to invite me to come to Russia for a year and then break up with me when I say no.

"Mel, here is what I know. When I'm making a movie, I'm involved in the movie. Absorbed. Not easily distracted. I don't want to lose you, and I love the idea of us communicating through e-mail and phone calls, and picking up where we left off when I get back."

"The store keeps me pretty busy. It doesn't sound too bad . . ."

"But . . ."

Oh shit. "But?"

"But. You and I have only been together a few short months. It seems weird to ask you to wait for me for a time that is exponentially longer than the amount of time we've been together. And I have no idea what other projects this film will bring. If you say yes, you'll wait, I want to know that it's with full understanding of who I am and what I do and how uncertain the future really is."

"You sound like you don't actually want us to wait for each other."

"No, honey, it isn't that. I want to stay together. I want to have you come visit me, and to sneak back a couple of times to visit you. I want to exploit the current advances in communication technology to sustain us. But I don't want you to lose out on any of your life waiting for me, I don't want to come back in a year to find that we have another few short months together before I ship out again, never getting enough sustained time to see if we should be together forever."

"Maybe you should make a film about a former fat girl who opens a healthy café instead." I'm trying to be flip, but I know that ultimately this decision is going to fall to me. And I don't know that I can wait for someone who may never be ready to be fully mine. And I don't know if I am ready to lose him so soon.

"Maybe next one."

The waitress comes back. "Everything okay? Can I get you anything?"

"Yeah," Nate says. "I'll take another order of bacon, please."

I look down. I have eaten all of his bacon without even thinking about it.

"Make it two," I call after her.

I pick up the phone and dial what seems to be an endless string of numbers.

"H'lo?" Yikes, that is one groggy voice.

"Gilly, it's me. I'm sorry, I know it's late there. . . ."

Her voice is immediately awake, lucid, and clear. "What is it, what's wrong?"

"I'm a mess."

"Tell me."

And I do. Everything. It pours out of me, all my anguish, all my fears, every piece of the backstory I never shared with her about Nathan and about my money troubles and Nadia. I tell her about how scared I have been, how conflicted about myself and my relationships with the people closest to me. I tell her about Nathan's offer and how much I love him and don't want to lose him, and yet, that there is a part of me that is somewhat relieved at the idea of him going away for a few months.

She listens. She prods here and there, but mostly umms and ahhhs in the right places. When I finish, she is quiet for a very short time.

"Can you hang in there for two days?"

"Gilly, it isn't like . . ."

"It is like. It is exactly like. And I don't want to do this over the phone. I don't want to give you pat answers or trite axioms. I want to think about it, process it all, and be present for you. Two days. I can be there Sunday. I'll come, and we'll stay up all night and hash it through, and we'll have Fakesgiving on Monday and hopefully have stuff to pretend to be thankful for."

"Gillian. I just needed to share, to vent. You're coming in the fall . . ."

"Either I'm coming there, or you're coming here. Full stop."

"Tell me what time your flight gets in Sunday and I'll come fetch you."

"I'll call in the morning with my travel stats. In the meantime, deep breaths and don't make any decisions, don't have any important conversations. Just do that thing from *Finding Nemo*."

"That thing from *Finding Nemo*?"

"Yeah. That Ellen fish thing. Just keep swimming."

I laugh, remembering the blue fish called Dory, endearing in her simplicity: "Just keep swimming."

"You got it. Love you, sis. I'm there in two days."

"I love you. Thank you."

"And I want your real stuffing, not that low-fat shit you make for your customers. And the brussels sprouts with the bacon."

"Done."

I hang up the phone and my neck unclenches.

Gilly is coming.

STUFFING

I was lucky in that my mother didn't relegate stuffing to a Thanksgiving side dish. She included it pretty regularly in the rotation of starchy side dishes we had for dinners. Mom believed strongly in the basic food groups, and dinners followed a pretty clear pattern. Salad with our choice of dressings. A protein with a starch and a vegetable. Steak and baked potatoes and broccoli, pork chops and stuffing and green beans, chicken and sweet potatoes and asparagus. I loved stuffing nights. Usually it was just boxed mix, but I didn't care. It was soft and salty with tiny bits of melting onions and crunchy pieces of celery. I used to love sneaking the leftovers out of the fridge, squishing it against my teeth, the slight gritty sense of the melted butter resolidified. Nothing beats a stuffing sandwich at midnight, snuck under the covers with your latest book and a flashlight.

* * *

"Hello, big sister." Gilly throws herself into my arms. She is a slip of a thing, lithe and sophisticated in her sleek traveling clothes, her hair is blonder and shorter than the last time I saw her, and it flatters her creamy skin and wide blue-gray eyes.

"Hello, little sister. You're looking wonderful."

"I'm looking knackered. Let's get home and order in and hunker down."

"Deal."

Kai is watching the store, and Nadia is staying at Daniel's tonight, so it is just the two of us for the evening. We've already prepped all the food for tomorrow's feast, the turkey is brining, the cranberry sauce is done, the stuffing is already assembled. We're doing it at the store for ease. My apartment is too small, and since Nadia has agreed to attend in spite of the fact that Nathan will be there, I think it will be easier on her to have it in a place that she feels strong and secure. I'm also seating her and Nathan at opposite ends of the table with Delia and Kai and Phil and Daniel buffering the space between them.

Gilly fills me in on her life in London, her fancy new office, and the nightmare of finding a decent assistant. She tells me about her best mates, about the guy she is sort of dating, but is thinking of dumping because the sex is only mediocre. We get to my place and I show her around, and she makes all the right noises at the changes since she was here last.

We order in sushi from Hachi's Kitchen and sit on the floor of the living room eating and talking.

"So you love him, but not enough to wait?"

I sigh. "I think that if we were further along, if it weren't still so close to my divorce, that maybe waiting would make sense. But the more I think about it, the more I think that my impulse to wait for him is a way of protecting myself. Because if I'm waiting for him, then I don't have to be open to the idea of anyone else. It makes it safe and keeps me cocooned in work, and I feel like, I don't know, it's just too soon to be limiting myself, you know?"

"I think if there is anything making you question the idea of waiting for him, then that is your answer."

"Yeah. I guess it is." The tears begin to come.

"But it doesn't mean that not waiting doesn't suck a little bit . . ." Gilly hands me her napkin, and I blow my nose.

"It was so hard and scary to open up to him, what if . . ."

"What if what? It's like anything else; if you can do the hard thing once, you can do it again. Look, I have nothing against him, I'm looking forward to meeting him tomorrow, truly, but he isn't the last man in the world who is going to find you amazing and lovable and desirable, and now that you know that you can be with someone new, the next time will be that much easier, you'll be that much stronger, and you and I can both be grateful to him for being the first."

I snuffle into the napkin. "You're sure he isn't the last?"

"If he is supposed to be the last, you'll end up there anyway."

"You sure?"

"I'm sure."

"Well, I'll start." Kai jumps up. "I'm fake thankful for the elliptical machine at the gym."

"I'm fake thankful for business lunches," Phil says.

"Easy, guys." Gilly laughs. "Fakesgiving isn't really fake;

we can be actually thankful. I, for example, am thankful for my big sister who loves me even though I am very neglectful of her." She leans over and kisses the top of my head.

"And I am thankful for my little sister who flew all this way to be with us and give me an excuse to make stuffing! I'm also thankful for all of you. I love each and every one of you, and am very blessed to know you."

"Here, here," Nathan says. "To our lovely hostess and the visiting guest of honor." He raises his glass, the group toasts, and the impulse to share around the table seems to dissipate.

We eat till near bursting, despite the summer heat outside, filling ourselves full of turkey and stuffing and mashed potatoes and all the trimmings. Nadia keeps herself well away from Nathan, and periodically Daniel eyes him warily. Gilly visits with Kai and Phil, who she fell in love with the last time she was here. Janey and Delia disappear next door to check out the progress on the new store.

Nathan comes up behind me. "So, can I help clean up?"

"Sure. Grab some plates." We head back to the kitchen, and I start rinsing dishes and silver and loading them into the powerful dishwasher. Nathan hands me another stack.

"You don't want to wait, do you." It isn't a question.

"Actually, I want to wait more than anything. But I don't think it would be healthy to wait. If that makes any sense."

He sighs. "I get it. I don't like it, and I hope you know that if you change your mind at any time, either about the waiting or about coming to join me, I'd be delighted."

"I know. Thank you."

"Do I at least get to keep in touch? To hope you'll still be available when I get back?"

"I think we should keep the communication to a moderate level. The rest will figure itself out." He leans over and kisses me.

"Do I get to at least spend as much time with you as possible before I go, or are we playing by the new rules already?"

I put my hand on the side of his neck, and pull him in for a deep, lingering kiss. "I expect you to do your level best to give me something to remember you by."

"That I can manage. One more thing?"

"Yeah?"

"Will you go to my folks for Passover? I'll never make it back for that, and they like you better than me anyway."

I laugh. "Well, we'll see. Lord knows when Ellie Gershowitz calls, I can refuse her nothing."

"I'm thankful for you every day, Mel. I hate that my work is coming between us."

"I think the universe works in magical ways. If we are supposed to end up together, we will. And if we weren't, then maybe this is the universe's way of letting us part friends, without acrimony or harsh words. Letting us part in a way that means we can still be in each other's lives."

"Well, if that is true, then it is another thing to be thankful for."

"Me too. Now go grab more dishes."

"Thank you for coming." I hug her, trying not to cry.

"Stop that. I'm a selfish cow and I should have come sooner. Promise that you'll come soon? My treat."

"I promise." After a long chat, I finally agreed to let her

fly me in on her abundant frequent flier miles. "London will be great for me, the food is so terrible, it won't undo my program!"

"Very funny. Love you, Mel. I'll talk to you soon." And I believe that she will.

"Love you too. Safe travels."

"Bye." She whizzes through the doors at O'Hare and is gone. I get back in the car.

"She's really nice," Nadia says.

"Thanks. I think so. And she liked you too."

"I was ready to be kind of jealous of her."

"Jealous, why?"

Nadia chews on a piece of pink hair. "Because she's your sister, and she always gets to be that to you. And because I never had a sister, but if I did, I would want her to be like you, and I kind of pretend sometimes that you are my sister and it makes me feel better. But I know I'm not, you know, not really."

I look over at her, and smile. "I'll tell you a secret. Someone like me, I can use all the family I can get. And I could sure use a little sister who is local."

Nadia starts to cry.

I reach a hand over and she takes it and squeezes.

"Mel, you're not breaking up with Nathan because of me, right?"

"Nathan and I aren't breaking up; we're just letting things go for the time being. And we're doing that because it is smart and the right thing for both of us. But I hope that in a year, when he comes back, if he and I end up giving it another try, that you will be ready to start over with him."

"Okay. I promise."

"Good girl. Let's go home."

"Yeah. Hey, do we have any leftover stuffing?"

"God, I certainly hope so!"

CHEESEBURGERS

When we were kids, there weren't that many vacations. Grandma and Grandpa Hoffman paid for day camp, and eventually overnight camp in the summers. We all loved to be home in Chicago during the winter break, with the white lights down Michigan Avenue, and the magical windows in Marshall Field's on State Street. But spring break Mom would always try to take us somewhere, usually a road trip with an educational bent. We loved those trips, just the three of us, driving through the country, radio on loud, having the conversations you only have on long drives. When we had time to stop and sit somewhere, we'd find someplace that seemed to have either trucks or Harleys parked in front, and order up whatever their "famous" burger was. Plain thin patties on sad buns, or juicy half-pound monsters on buttered, toasted pumpernickel. Basic American cheese and bacon, or fancy

*Swiss and sautéed mushrooms. We'd order them "bloody,"
with fries on the side. Skinny little pale fries, thick, extra-
crispy fries, wide steak fries with skin on. For food that was
invented for ease and speed, the pleasure it brings is simple
and pure. Food you eat with your hands, the tearing of meat,
grease on your chin and salt on your fingertips, and your
mom really deeply laughing.*

When I get to the store, Delia and Kai are there waiting
for me.

"Oh, crap, this feels like an intervention. What's up?"

"We are here to ask you again to partner with us in the
café next door," Kai says.

"Please, Mel. We need you. It isn't the same unless we have
you with us," Delia says.

"Oh, guys, I love you so much, but you know I just don't
have the financial wherewithal to do that right now. I'm really
lucky to own this place and my place outright, but I'm still
not making a huge amount of money, and it is just too risky in
this economy to take any loans against the store or my house.
I could lose everything. . . ."

"It is still possible, Little," Kai says with a wide smile.

"It appears that Kai's brilliant boyfriend has solved that
problem as well," Delia says, a grin splitting her round
cheeks.

Kai is practically hopping up and down. "Phil came up
with the perfect solution! Delia doesn't know shit about running a business."

"Boy, watch your mouth."

"Sorry, Delovely." He turns back to me. "She doesn't know fuck-all about running a business."

"KAI! I will wash your mouth out, don't think I won't." Delia walks over to get herself a cup of coffee.

"Anyway, you know all there is to know about putting a place together, sanitation regulations, permits and inspections, ordering, all that stuff. Phil and I don't know about that stuff. You know I was a mess with that crap at CHIC, barely passed those management classes, I just like to cook! So, we hire you as the consultant and manager for the place. You work with us to design the kitchen, to set up the business end, and do all the ordering, centralized out of Dining by Design and run by you. Essentially, next door becomes a satellite of this place. We'll be ordering larger amounts, so we'll get better deals from vendors, and the savings will help both businesses. We'll do all of the insurance and so on through your company, keeping the thing as streamlined as possible. Plus, if Delivery by Design gets off the ground, again, we can deliver food from both stores . . . so the busy couple who wants the convenience can have broader choices. We figured that if we had to hire an outside consultant on all of this it would cost about fifteen to twenty thousand dollars to get the place set up, plus about another grand a month or so to manage it. What we do is give you an initial share of the place valued at twenty thousand dollars in exchange for your services, and the first two years of your thousand dollars a month also coming to you as credit toward the partnership. By the end of the second year, you'll own fifteen percent of the business, and you can decide whether you want to continue to serve as manager. If you do, the thousand dollars a month can come to you as income, or you can continue to put it back into the business up to a maximum partnership of twenty-five percent. If the business starts turning a profit earlier than we anticipate, you can flip your profits to get to that twenty-five percent share quicker."

I'm floored. "You really have worked all this out, haven't you?"

Kai comes over and sits on my lap, putting an arm around my shoulder, the weight of him barely registering on me. "We wanted to be sure it would work, and we wanted to be sure that it would be attractive enough for you to say yes. Say yes, Ittle Bittle. It won't be any fun without you."

"I'll have to talk to my accountant, and we'll have to come up with a good business plan, but I think it sounds wonderful. I think it sounds better than wonderful, I think it sounds like the best news I've had in ages. I love you guys!"

The three of us fall into a group hug of the motliest sort. Three people who in a million years would never have met, except that the universe, for all its nastiness, sometimes sends you exactly what you need, exactly when you need it. And when what you need is family, because you are bereft of yours, or because the one you have is broken or doesn't appreciate you, there is always family to be created.

"How on earth are we going to carry all this?" Delia asks, looking at the stack of coolers and cooking equipment around us.

"Phil has a friend with connections, so we get special parking, and access to a golf cart."

It's July third, and we are going to Navy Pier to picnic and watch the fireworks. We've packed a small grill for burgers, luscious three-to-a-pound prime babies we made today. Coolers hold cheese and crackers, potato and pasta salads, fruit and cookies, champagne and beer. We have fold-up chairs and a portable picnic table. We are celebrating the official launch of our new venture. Dining by Design and Delivery by Design and Comfort Food! The contractor starts the build-out next door right after the holiday, and our first deliveries will begin the same day. Delia moved into her new place on the first, and I helped the shelter throw her a big party. It feels like she's grown a foot in the last month, she feels taller somehow. It's amazing to see how something so simple as your own place to live and a sense of work pride can make all the difference in the world.

"Hey, what can we carry?" Nadia comes into the kitchen, trailed by Daniel.

"It all goes, child, grab whatever you can." Delia gestures at the pile.

Nadia picks up a cooler, and Daniel grabs two chairs under each arm and they head out to start loading up.

"He's a nice boy."

"Yes, D, he is."

"She's moving in with him?"

"Soon. She wants to wait till you open, since then she'll have full-time hours and can contribute more to the household expenses."

"You don't mind my stealing her?"

"I think it's a good fit. You guys work well together, and she'll still be coordinating the delivery business with me.

Besides, I get Kai, and I have to start having externs again in the fall. When we get you open I can hire someone to work afternoons with me."

"And you don't mind Daniel stealing her?"

"I think it's good for us to know that our time together has an official expiration date. Takes the pressure off."

"Seems like a lot all at once."

"No more than I can handle."

"Child. The good lord will never send you more than you can handle." She picks up a large cooler, as if to put a point on it.

I grab the cooler nearest me. "Let's hope so."

I'm locking up the front door when suddenly I'm engulfed in shadow.

"Are you closed?" I turn to see a large woman standing behind me. She looks somewhat stricken.

"Just getting ready to go, was there something you needed?"

Her shoulders slump. "No, it's okay, never mind. Have a good holiday." She is a pretty girl, porcelain skin and wide brown eyes and a little rosebud mouth. She's probably five-six or -seven, and looks like a Swiss milkmaid. I'd peg her at around 240, maybe 250.

She turns to go, and despite the fact that I want to go meet up with my friends, something makes me hesitate.

"Are you sure?"

"I just, I thought, it's silly, but . . ."

I unlock the door and pull it open. "Come in."

I turn on the light and she looks around. "It's a really nice place."

"Have you been in before?"

"No. But I read the article in *Time Out* a few weeks ago, and I've been meaning to come. I walk by all the time on my way to my sister's house, she lives near here."

"I see. Well, I'm glad you finally came in. I'm Melanie. What can I do for you?"

"I'm Beth. I, um, well, it's just . . . usually I'm out of town with my family for the weekend of the Fourth, you know? My folks rent a place in Michigan, and we all go, but this year they didn't, they went to Vegas instead, and my sister and her husband decided to go see some of their friends in the Dunes, and none of my friends even would think to call, because I've been declining barbecue invites for the Fourth my whole life, so I just, I have no plans, which is fine, except . . ."

"Except all you can think about is four days on the couch watching TV and eating everything in sight."

She smiles. "Yeah. I know it's stupid, but I thought if I came here and bought enough good food to get me through the weekend . . ."

"I know the feeling. On the one hand having no plans for a few days seems like such a luxury. But then you end up sopping up the dregs at the bottom of a gallon of mint chocolate chip with a Twinkie, and suddenly home alone isn't such a good idea."

"Rocky road."

"Excuse me?"

"Rocky road, not mint chocolate chip. Was your mom fat or something? You seem to know a lot about how we think."

"I was fat."

"Yeah, right. What, like fifteen, twenty pounds? You're tiny."

"I was two-ninety at my heaviest, four years ago."

Beth's mouth drops open. "No way."

"Way. I've been there, sister, bigger than you. And I know exactly what you are going through. So how about this. Let's set you up for some good delicious healthy eating this weekend, and then maybe next week, if you want, you can come back and we can talk some more."

"Really?"

I smile. "Really."

"Thank you."

"It's what I'm here for."

"More bubbles?" Kai asks, shaking the bottle at me after refilling Janey's, Nadia's, and Daniel's glasses.

I hesitate. "Go on," Nate says. "I'm driving."

"Okay, thanks."

Kai fills my glass, and his own. "When do you leave?" he asks Nate.

"A week from tomorrow."

"And when are you back?" Phil asks, plopping down at Kai's feet. Kai starts rubbing his neck.

"A year. I'll be back once or twice to check in with things here."

"That's a long time to be gone." There is a world of meaning in Kai's voice.

"True enough," Nate says.

"That must be hard," Phil offers.

"It's what I know, it's what I do. But yes. Sometimes it is harder than other times." He reaches for my hand and squeezes.

"So what are you going to do about Melanie?" Kai asks.

"Kai!" Phil snaps his head around.

Nate laughs. "It's okay, he has every reason to be protective. I tried to get her to come with me, but apparently she prefers hanging out with you in the kitchen to hanging out in a Moscow apartment waiting for me to come home."

"Well, she's no idiot," I say.

Nate leans over and kisses me. "No, she certainly isn't."

"We're not up for the long-distance commitment thing, so we're taking a break. When Nate comes home, if neither of us is involved with anyone else and we want to see each other, we'll see if we think that makes sense. In the meantime, friends."

"Sounds like a very wise way to look at things," Phil says.

"Hey, guys! It's starting!" Nadia calls over, pointing straight over our heads, where the first flashes are appearing.

And the eight of us turn our faces skyward and celebrate independence.

FROM MELANIE'S
RECIPE FILES

Here are the basics, both the original decadent versions and the healthier Dining by Design versions of the central recipes from the book.

Mashed Potatoes—Dining by Design Style

SERVES 6

2 pounds Yukon gold potatoes
2 tablespoons salt
½ to 1 cup skim milk
4 tablespoons light sour cream
1 tablespoon butter, melted

2 tablespoons chives, chopped

Salt and pepper, to taste

Peel potatoes and cut into large chunks. Put in pot and cover with cold water. When water comes to a boil, add 2 tablespoons salt and cook until potatoes are tender. Mash with ½ cup milk and the sour cream. Add more milk to get the texture you prefer. Add melted butter and chives, and season to taste.

Mashed Potatoes—Decadent Version

SERVES 6

2 pounds Yukon gold potatoes

2 tablespoons salt

½ to 1 cup whole milk or half-and-half

4 tablespoons sour cream or crème fraîche

4 tablespoons butter, melted

2 tablespoons chives, chopped

Salt and pepper, to taste

Peel potatoes and cut into large chunks. Put in pot and cover with cold water. When water comes to a boil, add 2 tablespoons salt and cook until potatoes are tender. Mash with ½ cup milk and the sour cream. Add more milk to get the texture you prefer. Add melted butter and chives, and season to taste.

Add-ins
½ cup shredded sharp cheddar cheese or crumbled goat cheese
½ cup crumbled bacon
¼ cup fried sage leaves

Guilt-Free Chocolate Cupcakes
with Vanilla Cream-Cheese Frosting

MAKES 16 CUPCAKES

Cupcakes
1 cup granulated sugar
½ cup egg substitute
¼ cup canola oil
½ teaspoon vanilla extract
1½ cups all-purpose flour
½ cup unsweetened cocoa powder
1 teaspoon baking soda
1 teaspoon instant espresso granules
½ teaspoon baking powder
¼ teaspoon salt
1 cup fat-free Greek yogurt

Frosting
1 cup powdered sugar
½ teaspoon vanilla extract
Dash salt
1 8-ounce block ⅓-less-fat cream cheese, softened

Preheat oven to 350°F.

To prepare cupcakes, place the first 4 ingredients in a large bowl; beat with a mixer at medium speed until well blended, about 2 minutes.

In a separate bowl, sift together the flour and the next 5 ingredients. Stir flour mixture into sugar mixture, alternating with Greek yogurt; begin and end with flour mixture. Mix after each addition just until blended.

Place 16 paper muffin cup liners in muffin pans; spoon about 2½ tablespoons batter into each cup. Bake 18 minutes or until a skewer inserted in the center of a cupcake comes out with moist crumbs attached (do not overbake). Remove cupcakes from pans; cool on a wire rack.

To prepare frosting, combine powdered sugar and remaining ingredients in a medium bowl. Beat with a mixer at medium speed until combined. Increase speed to medium-high, and beat until smooth. Spread about 1 tablespoon frosting on top of each cupcake.

Decadent Dark Chocolate Cupcakes

MAKES 12 CUPCAKES

Cupcakes
  8 tablespoons unsalted butter, cubed
  2 ounces high-quality bittersweet chocolate (Valrhona or
      Callebaut), chopped
  ½ cup Dutch-processed cocoa powder

¾ cup all-purpose flour

½ teaspoon baking soda

¾ teaspoon baking powder

2 large eggs

¾ cup sugar

1 teaspoon vanilla extract

1 tablespoon white vinegar

½ teaspoon salt

½ cup sour cream

Frosting

10 tablespoons unsalted butter, softened

½ vanilla bean, halved lengthwise

1¼ cups confectioners' sugar, sifted

Pinch salt

½ teaspoon vanilla extract

1 tablespoon heavy cream

Adjust oven rack to lower-middle position; heat oven to 350°F. Line standard-size muffin pan with paper muffin cup liners.

Combine butter, chocolate, and cocoa in medium heatproof bowl. Set bowl over saucepan containing barely simmering water; heat mixture until butter and chocolate are melted, and whisk until smooth and combined. Set aside to cool until just warm to the touch.

Whisk flour, baking soda, and baking powder in small bowl to combine.

Whisk eggs in a second medium bowl to combine; add sugar, vanilla, vinegar, and salt, and whisk until fully incorporated.

Add cooled chocolate mixture to egg mixture, and whisk until combined. Sift about ⅓ flour mixture over chocolate mixture, and whisk until combined; whisk in sour cream until combined, then whisk in remaining flour mixture until batter is homogenous and thick.

Divide batter evenly among baking cups. Bake until a skewer inserted into center of cupcakes comes out clean, 18 to 20 minutes.

Cool cupcakes in muffin pan on wire rack until cool enough to handle, about 15 minutes. Carefully lift each cupcake from muffin pan and set on wire rack. Cool to room temperature before icing, about 30 minutes.

To make the frosting: In standing mixer fitted with whisk attachment, beat butter at medium-high speed until smooth, about 20 seconds. Using paring knife, scrape seeds from vanilla bean into butter, and beat mixture at medium-high speed to combine, about 15 seconds. Add confectioners' sugar and salt; beat at medium-low speed until most of sugar is moistened, about 45 seconds. Scrape down bowl and beat at medium speed until mixture is fully combined, about 15 seconds; scrape bowl, add vanilla extract and heavy cream, and beat at medium speed until incorporated, about 10 seconds, then increase speed to medium-high and beat until light and fluffy, about 4 minutes, scraping down bowl once or twice.

To frost cupcakes: Mound about 2 tablespoons icing on center of each cupcake. Using small icing spatula or butter knife, spread icing to edge of cupcake, leaving slight mound in center.

Macaroni and Cheese for Every Day

SERVES 2

1 8-ounce package elbow macaroni, preferably whole wheat
  or Jerusalem artichoke pasta
½ cup skim milk
8 triangles Laughing Cow Light cheese
3 tablespoons light sour cream
1 ounce reduced-fat extra sharp cheddar, shredded
¼ teaspoon nutmeg
Salt and pepper, to taste

Boil pasta according to package directions. Heat milk and
Laughing Cow cheese in a saucepan over medium heat, whisk-
ing as the cheese melts to combine. Remove from heat and stir
in the sour cream and cheddar. Season with nutmeg, salt, and
pepper, and stir in cooked pasta.

Macaroni and Cheese for Special Occasions
(if you are skipping the famous blue box)

SERVES 2 AS A MAIN COURSE OR 4 AS A SIDE DISH
(OR 1 REALLY DEPRESSED PERSON)

1 pound elbow macaroni
5 tablespoons unsalted butter
6 tablespoons flour

1 tablespoon mustard powder

½ teaspoon grated nutmeg

5 cups whole milk

4 ounces fontina, grated

4 ounces smoked Gouda, grated

8 ounces extra sharp cheddar, grated

Salt and pepper, to taste

Topping

½ cup bread crumbs tossed with 3 tablespoons melted butter

Preheat broiler. Cook pasta according to package directions.

Heat butter in pan over moderate heat until foaming subsides, then whisk in flour, mustard, and nutmeg, combining for about 1 minute. Add milk and whisk to combine, heating and stirring until mixture thickens, about 5 minutes. Remove from heat, stir in cheeses until melted, add pasta, and season to taste. Pour into a baking pan and top with bread crumbs. Broil to brown bread crumbs, about 3 minutes, then serve.

Turkey Meat Loaf from Dining by Design

SERVES 8 TO 10

1 tablespoon unsalted butter

1 medium onion, chopped

1 rib celery, chopped

1 clove garlic, minced

2 teaspoons fresh thyme leaves

1 teaspoon smoked paprika

¼ cup tomato juice

½ cup chicken stock

2 large eggs

1 tablespoon soy sauce

1 teaspoon Dijon mustard

½ teaspoon ground cumin

⅔ cup bread crumbs

2 tablespoons fresh flat-leaf parsley, minced

¾ teaspoon salt

½ teaspoon ground black pepper

1 pound ground turkey, white and dark meat mixed

1 pound ground turkey, white meat only

Glaze

½ cup chili sauce

3 tablespoons brown sugar

¼ cup sherry vinegar

Adjust oven rack to middle position; heat oven to 375°F.

Heat butter in a 10-inch skillet over medium-high heat until foaming; add onion and celery and cook, stirring occasionally, until beginning to brown, 6 to 8 minutes. Add garlic, thyme, and paprika and cook, stirring, until fragrant, about 1 minute. Reduce heat to low and add tomato juice. Cook, stirring to scrape up browned bits from pan, until thickened, about 1 minute. Transfer mixture to small bowl and set aside to cool.

Whisk stock and eggs in large bowl until combined. Stir in soy sauce, mustard, cumin, bread crumbs, parsley, salt, pepper, and onion mixture. Add ground turkey; mix gently with hands until thoroughly combined, about 1 minute. Transfer meat to sheet pan and shape into a 10 x 6 inch oval about 2 inches high. Smooth top and edges of meat loaf with moistened spatula. Bake until an instant-read thermometer inserted into center of loaf reads 135 to 140 degrees, 55 to 65 minutes. Remove meat loaf from oven and turn on broiler.

While meat loaf cooks, combine chili sauce, brown sugar, and sherry vinegar in small saucepan; bring to simmer over medium heat and cook, stirring, until thick and syrupy, about 5 minutes. Spread half of glaze evenly over cooked meat loaf with rubber spatula; place under broiler and cook until glaze bubbles and begins to brown at edges, about 5 minutes. Serve with remaining glaze on the side.

Grandma's Texas Barbeque Meat Loaf

SERVES 8

Glaze

    1 bottle favorite barbeque sauce

    2 tablespoons brown sugar

    1 tablespoon tomato paste

    1 tablespoon maple syrup

Meat Loaf

    2 teaspoons vegetable oil

    1 medium onion, chopped

2 cloves garlic, minced

2 large eggs

2 teaspoons fresh thyme

1 teaspoon salt

½ teaspoon black pepper

2 teaspoons Dijon mustard

2 teaspoons Worcestershire sauce

½ cup whole milk

1 pound ground beef chuck

½ pound ground pork

½ pound ground veal

⅔ cup saltine crackers, crushed

½ cup French's french fried onions, chopped

⅓ cup fresh parsley, minced

8 ounces bacon, sliced thin

For the glaze: Mix ½ bottle barbeque sauce, brown sugar, tomato paste, and maple syrup in saucepan; set aside.

For the meat loaf: Heat oven to 350°F. Heat oil in medium skillet. Add onion and garlic; sauté until softened, about 5 minutes. Set aside to cool while preparing remaining ingredients.

Mix eggs with thyme, salt, pepper, mustard, Worcestershire sauce, and milk. Add egg mixture to meat in large bowl along with crackers, fried onions, parsley, and cooked onion and garlic; mix with fork until evenly blended and meat mixture does not stick to bowl. (If mixture sticks, add additional milk, a couple tablespoons at a time, until mix no longer sticks.)

Turn meat mixture onto work surface. With wet hands, pat mixture into an approximately 9 x 5 inch loaf shape. Place on foil-lined (for easy cleanup) shallow baking pan. Brush with half the glaze, then arrange bacon slices, crosswise, over loaf, overlapping slightly and tucking only bacon tip ends under loaf.

Bake loaf until bacon is crisp and loaf registers 160 degrees, about 1 hour. Cool at least 20 minutes. Simmer remaining glaze over medium heat until thickened slightly. Slice meat loaf and serve with extra glaze passed separately.

Andrew's Sunday Pancakes

SERVES 2

1 cup all-purpose flour
2 teaspoons sugar
½ teaspoon salt
½ teaspoon baking powder
¼ teaspoon baking soda
¾ cup buttermilk
¼ cup whole milk
1 large egg, separated
2 tablespoons butter, melted
Vegetable oil for brushing skillet or griddle

Mix dry ingredients in medium bowl. Pour buttermilk and milk into 2-cup Pyrex measuring cup. Whisk in egg white; mix yolk with melted butter, then stir into milk mixture. Dump wet ingredients into dry ingredients all at once; whisk until just mixed.

Meanwhile, heat griddle or large skillet over medium-high heat. Brush griddle generously with oil. When water splashed on surface confidently sizzles, pour batter, about ¼ cup at a time, onto griddle, making sure not to overcrowd. When pancake bottoms are brown and top surface starts to bubble, 2 to 3 minutes, flip cakes and cook until remaining side has browned, 1 to 2 minutes longer. Re-oil the skillet and repeat for the next batch of pancakes.

Serve with warmed maple syrup, melted butter, and crispy bacon or sausage.

Healthy Apple Pancakes

SERVES 4 TO 6

2½ cups all-purpose organic flour

1 cup whole wheat pastry flour

1 tablespoon baking powder

2 teaspoons baking soda

⅛ teaspoon cinnamon

2 eggs

2 egg whites

2 cups buttermilk

¼ cup agave nectar

2 tablespoons margarine, melted

3 medium apples (preferably Honeycrisp, Fuji, or Gala), peeled and diced

Cooking spray

Combine dry ingredients in a bowl and mix well.

In a separate bowl, lightly beat eggs and egg whites together; add buttermilk and agave nectar.

Add wet ingredients to dry and stir until just moistened; do not overbeat. Add melted margarine and apples and mix until just combined.

Spray hot skillet with cooking spray. Pour 3 tablespoons of batter per cake, and flip when top of each cake is covered with tiny bubbles and bottom is browned. Brown other side and serve hot.

Risotto à la Melanie

SERVES 4 TO 6

10 cups chicken stock

2 tablespoons butter

1 tablespoon olive oil

2 shallots, chopped

2 cups Carnaroli or Arborio rice

½ cup dry white wine or champagne

Pinch saffron threads

2 chicken breasts, cooked and shredded

4 artichoke bottoms (preferably fresh), cooked and diced

Zest of 1 lemon

Salt and pepper, to taste

¼ cup grated Parmigiano-Reggiano

2 tablespoons flat-leaf parsley, chopped

Put stock in small saucepan over medium heat. Melt 1 table-spoon butter in pan with olive oil. Add shallots and cook until translucent. Add rice and stir until each grain is coated. Add wine and saffron threads and stir until wine is totally absorbed. Add stock one ladle at a time until absorbed, and then add next ladle. Stir continuously. When it begins to take longer for stock to be absorbed, taste rice. You are looking for al dente, not mushy or gummy. When you are getting close to al dente, add chicken and artichokes to heat through, along with lemon zest, salt, and pepper. When rice is perfectly cooked, stir in remaining 1 tablespoon butter, cheese, and parsley, and do a final taste for seasonings.

This dish is actually not too bad for you. To make it deca-dent, add 2 more tablespoons butter and another ¼ cup Par-mesan at the end, swap the chicken for cooked sweet Italian sausage chunks, and stir in ¼ cup mascarpone just before serving.

Dad's Chicken Soup

SERVES 8 TO 10

2 tablespoons vegetable oil or chicken fat
1 whole chicken, cut into pieces, plus 4 wings or 4 drum-sticks (and 2 to 4 chicken feet if you can handle it)
2 medium onions, quartered
2 large carrots, peeled and cut into 2-inch chunks
2 ribs celery

6 whole peppercorns

1 tablespoon fresh thyme leaves

2 quarts water

2 teaspoons salt

2 bay leaves

2 cups egg noodles (preferably wide)

Salt and pepper, to taste

¼ cup fresh flat-leaf parsley, minced

Heat oil in large soup kettle over high heat. When oil shimmers and starts to smoke, add chicken in batches; sauté until brown on both sides, about 5 minutes. Put all chicken pieces back in pot, with vegetables, peppercorns, and thyme. Fill with water to just cover. Reduce heat to low, cover, and simmer about 40 minutes. Add 2 teaspoons salt and bay leaves. Barely simmer until chicken is cooked and broth is rich and flavorful, about 20 minutes.

Remove chicken from kettle; set aside. When cool enough to handle, remove skin, then remove meat from bones and shred into bite-size pieces; discard skin and bone. Strain broth; skim fat from broth, reserving 2 tablespoons. (Broth and meat can be covered and refrigerated up to 2 days.)

Cook new vegetables, if desired, in reserved chicken fat (or butter), and cook noodles according to package directions. Combine chicken, broth, new vegetables, and noodles. Adjust seasonings, stir in parsley, and serve.

Turkey Tetrazzini

SERVES 8

1 can condensed cream of chicken soup

1 cup sour cream

¼ cup Parmesan, grated

¼ cup sherry

1 teaspoon celery salt

1 pound linguini, cooked

2 cups turkey or chicken, cooked and cubed

½ cup bread crumbs

4 tablespoons butter, melted

Preheat oven to 350°F.

Whisk together soup, sour cream, cheese, sherry, and celery salt. Pour over noodles and turkey, and mix until all noodles are coated and turkey is mixed throughout. Pour into buttered 9 x 13 inch pan. Sprinkle bread crumbs evenly over top, and drizzle with butter. Bake 30 to 40 minutes until top is golden brown.

Serve with caution; people will fall in love with you.

For a healthier version, use all-white-meat turkey or chicken, reduced-fat soup, light sour cream, and whole wheat noodles, and replace the butter with 2 tablespoons olive oil.

Susan's Banana Cake with Chocolate Frosting

MAKES 1 8-INCH CAKE

Cake

  ½ cup (1 stick) unsalted butter

  1½ cups sugar

  2 large eggs

  2 cups flour, sifted

  1 teaspoon baking powder

  ¾ teaspoon baking soda

  ½ teaspoon salt

  1 cup overripe bananas, mashed (I let mine go brown and
    then store in the freezer)

  ½ cup sour cream

  1 teaspoon vanilla extract

Frosting

  3 squares unsweetened baking chocolate, melted

  1 stick butter, softened

  1 teaspoon vanilla extract

  1 box confectioners' sugar, sifted

  Pinch salt

  4 ounces chocolate milk mixed with ½ tablespoon instant
    espresso powder (or 2 ounces leftover coffee mixed with
    2 ounces milk)

  2 tablespoons sour cream

Preheat oven to 350°F. Grease two 8-inch round cake pans (or
spray with cooking spray). Cream butter and sugar until fluffy;

add eggs one at a time and beat until smooth. Sift remaining dry ingredients together. Mash bananas in a bowl with sour cream and vanilla. Add dry ingredients and banana mash alternately to egg mixture in thirds, blending to combine each time but trying not to overbeat. Divide between the two cake pans and bake 27 to 34 minutes, until a skewer inserted in the center comes out clean. Cool on a rack completely before frosting.

To make the frosting: Blend melted chocolate with butter and vanilla, and then mix with sugar and salt, adding 1 teaspoon of coffee milk at a time until you reach a fluffy, spreadable consistency that holds a soft peak. Blend in sour cream and hold at room temperature until frosting the completely cooled cake.

Healthy Banana Muffins with Chocolate Chips

MAKES 12 MUFFINS

1¼ cups plus 1 tablespoon all-purpose flour, divided

1 cup whole wheat flour

⅓ cup sugar

2 teaspoons baking powder

½ teaspoon baking soda

2 teaspoons cinnamon

½ teaspoon salt

½ cup low-fat buttermilk

⅓ cup vegetable oil

1 egg

3 really ripe bananas, mashed

¼ cup walnuts, chopped

¼ cup mini dark chocolate chips

Preheat oven to 375°F. Line a 12-cup muffin pan with paper muffin cups or spray with nonstick cooking spray. Sift dry ingredients together, reserving 1 tablespoon of flour. Mix in buttermilk, oil, egg, and bananas, being careful not to overmix. Toss walnuts and chips with reserved tablespoon of flour and fold into muffin mix. Fill muffin cups three-fourths full. Bake 15 to 20 minutes.

First-in-Class Braised Brisket

SERVES 12

¼ cup water

1 5-pound beef brisket

2 teaspoons salt

¼ teaspoon pepper

2 yellow onions, sliced

4 ribs celery, sliced

1 cup chili sauce (Heinz is good)

1 bottle beer

Preheat oven to 350°F. Put enough water in the bottom of a heavy roasting pan to reach a depth of about 1 inch. Season brisket with salt and pepper, and place in roasting pan with water. Put onion and celery on top of meat, then distribute chili sauce evenly over vegetables. Cook uncovered 90 minutes. Remove brisket from oven, pour beer over meat, cover tightly with foil, return to oven, and braise 45 minutes per pound of meat. Remove meat from gravy, defat liquid, and puree juices with vegetables. Put juice in container, and chill meat overnight in fridge. The next day, slice meat across the grain and place in a baking dish. Cover with gravy, and put back in fridge. Reheat at 350°F to serve (1 hour to indefinitely!).

Doug's Peanut and Sesame Noodles

SERVES 4 AS A MAIN COURSE OR 8 AS A SIDE DISH

1 pound linguini

4 tablespoons peanut oil

½ cup soy sauce

½ cup rice vinegar

6 tablespoons creamy peanut butter

2 teaspoons sesame oil

½ teaspoon powdered ginger

1 teaspoon sugar (optional)

6 tablespoons sesame seeds

3 garlic cloves (or more), finely minced

1 teaspoon hot red pepper flakes, to taste

Green onions and cucumber for garnish

Cook the noodles according to package directions. Toss with 2 tablespoons peanut oil and set aside.

Mix together soy sauce, vinegar, peanut butter, sesame oil, ginger, and sugar. (I often skip the sugar. Actually, I forgot it completely once and didn't really miss it.)

Toast sesame seeds in large pot. Remove and set aside to cool. In same pot, sauté garlic in 2 tablespoons peanut oil; add red pepper flakes and sauté for 1 to 2 minutes. Add noodles and soy mixture. Toss and mix over medium heat just until heated through. Cool to room temperature. Garnish with chopped green onions and sliced, seeded cucumbers. Sprinkle with toasted sesame seeds. If serving as a main course, shredded chicken is really good mixed in.

Peanut Butter Cookies

MAKES 2 DOZEN COOKIES

2½ cups all-purpose flour

½ teaspoon baking soda

½ teaspoon baking powder

½ teaspoon salt

½ pound (2 sticks) salted butter, softened

1 cup dark brown sugar, packed

1 cup granulated sugar

1 cup super-chunky peanut butter

2 large eggs

2 teaspoons vanilla extract

1 cup roasted salted peanuts, ground in processor to
resemble bread crumbs

Adjust oven rack to low center position; heat oven to 350°F. Sift flour, baking soda, baking powder, and salt in medium bowl.

With electric mixer or by hand, beat butter until creamy. Add sugars; beat until fluffy, about 3 minutes, stopping to scrape down bowl as necessary. Beat in peanut butter until fully incorporated, then add eggs one at a time, then vanilla. Gently stir dry ingredients into peanut butter mixture. Add ground peanuts; stir gently until just incorporated.

Working with 2 tablespoons of dough at a time, roll into large balls, placing them 2 inches apart on a parchment-covered cookie sheet. Press each dough ball with back of dinner fork dipped in cold water to make crisscross design. Bake until cookies are puffed and slightly brown along edges but not on top, 10 to 12 minutes (they will not look fully baked). Cool cookies on cookie sheet until set, about 4 minutes, then transfer to wire rack to cool completely. Cookies will keep, refrigerated in an airtight container, up to 7 days.

Spaghetti and Meatballs

SERVES 4

Meatballs

    2 slices white sandwich bread, torn into small cubes

    ½ cup half-and-half

    ½ pound ground veal

    ¼ pound ground pork

¼ pound ground chuck

¼ cup Parmesan, grated

2 tablespoons fresh flat-leaf parsley, minced

1 large egg yolk

1 small clove garlic, grated

¾ teaspoon salt

¼ teaspoon pepper

3 tablespoons vegetable oil (for frying)

Simple Tomato Sauce

2 tablespoons extra-virgin olive oil

1 teaspoon garlic, grated

1 28-ounce can crushed tomatoes (San Marzano if available)

1 tablespoon fresh basil, chopped

Salt and pepper, to taste

Pasta

4 quarts water

1 tablespoon salt

1 pound spaghetti

For the meatballs: Combine bread and half-and-half in small bowl, mashing occasionally with fork, until smooth paste forms, about 10 minutes.

Mix all meatball ingredients, including bread mixture, in medium bowl and pepper to taste. Lightly form meatballs, ½ tablespoon at a time; you can make these larger if you like, or even smaller. A good way to prevent the meatballs from sticking together is to cover the top of a large sheet pan with a layer of cling film. Resting the meatballs on this will cushion them and prevent them from getting flat on the bottom. Chill them in the refrigerator at least 30 minutes, covered, before frying.

Bring 4 quarts water to a boil in large pot for cooking pasta. Meanwhile, heat ¼-inch vegetable oil over medium-high heat in large sauté pan. When edge of meatball dipped in oil sizzles, add meatballs in a single layer. Fry, turning several times, until nicely browned on all sides, about 5 to 10 minutes depending on the size of the meatballs, regulating heat as needed to keep oil sizzling but not smoking. Transfer browned meatballs to paper towel–lined plate; set aside. Repeat, if necessary, with remaining meatballs.

For the sauce, discard oil in pan, leaving behind any browned bits. Add olive oil along with garlic; sauté, scraping up any browned bits, just until garlic is golden, about 30 seconds. Add tomatoes, bring to boil, and simmer gently until sauce thickens, about 10 minutes. Stir in basil; add salt and pepper to taste. Add meatballs and simmer, turning them occasionally, until heated through, about 5 minutes. Keep warm over low flame.

Meanwhile, add salt and pasta to boiling water. Cook until al dente, drain, and return to pot. Ladle several large spoonfuls of tomato sauce (without meatballs) over spaghetti and toss until noodles are well coated. Divide pasta among individual bowls and top each with a little more tomato sauce and 2 to 3 meatballs. Serve immediately with grated cheese passed separately.

For a healthier version, substitute fat-free buttermilk or plain yogurt for half-and-half, ¾ pound ground white-meat chicken plus ¼ pound ground pork for the meat, and 1 egg white for the egg yolk. Instead of panfrying the meatballs, place in a single layer on an oiled sheet pan, lightly spritz with olive oil spray, and broil for 3 to 5 minutes until browned on top. Turn meatballs over and brown again, and then heat through in sauce as above. Substitute whole wheat or Jerusalem artichoke pasta for the spaghetti.

Famous Super Bowl Chili

SERVES 12

¼ cup olive oil

2 cups onion, diced

6 cloves garlic, minced

2 pounds ground veal

1 pound sweet Italian sausage, removed from its casing

7 tablespoons chili powder

2 tablespoons ground cumin

1 tablespoon dried thyme leaves

1 tablespoon dried oregano

2 14.5-ounce cans crushed tomatoes (San Marzano if available)

12 ounces beer

¼ cup tomato paste

3 15-ounce cans cannellini beans, drained and rinsed

Heat oil in large pot until shimmering, then add onions and cook until translucent. Add garlic, veal, and sausage, and cook until lightly browned. Add spices and herbs, and cook additional 10 minutes. Add tomatoes with juice, beer, and tomato paste, and cook over medium heat for 30 minutes. Add beans and cook 10 minutes to heat through.

Healthy Chili

SERVES 12

¼ cup olive oil

2 cups onion, diced

1 cup celery, diced

6 cloves garlic, minced

2 pounds ground chicken, light and dark meat

1 pound ground chicken, white meat only

1 can diced green chilies

2 tablespoons ground cumin

1 tablespoon dried thyme leaves

1 tablespoon dried oregano

24 ounces chicken stock

12 ounces beer

3 15-ounce cans cannellini beans, drained and rinsed

Heat oil in large pot until shimmering. Add onions and celery, and cook until translucent. Add garlic and chicken, and cook until lightly browned. Add chilies and spices and herbs, and cook additional 10 minutes. Add chicken stock and beer, and cook over medium heat for 30 minutes. Add beans and cook 10 minutes to heat through.

Gillian's Apple Pie

MAKES 1 9-INCH PIE

Pie Dough

    2½ cups unbleached all-purpose flour, plus extra for dusting

    1 teaspoon salt

    2 tablespoons granulated sugar

    12 tablespoons unsalted butter, chilled and cut into ¼-inch
        cubes

    8 tablespoons lard (or vegetable shortening), chilled

    6 to 8 tablespoons ice water

Apple Filling

    2 pounds sweet apples, about 4 medium (Honeycrisp, Fuji,
        or Mutsu are good here)

    2 pounds Granny Smith apples, about 4 medium

    ¾ cup Sugar in the Raw or demerara sugar

    1½ tablespoons lemon juice

    1 teaspoon lemon zest

    ¼ teaspoon salt

    ¼ teaspoon cinnamon

    ⅛ teaspoon ground nutmeg

    1 egg white, lightly beaten

    1 tablespoon granulated sugar

To prepare dough, put flour, salt, and sugar in a food processor and pulse a couple of times to combine. Add butter and
pulse in five 1-second bursts. Add lard and continue pulsing

until flour is pale yellow and resembles coarse cornmeal, four or five more 1-second pulses. Add 6 tablespoons ice water, 1 tablespoon at a time, pulsing after each addition. Test dough to see if it will hold together. If it doesn't, add another tablespoon water, and pulse again. Repeat if necessary. Turn dough onto a board, and squeeze together. Divide in half and make two flat disks. Wrap each disk in plastic wrap and chill in fridge at least 30 minutes.

Remove dough from refrigerator. It should be cool but still rollable. Adjust oven rack to center position and heat oven to 425°F.

Roll one dough disk on a lightly floured surface into a 12-inch circle. Place dough in 9-inch Pyrex regular or deep-dish pie pan.

Gently press dough into sides of pan, leaving portion that overhangs lip of pie plate in place. Refrigerate while preparing fruit.

Peel, core, and cut apples into ½- to ¾-inch slices and toss with ¾ cup sugar and lemon juice. Add zest, salt, cinnamon, and nutmeg. Turn fruit mixture, including juices, into chilled pie shell and mound slightly in center. Roll out other dough round and place over filling. Trim top and bottom edges to ½ inch beyond pan lip. Tuck this rim of dough underneath itself so that folded edge is flush with pan lip. Flute edging or press with fork tines to seal. Cut four slits at right angles on dough top. Brush egg white onto top of crust and sprinkle evenly with remaining 1 tablespoon sugar.

Bake until top crust is golden, about 25 minutes. Reduce oven temperature to 375°F; continue baking until juices bubble and crust is deep golden brown, 30 to 35 minutes longer. Transfer pie to wire rack; cool to almost room temperature, at least 4 hours.

For a healthier version, replace 1½ cups of flour with whole wheat flour, and freeze half of the dough for use at a later time. Take the sugar in the filling down to ½ cup. Make a topping of ½ cup rolled oats, ¼ cup sliced toasted almonds, and ¼ cup demerara sugar, mixed with 2 tablespoons melted butter, and sprinkle this on top of the filling instead of a top crust.

Classic Tomato Soup and Grilled Cheese

SERVES 1

1 can Campbell's tomato soup
1 can whole milk
1 tablespoon butter
2 slices white bread (Wonder or Butternut; do not use nice
   bakery bread!)
2 slices Kraft Singles American cheese slices

In small saucepan, heat contents of can of soup with can of milk over medium heat, stirring to combine. When bubbles start to appear, turn heat to low and keep saucepan on heat while making sandwich. In skillet, melt butter over medium-high heat. Place slices of bread in butter, sliding them around to coat. Place cheese slices on top of bread slices and let cook until cheese begins to melt around the edges. Flip one slice of bread on top of the other slice of bread, taking care not to press down on the sandwich. Flip once or twice to ensure even browning and that the cheese is completely melted. Cut sandwich in half diagonally, which makes for easier dunking.

Healthy Roasted Tomato Soup and Grilled Cheese

SERVES 6

Soup

4 pounds tomatoes (I use a mix of plum and cherry for
   depth of flavor, but will work with almost any type.
   It is only essential they be fresh and ripe.)
¼ cup olive oil
1 medium sweet onion or 4 large shallots, diced
2 tablespoons Herbes de Provence
Salt and pepper, to taste

Sandwiches (per sandwich)

1 ounce sharp white cheddar, grated
1 ounce fontina, grated
1 tablespoon butter, softened
2 slices sourdough bread
⅛ teaspoon grains of paradise, ground

Preheat oven to 250°F.

Cut tomatoes in half, toss in olive oil to coat, and arrange cut side down on oiled sheet pans.

Add onion or shallot on top of tomatoes. Sprinkle with herbs and liberally salt and pepper. Roast approximately 1½ to 2 hours until skins are loose and flesh is soft.

Peel skins off tomatoes and discard. Dump the contents of the sheet pans into a large bowl and, using an immersion blender, blend into chunky soup. Adjust seasonings.

Serve either warm or cold with a dollop of crème fraîche or sour cream and some chopped fresh mint for grown-ups. Add alphabet noodles or cooked rice for kids. Stir in toasted croutons and drizzle with olive oil and Parmesan for a classic Pappa al Pomodoro. Add fresh basil and garlic, and you have a chunky pasta sauce. Add fresh oregano, and it becomes pizza sauce. Freezes beautifully, can be canned if you are ambitious, and lasts up to a week in the fridge.

To make a sandwich: In a bowl, mix the two grated cheeses until well combined. Butter one side of each slice of bread with half the butter. Heat a skillet over medium-high heat. Add the bread slices, buttered sides down, and divide the cheese mixture equally between the two slices of bread and sprinkle with grains of paradise. Cook until cheese begins to melt, covering with a lid if necessary. Flip one piece of bread onto the other, and cook until crisp on outside and completely melted within.

Delia's Fried Chicken

SERVES 4 TO 6

1 gallon whole milk

1 tablespoon salt

2 tablespoons dried thyme leaves

¼ teaspoon ground nutmeg

2 cloves garlic, whole

1 whole fryer, cut into 8 pieces

2 cups flour mixed with 1 tablespoon seasoning salt

4 eggs, beaten

Peanut oil for frying

Bring milk, salt, thyme, nutmeg, and garlic to simmer in large pot. Add chicken and maintain gentle heat until almost cooked through, about 15 minutes. Cover, turn off heat, and leave in milk for another 30 minutes. Remove chicken from milk and pat dry. Dip pieces in flour, then in egg, then in flour again, and set on rack until all chicken is coated. Heat oil to 350°F, and fry chicken in batches until coating is golden and crisp and chicken is hot, about 5 minutes per batch.

Healthy Baked Fried Chicken

SERVES 4

1 cup bread crumbs

½ cup Parmesan, grated

4 boneless, skinless chicken breasts
½ cup fat-free buttermilk
4 tablespoons olive oil

Preheat oven to 375°F. Mix bread crumbs with Parmesan in shallow dish. Dip chicken in buttermilk, let excess run off, and then coat chicken in crumb mixture. Arrange chicken on tray, and drizzle each breast with 1 tablespoon olive oil. Bake 15 to 18 minutes until done.

Corned Beef Hash

SERVES 6 TO 8

5 tablespoons vegetable oil
¾ cup onion, minced
5 cups good-quality corned beef, chopped fine
4 cups potatoes, cooked and diced small
2 tablespoons beer
Salt and pepper, to taste

Heat 2 tablespoons of the oil to shimmering in a wide skillet, and sauté onions until translucent, but not caramelized. Mix corned beef, potatoes, onions, and beer in a large bowl and taste for seasoning. Heat remaining oil in the skillet and place hash mix in an even layer, pressing down to make a solid mass. Let cook a few minutes until the underside is browned and very crispy. Flip over, in sections if necessary, and cook other side until crispy as well (this can be done in two skillets or in batches, depending on whether you have one large enough for the whole recipe). Hash should be only about ½-inch thick in skillet. Serve with poached, scrambled, or fried eggs and hair of the dog.

Healthy Hash

SERVES 4 TO 6

2 tablespoons chicken stock

1 cup onion, chopped

1 cup celery, chopped

2 cups canned kidney beans, 1 cup slightly mashed
   with fork

1 cup smoked turkey, chopped

1 cup broccoli, cooked and chopped

4 cups potatoes, cooked and diced

Salt and pepper, to taste

3 tablespoons olive oil (for cooking)

In a nonstick skillet, heat chicken stock and add onions and celery and cook until translucent. Add onions and celery to rest of ingredients; mix well. Heat oil in skillet and place hash mix in an even layer, pressing down to make a solid mass. Let cook a few minutes until the underside is browned and very crispy. Flip over, in sections if necessary, and cook other side until crispy as well (this can be done in two skillets or in batches, depending on whether you have one large enough for the whole recipe).

Hash should be only about ½-inch thick in skillet. Serve with scrambled egg whites, poached eggs, or tofu scramble.

Covenant Club Creamed Spinach

SERVES 4

5 tablespoons butter
4 tablespoons flour
1¼ teaspoons salt
1 cup whole milk
½ teaspoon ground nutmeg
2 tablespoons onion, minced
20 ounces frozen spinach, chopped
¼ cup water
1 cup sour cream
¼ cup Parmesan
Salt and pepper, to taste

Melt 3 tablespoons butter in a small saucepan over medium-low heat. Stir in flour and salt until creamed together, and cook for 1 minute. Stir in milk a little at a time. Increase the heat to medium. Add nutmeg. Constantly stir with a whisk until mixture is thick and smooth.

Remove sauce from heat and set aside.

Melt 2 tablespoons butter in a 2-quart saucepan over medium heat, add onions and cook until translucent. Add spinach and water to pan, lower the heat, and cover. Stir several times until spinach is heated through.

When spinach is almost done, add white sauce, sour cream, and Parmesan. Stir well and simmer until completely blended. Add salt and pepper to taste.

For a healthier version, substitute reduced-fat margarine for the butter, skim milk for the whole milk, and reduced-fat sour cream for the regular sour cream.

Classic Chocolate Chip Cookies

Really? C'mon. Just buy the Nestlé chips and make the recipe on the back of the bag.

Healthier Chocolate Chip Cookies

MAKES 2 DOZEN COOKIES

1 cup whole wheat flour
1 cup all-purpose flour
2 teaspoons baking powder
½ teaspoon salt
¼ teaspoon nutmeg
¼ teaspoon cinnamon
½ cup butter, softened
¾ cup organic brown sugar
1 egg
¼ cup skim milk

5 ounces dark chocolate chips or bittersweet chocolate
   chips
½ cup rolled oats

Preheat oven to 350°F. In a medium bowl, mix the flours, baking powder, salt, nutmeg, and cinnamon with a whisk to combine. In the bowl of an electric mixer, cream butter and sugar until light and fluffy. Add the egg and milk, and combine well. Mix in flour mixture. Add chocolate chips and oats. Drop rounded teaspoons on greased cookie sheets, and bake 12 to 14 minutes until browned around the edges.

Bacon

I like to cook my bacon on a sheet pan in a 400°F oven
for 15 to 20 minutes until crisp. And here is some of
what I like to do with it.

Bacon PB&J

MAKES 1 SANDWICH

¼ cup creamy peanut butter
2 slices white bread
2 tablespoons strawberry jam
2 slices crisp bacon

Spread peanut butter on one side of a piece of bread and jam on one side of the other piece. Put bacon on top of peanut butter and close sandwich.

Honey Bacon Butter

½ pound unsalted butter, softened
4 tablespoons honey
½ cup crisp bacon, crumbled

Blend well and put on pancakes and French toast.

Healthy Bacon

Eat in moderation. There is no substitute.

Basic Stuffing

SERVES 12

1½ cups onion, chopped
1½ cups celery, chopped
Celery leaves from 2 heads, chopped
¼ cup flat-leaf parsley, chopped

1 tablespoon dried sage

1 tablespoon dried thyme

1 tablespoon dried marjoram

2½ sticks butter

1 extra-large loaf (about 2 pounds) country bread or French
   bread, cubed and toasted until totally dry

1 package soft rolls or hot dog buns, torn coarsely

1 16-ounce box or can chicken stock (as necessary to
   moisten)

Salt and pepper, to taste

4 large eggs, beaten

Sauté onions, celery, and herbs in 1½ sticks butter. Toss with bread. Add stock slowly until moist but not overly soggy. Taste for seasoning. Stir in eggs and mix well. Put in deep foil pan. Melt remaining stick of butter and drizzle on top of bread crumbs.

Bake at 400°F for 25 minutes covered. Uncover and bake another 20 minutes. If you want extra moistness, melt another 4 to 8 tablespoons butter in 1 cup chicken stock and pour over top when you uncover the stuffing, then continue cooking.

For a healthier version, substitute whole wheat bread for the country bread, use 2 tablespoons butter and 3 tablespoons olive oil to sauté the veggies, and drizzle with 2 tablespoons of olive oil. Use 4 egg whites instead of whole eggs. For extra moistness, just use the chicken stock and omit the extra butter.

Cheeseburgers

SERVES 4

1½ pounds 80 percent lean ground chuck
1 teaspoon kosher salt
½ teaspoon ground black pepper
4 slices cheese of your choice
4 buns
Condiments of your choice

In a bowl, break up meat with your hands and distribute seasoning evenly. Toss lightly with your fingertips to mix. Divide meat into four equal portions. Toss meat back and forth between hands to form a ball, and then gently press to make a patty. Depress patty in center slightly. Grill over direct heat without pressing down on patties 2½ minutes on first side. When well seared and brown, flip burger and cook additional 1½ minutes, uncovered. Cover patties with cheese and cook additional minute for medium rare, up to 2½ minutes for medium well. Serve on buns and top with preferred condiments.

Turkey Burgers

SERVES 4

1½ pounds ground turkey (lean but not all white)
½ teaspoon kosher salt

½ teaspoon ground black pepper

2 teaspoons Dijon mustard

2 teaspoons Worcestershire sauce

1 tablespoon canola oil (for cooking)

Mix all ingredients lightly until well blended. Follow directions in cheeseburger recipe for forming patties. Heat oil and cook patties to internal temp of 160 degrees, then let rest, covered, for 5 to 10 minutes, before serving.

PRAISE FOR

Good Enough to Eat

"*Good Enough to Eat* is like a perfect dish of macaroni and cheese—rich, warm, nuanced, and delicious. And like any great comfort food, Stacey Ballis's new book is absolutely satisfying."

—Jen Lancaster, *New York Times* bestselling author of
Such a Pretty Fat

"Witty and tender, brash and seriously clever, Stacey Ballis's characters are our friends, our neighbors or, in some cases, that sardonic colleague the next cubicle over . . . Her storytelling will have you alternately turning pages and calling your friends urging them to come along for the ride. And in Stacey Ballis's talented hands, oh what a wonderful ride it is."

—Elizabeth Flock, *New York Times* bestselling author of *Me & Emma*

"A toothsome meal of moments, gorgeously written, in warmth and with keen observation, *Good Enough to Eat* is about so much more than the magic of food; it's about the magic of life. Pardon the cliché, but you'll devour it and wish there was more to savor."

—Stephanie Klein, author of
Straight Up and Dirty and *Moose: A Memoir*

The Spinster Sisters

"Readers will be rooting for Ballis's smart, snappy heroines."

—*Booklist*

"Stacey Ballis provides a wonderful, deep family drama."

—*The Best Reviews*

continued . . .

"A laugh-out-loud hoot of a book. Jodi and Jill are amazing characters. They are challenged by balancing their business lives with style, charm, and grace. A must-read."   —*A Romance Review*

"Ballis addresses the dilemmas of empowered, independent women who are proud of their single status, but also looking hopefully toward settling down with someone special with grace and eloquence."   —*Fresh Fiction*

"With good-natured insight, this is an honest look at family, personal, and business relationships and how women deal with their need for independence and companionship. Strong, caring main characters are compassionate and well developed, giving each a convincing voice . . . For a terrific treat, pick up a copy of *The Spinster Sisters*."   —*Romance Reviews Today*

Room for Improvement

"Self-proclaimed home improvement junkie and author Ballis has written a laugh-out-loud novel that will appeal to HGTV devotees as well as those who like their chick lit on the sexy side."
     —*Booklist* (starred review)

"This book is frequently laugh-out-loud funny."
     —*Romantic Times*

Sleeping Over

"Ballis presents a refreshingly realistic approach to relationships and the things that test (and often break) them. Ballis's sophomore effort will please readers who want something more than fairy-tale romance."   —*Booklist*

"*Sleeping Over* is a snappy tale of love lost, gained, revamped, rehashed, and true friendship through thick and thin . . . a remarkable chick lit novel . . . Don't let this entertaining tale pass you by."   —*Romance Reviews Today*

"Fans of relationship dramas will appreciate this fine, character-driven tale." —*The Best Reviews*

"*Sleeping Over* will have you laughing, crying, and planning your next girls' night out. This is the first novel I have read by Stacey Ballis, but I guarantee it won't be the last!"
—*Romance Reader at Heart*

"This engaging story delivers everything you ask from a great read: it makes you laugh, it makes you cry, it makes you *feel*. *Sleeping Over* gets my highest recommendation." —*Romance Divas*

Inappropriate Men

"Ballis's debut is a witty tale of a thirtysomething who unexpectedly has to start the search for love all over again." —*Booklist*

"Cheekily comic . . . Sidney Stein is a heroine to cheer lustily for, because that is how she lives her life: in grand style, and refusing to settle." —*BookPage*

"Without a doubt, *Inappropriate Men* is one of the best books of 2004. Stacey Ballis has a way with words. Effortlessly, she makes them exciting and pulls the reader into the life of one of the most engaging characters ever created, Sidney Stein."
—*A Romance Review*

"For an insider's look at dating and relationships, with all the laughs and wit you could want, *Inappropriate Men* by Stacey Ballis is a wonderful choice for your reading pleasure."
—*Romance Reviews Today*

Berkley Books by Stacey Ballis

ROOM FOR IMPROVEMENT
THE SPINSTER SISTERS
GOOD ENOUGH TO EAT